LOVE
IN AN
EMPTY NEST

A Story By

Sarah Frederick

authorHOUSE®

AuthorHouse™
1663 Liberty Drive
Bloomington, IN 47403
www.authorhouse.com
Phone: 1-800-839-8640

Published by AuthorHouse   04/12/2012

ISBN: 978-1-4685-8352-6 (sc)
ISBN: 978-1-4685-8353-3 (e)

Library of Congress Control Number: 2012906895

JOLYN

"*G*WAMPA!" LITTLE JOE'S short legs pumped mightily, propelling him across the well-kept lawn and into the arms of his favorite person . . . after his mother and father, of course. "What'd you bwing me?" he asked, smiling when he was rewarded with a chocolate chip cookie. Engrossed in his treat, he didn't complain when his grandfather set him on the grass, leaving the toddler to munch his goodie while he wandered over to the patio where his daughter waited.

"Hi, Kitten," he said, ruffling her hair as he always did. Giving her a kiss on the cheek, he sat heavily on a chaise lounge and sighed.

"That bad?" she asked sympathetically, seeing the glum look on his face. She knew how difficult it was for him to admit that everything wasn't quite as perfect in his life as most people believed, although, besides sex, perfect wasn't too far from the truth. Her mother and father were still as crazy about each other as two people could be. "What did Dr. Summers say?"

1

"I don't know if it's bad or not," he said. "He said about the same things you told me. He showed me the facility. It looks really swanky. I just don't know if I can do this. I don't know how your mother will react and I don't know if I can do all the things he said I'll have to if we want to make it work."

"I'm sure she'll be terrified at first," Jolyn agreed, understanding his reluctance. She had seen some of the couples who had been treated at the luxurious clinic, indeed, had been the one to monitor a few, and understood how traumatizing the treatment could be. Still, she believed in Dr. Summers and what he and her husband, Tom, were doing. She'd seen the results firsthand. "But, if you do everything he tells you to, it can make all the difference in both your lives."

"But what happens if it doesn't work?" he argued, half-heartedly. He'd already made up his mind, but wanted her to talk him into it one more time, just as she had in the first place.

"Will it really be any different?" his daughter asked. "You know she'd forgive you. She loves you, Dad. She'd forgive you anything." She stood and walked over to where he sat, kneeling in front of him. "You two have everything going for you except sex. You're both tenured college professors. You're an awesome coach. She's a world class artist. If you can get her to enjoy sex, you'll have it all."

He gave her his endearing, lopsided grin. "Do you really believe God wants us to have it all?"

"I believe He wants us to live up to our potential," she answered, hoping to convince him to give the clinic a try. "He gave us sex, Dad. He must want us to enjoy it. It's just our Victorian mores that make us so inhibited about it."

"I can't believe I'm sitting here talking about sex with my own daughter," he groaned.

"We're not discussing sex, Dad. We're discussing whether you and Mom should enter a clinic that teaches you how to enjoy it."

"I don't need any help." He laughed. "I already enjoy it."

She laughed with him, then said soberly, "Yes, but she doesn't. Don't you think it would be better for you if she did, too?"

"Absolutely," he agreed, sighing. He could think of nothing he'd like more than to have his wife enjoy touching him as much as he enjoyed touching her. He had never lost the desire for her that had hit him like a lightening bolt the first time he'd seen her, but, while she undoubtedly cherished him, there had never been a hint of sexual longing. "But you can never, ever tell her that it was all your idea in the first place. She'd never forgive either one of us."

"Don't worry. Dr. Summers said he would personally monitor you two. Neither Tom nor I will have anything to do with your therapy." That had been one of the very first conditions her father had made, knowing just how embarrassed her mother would be throughout the whole ordeal. It would be mortifying for her if she had any inkling that her daughter knew everything that transpired. She was just too self-conscious about anything that had to do with her body, especially when it came to sex.

Jolyn looked over at her toddler, giving her dad a moment. "Little Joe is sure gonna miss his grandpa for the next month," she murmured.

"I'll miss him, too," he said. "But I'll see him once or twice, won't I? I mean I'll be coming back to the house to work on the den." One of the concessions he had made to his conscience was to remodel the unused den for a studio for his wife, hoping that would help her forgive him if the need arose. "And the boys have promised to help. You can bring him by, can't you? He is my favorite grandson, you know."

She smacked him on the arm, laughing. "He's your *only* grandson."

"I know," he chuckled, rising, he ambled over to the little tyke, who was now covered in chocolate. "C'mere," he said, catching the boy under the arms and tossing him high into the air. He waited until the very last possible second to catch him, giving the child a true rush while he whooped and cackled with glee. "Do 'gain," he said and went off into gales of laughter when his grandfather scooped him up once again, lofting him skyward.

Jolyn watched fondly while the big man played with her son. She remembered him tossing her into the air in just the same way and she remembered how she had always loved her 'wooly teddy bear', as she called him. Not that she didn't adore her mother. There weren't many people as put together as her parents, and she had always worked very hard to be as good a person as she knew them to be.

His grandson tucked safely under his arm, he returned to his daughter's side. Handing her the little boy, he nodded. "You promise you'll square everything with your brothers and sister?"

"Kate and Kyle already know. I haven't been able to get a hold of Jack, yet. But I will, if I can track him down."

"You're right, you know," he started.

"Yes, I know," she said before he could go on.

"Women!" he muttered, giving her another kiss and a pat on the cheek. "We have an appointment tomorrow morning and it'll all start tomorrow night."

"So soon?"

"Figured we might as well get started as soon as possible, before I lose my nerve. It took me weeks to talk her into visiting him in his office and that was his first available appointment. I've already squared it with our insurance, too. Since it's in the clinic, it's considered therapy, so they'll pay most of it. I'll be sleeping there, too, but I'll be at the house quite a bit. It just seems so extreme. Are you sure it'll work?"

"No one can say that for sure," she replied. "Didn't Dr. Summers explain that?" She could have added that it only worked when the man involved was willing to put aside a lifetime of habit and learn a whole new approach to just about everything, including sex.

"He said it works for some, but not for others. He thinks we have a pretty good chance to make it work, though. That's why I decided to go through with it."

"Good luck, Dad," she called as he let himself out the gate. "You're going to need it," she said softly to herself when he was out of sight.

JILLIAN

"*I*T'S DARK. REALLY, really dark." Jillian thought as she tried to rouse herself, but sleep was loath to relinquish its hold on her. "The power must be out," she muttered groggily, trying to reach for the lamp to prove her theory. When her arm refused to obey her commands, she panicked, thrashing until she came fully awake, still unable to see or to raise her arms.

Terror claimed her. Fear preyed upon her now alert mind, driving screams from her in wave upon wave. Tears threatened to drown her, pouring from under her eyelids, but unable to roll down her cheeks, impeded by the mask that covered her eyes. She was unable to hear her own screams because of the tiny ear buds nestled within her ear canals, streaming a steady white noise that drowned out any other sound.

After a few minutes that seemed like years, Jillian's screams turned to muffled sobs, her intense emotions unsustainable, her fear unabated. As coherent thought returned, she tried to gather her wits, to garner the facts of her captivity. "Captivity?" she thought. "Yes, that's the word for it." One part of her mind tried to find some logical answer for the absence of light or the unremitting sound, while another part wandered over and over again into the minefield of sheer terror.

At last she was calm enough to be able to assess the situation, taking stock of everything she could feel. Her wrists and ankles were bound, but not with handcuffs or rope. The material holding her seemed to be softer, padded, for there was no pain where she had fought against her bonds. Soft, too was whatever was over her eyes, closing out even a hint of light without hurting her. She must be on a bed, she thought. She couldn't reach the edges with her bound hands, which were at right angles to her body. Nor could she reach anything above her head but pillowy softness, silky and warm.

"Okay," she said to herself. "I'm comfortable within the bounds of my bounds." Then she giggled at the double use of the word. "I'm totally losing it," she thought. "First I'm frantic, now I'm laughing. Must be hysteria. Yes, that's it. I'm hysterical. Or I'm dreaming. I'll wake up any minute now and this will all be a dream."

She waited, hoped, gave up hope. "I'm awake," she admitted to herself. "But, why? Why would anyone want to tie me up like this? I'm sure no prize to look at. No one would want to rape me. Would they?" At that thought, she felt the terror rise in her again. Rape! She'd been married for twenty-six years. In all that time she had never enjoyed sex, but she'd never been afraid of it. It was just one of those things you had to do to get children or keep a husband. Now she couldn't think beyond the imposition on her body of an unwanted male, the rutting and grunting that would accompany it, the barbarity of the act, the cruelty associated with it.

Her sobs renewed, now more sorrow than fear, as shame took a foothold within her heart, and disgust became only a secondary emotion. "Rape." Wasn't that what happened between her and Joe every time they had sex? "No, it isn't. Just because I don't like it, doesn't mean it's rape," she chided herself. "Joe's a good man and he doesn't make too many demands on me. He calls it making love. It's not the same."

In her own personal darkness, she wept, not the sobs of terror as before, but the sorrow of a life spent doing what she thought was right without ever having found pleasure in the act. Then the thought hit her. "Joe! Where was Joe?" She tried to think, to understand what had happened.

"The restaurant parking lot," she whispered into the softly scented air. "The two men! Did they hurt him? Is he all right? Oh, Lord, help us," and she wept once more. This time, she succumbed to the adrenal down that follows intense emotion, and she slept once again.

JOE

"**I**S SHE OKAY?" Joe asked the young doctor who was making notes about the scene that was repeated on numerous monitors, the feeds coming from the next room where his wife lay bound hand and foot on the elaborate king-sized bed.

"Yes, she's fine. It's a typical response. First fear, then acceptance, then trying to figure out where she is and, finally, worrying about her husband. It usually follows that general path."

"She's going to be really pissed when we finally let her go," Joe said.

"Not if you do exactly what I tell you and nothing else," Dr. Summers cautioned. "And she'll only be bound like this until you're sure you can trust her not to hurt herself."

"Or me." Joe's chuckle was forced.

"Oh, she'll probably do a little bodily damage before it's all over," the doctor assured him. "But it'll be minimal and, believe me, it'll be worth it."

"I sure hope you're right," Joe said.

"Me, too," he said with a twinkle, his somber face becoming almost beautiful with the addition of his generous smile.

Joe had come to trust this man as he had never trusted anyone before, but he couldn't for the life of him tell anyone why. Maybe it was the twinkle in his eye, or the ready smile. If anything, he should hate him with his dark shiny hair and deep blue eyes. He'd been sure the lean, good-looking younger man would scare off his wife, but Jillian had fallen under his spell with their first appointment. He'd had to all but drag her there for their initial consultation, but, once she'd met their new therapist . . . their sex therapist . . . she'd made their next appointment without argument.

"Now. Do you remember what I told you to do?"

Joe nodded, swallowed, nervous and very unsure. "What if it doesn't work?" he asked.

"Has she ever been receptive to your advances?" Dr. Summers asked gently.

"You know she hasn't." Joe's anxiety showed in his eyes and the tight way he held his big body. "That's why we came to you in the first place."

"But she didn't want to come, did she?"

"No, she didn't," Joe replied, his eyes on one of the screens in front of them.

"Joe, don't feel so guilty. It's not that unusual. So many women her age, and older, spend their whole lives missing one of the finest joys in life. But teaching her to like sex, awakening her libido, is something *you* have to do. No one else can do it for you . . . or her."

"It's just that I'm so damn clumsy."

"That's what you're going to learn. And the more you learn the better it will be both for you and for her." He turned back to the controls, adjusting the angle of the hidden camera. "Did you enjoy the manicure?"

Joe looked at his newly cleansed and filed nails, the calluses in his palms sanded to softness. "It was embarrassing," he replied. "I couldn't go all the way and let them put polish on, but my hands really do feel softer. Do you think it'll make a difference?"

"Of course it will. And so will the short haircut and your beard when it grows out. She won't know it's you. That's important."

"I still don't understand why," Joe's querulous voice came close to a whine. He blushed, not wanting the younger man to think he was some kind of wimp. "I mean . . ."

"I know what you mean," Dr. Summers said, nodding, understanding. "So I'll explain it one more time. Right now, she thinks she's been kidnapped. And, considering the position she's found herself in, she's pretty sure she's about to be raped. What we're trying to do is make her anticipate something that, at this point, she fears."

"But she isn't afraid of sex, she just doesn't like it. She thinks it's disgusting."

"And we're trying to make her change her mind." He turned back to the monitors. "Okay, she's asleep, but just lightly. Go inside, sit beside her, and remember, only five minutes. All you're going to do is touch her very gently at the waist and across the belly, and down her arm. Then get up and leave. She might not wake up this time. But her body will remember the sensations even if her mind doesn't." He stood and led the way down the hall to the door, towing a reluctant Joe, his hand clasped around his bicep. "Ready?"

Joe swallowed, nodded and stepped through the portal into the dim light of the bedroom, almost as afraid as Jillian had been on awakening. He lowered his big body onto the mattress as gently as he could, but nothing could prevent the sag caused by his weight. He sighed deeply, trying to remember the doctor's admonitions. Softly, he lifted the sheet, pulling it down below her waist. He spread his hand across her belly, pressing slightly, moving up across her middle and over the curve of her ribs. He did the same with the other hand until he held her trapped between his big hands, his long fingers rubbing small circles, his thumbs kneading her, his palms and the heel of his hands maintaining a small amount of pressure. He repeated the motions several times before he felt the change in her breathing that signaled awareness.

He could feel her stiffen, could sense the revulsion that had always accompanied their sexual encounters, but he continued moving his hands across her abdomen and around her waist. After a while, he skimmed the backs of his fingers up her sides to her arms and began kneading the tense muscles there until the voice in his ear told him that time was up. His fingertips retraced her ribs as he lifted himself from the bed, ending where he'd begun. At the last, he pulled the sheet back over her breasts and left the room, his heartbeat and breathing as elevated as though he'd run a mile.

JILLIAN

THE SENSATIONS THAT coursed through her middle brought her to unwelcome awareness. "I was right," she cried inside her mind, tensing her body, expecting the usual thrusting that had always been the main focus of Joe's lovemaking. The hands were gentle, smooth as they massaged her middle, not rough and calloused. "Not Joe!" she thought, embarrassed and afraid at having some man other than her husband touch her. Oddly, the first thing that raced through her mind was that someone other than her husband would see the stretch marks left by four pregnancies or would touch her thickened waistline.

Strange feelings accompanied the movements of the hands, feelings that were as unfamiliar as the hands themselves. Not unpleasant, indeed soothing, their steady rhythm was almost tender, the subtle pressure sending shudders through her body. The tickle up her ribs followed by the kneading of her upper arms, while pleasant, didn't compare to the feelings the stroking had created in her middle.

It took a moment for her to realize the white noise had changed to music. No, not just any music, but the dulcet tones of Andrea Bocceli, her favorite. "How?" was followed instantly by "Why?" She had no idea what the answers might be, indeed had only realized the question when the music ceased, the white noise returned, the weight of the man lifted from the bed and something covered her breasts once more.

"What do you suppose that was all about?" she asked herself. She went over the last five minutes in her mind, trying to comprehend everything, but found no answers. She still didn't know where she was or why, and she didn't know what had happened to Joe. "Joe?" She whispered his name in the darkness, but got no response. "I'm sorry, Joe," she said to the air. "I can't stop him. Please forgive me."

JOE

"*Y*OU DID JUST fine," Dr. Summers told him, holding the door open just long enough for Joe to slip through. He looked closely at the big man, knowing pretty much what was going through his mind. "She didn't fight, Joe," he said. "That's a plus."

"She really didn't have time," Joe said, shaking his head. "What am I doing, Doc. She's terrified. I could feel it in every fiber of her body."

"We already knew that, Joe. You heard it when she woke up the first time."

"Yeah, but I didn't know it would be this hard."

"It won't do you any good to quit now," Dr. Summers told him. "When you and I talked about doing this, I warned you about the risks. I know it's really extreme, but I've never known this particular therapy to fail. You've come this far, Joe. Don't give up now."

Joe shook his head. "No, I know I can't. I'm not doing this for me, Doc. She'll let me make love to her any time I ask. But . . ."

"But to her it isn't making love, is it?"

"No. To her it's a chore, just like vacuuming or doing the laundry."

"And you said you want to teach her to enjoy the experience as much as you do, right?"

"Right," he agreed with a wry grin. "But, you know, when you and I talked about this, I really had no idea what it would be like." He held up a hand, staying the doctor's comment. "I know, I know. You showed me the facility, you told me what to expect and you've explained what I need to learn to do to please her. I just hate to see her in pain."

"She's afraid," Dr. Summers argued. "But there's no physical pain. She's not being harmed in any way."

"Okay, all right. You're right. I know, I know." He sat heavily in one of the office chairs. "How long before I go back in there?"

"Not just yet. We're going to let her take a potty break."

"How? If you untie her she'll bolt."

"Watch," the young doctor pointed to the consoles.

On the screen, the lights came up a bit, allowing them to see the furnishings around the room. The big bed with the pillow soft mattress took up most of the room. There was nothing sharp, no wooden or metal headboard, no long legged furniture, only a single large overstuffed, pillowed chair. Everything was soft, opulent, richly covered in silky, comforting fabric. The colors too were soft, subtle, a hint of blue, a touch of lavender.

Three women, dressed from chin to toe in soft white sheaths, entered the room and approached the bed. One on either side undid her bindings, lifting her by the wrists and upper arms, turning her until she was seated on the side of the bed. The third folded the sheets to the foot of the bed before settling a silky toga-like wrap over Jillian's left shoulder and wrapping it loosely around her torso, covering her to her toes in satiny luxury. Raising her to her feet they guided her out of sight into the adjoining bathroom.

"This is for her sake when it's all over," Dr. Summers explained. "There are some things no woman wants to share, not even with her husband and she'll be thankful that she has privacy when she has to use the bathroom."

Joe chuckled. "You have no idea," he said. "She still locks the bathroom door at home."

"Figured that out. She's embarrassed, both by her bodily functions and by the way she perceives her appearance. It's all part of the same problem, Joe. I don't think we'll ever get her to the point she wants to allow you in the bathroom when she needs to use the john, but you might be allowed to join her in the tub. No promises, yet. We'll just have to wait and see how she progresses. If that happens we'll be able to tape it, but until then we'll give her her privacy."

JILLIAN

THE HANDS THAT released her restraints were encased in soft gloves, but they were rigid and strong and she knew she couldn't fight. They didn't exactly pull her to her feet, but there was nothing she could do but rise from the bed. She was surprised at the feel of richly sheer fabric that settled over her body and the plush carpet beneath her feet. She didn't ask questions, although there were thousands flitting through her mind. She knew with certainty that these people wouldn't answer and she wouldn't be able to hear the answers, anyway.

A toilet? "Oh, thank God," she said aloud, sighing with relief, even with her arms held on both sides by her warders. "How am I going to . . . ?" she asked them, but found herself lifted once again, this time settling over a bidet where the warm water cleansed her bottom and one of her warders dried her with a warm towel. Still being held by her wrists and arms, she was led once more into the bedroom where she was seated in a roomy chair, unable to stop herself from sinking into the luxurious softness.

Her arms were placed on the arms of the chair and she realized that she was once again shackled.

She sat quietly, not understanding, but grateful that she hadn't been harmed. Somewhere deep in her mind, she came to terms with her captivity, still afraid, still worried about her husband, but no longer frantic. What she did understand was that it would do no good to fight her bonds or the people who had so far come into contact with her. Sitting there, comfortable and essentially pampered, despair gave way to curiosity. "Why?" she asked herself over and over.

She sensed rather than felt another presence. Tensing, she sat up straighter, once again afraid. At almost the same time, her other senses took over. Romantic music filled her ears as delicious aromas wafted on the still air. "Food?" she thought and was instantly embarrassed by the hungry rumble of her stomach. Her blush was unbidden, but not unnoticed. She could feel the warmth rising from her neck and up over her cheeks, and that embarrassed her even more. "Why would it embarrass me for kidnappers to hear my stomach grumble," she thought to herself. "What do I care what they think?"

Gentle caresses, a soft touch on her forearm, another along her jaw line, surprised her and she jerked away as far as her bonds permitted. The touch was repeated. This time the fingers followed her jaw, slipped down her neck to her one bare shoulder. Knowing she couldn't escape, she shuddered but sat still, permitting the caress without welcoming it.

JOE

"REMEMBER TO WAIT until she's finished chewing every last morsel before giving her the next bite," Dr. Summers had cautioned Joe before opening the door for him to enter the bedroom once again, this time burdened with a tray of food for his wife and a short, padded stool.

Joe just nodded and carried the tray into the room, setting it on its own legs beside the chair where his wife waited. He placed the stool immediately in front of her and sat facing her. He wanted to talk to her, but knew he wasn't allowed to say anything. It wouldn't have made any difference. With the little ear buds, she couldn't have heard him, anyway. He sat immediately in front of her, reaching out to touch her arm, her jaw, flinching as she did, smiling when her stomach rumbled.

He reached out once again, tracing her jaw line, then from her chin to her neck and beyond, down her throat to her one bare shoulder. He retraced the line, ending once again at her chin and on up, outlining with his fingertips the curve of her lips.

"Will she ever forgive me," he thought. "Will she ever understand that I did this for her? Will she ever comprehend the depth of love I have for her?" He shrugged and bent to his task.

The tender steak was already cut into bite-sized morsels, as was the baked potato. Already smothered in butter and sour cream with a trace of cheese and bacon bits, just the way she liked them, a taste of potato was his first offering. He touched her chin once again, his fingers moving to her lips, lightly pushing down on her lower lip while offering the tiny portion of potato on the tip of the fork. He was relieved when she reacted to the food, opening her mouth slightly, just enough for him to be able to slide the tasty treat into her mouth.

A second bite of potato followed the first. This time he had only to touch her full lower lip before she opened up once again. One tiny bite of steak on the fork was his next offering and she accepted it as she had the last. Now he put the fork down, freeing his hands to once again trace the fine line of her neck, his thumb feeling her heartbeat, his fingertips moving up behind her ear, caressing, pressing, loving.

She sat perfectly still, allowing the caress without welcoming it. Again she shuddered, reacting as she always had to his touch. "What did you expect?" he asked himself, chagrinned. "She's not going to change. At least not this quickly." He offered her another bite of dinner which she took as she had the others, chewing thoroughly before ready for another.

And so it went. A little food, a gentle touch, caresses along her throat and shoulder. After a while, the shudders stopped when she came to accept the nonthreatening stroking of her neck as she had the touch on her lower lip. He held a glass to her lips, his hand cupping her chin. She sipped the cool lemonade, licking her lips for the very last pearly drop and setting her husband on fire.

"Doesn't she know how exciting that is?" he asked himself. This time he moved his hand up her arm, inside her upper arm, kneading, gently squeezing as he went. It took all of his self-control not to grab her and throw her on the bed. "I don't think I can do this," he said to himself. His body was so tense he felt like a rubber band and his crotch throbbed painfully. "Slowly," the voice in his ear reminded him.

He sat back in his chair, away from the temptation of his life's companion. "I should never have agreed to this," he told himself, watching her tiny movements, her head cocked as though she could hear his thoughts, waiting.

He gave her the last bite of green beans and another sip of lemonade. This time, when he took her chin in his hand, she leaned forward, into his grasp, setting him on fire once again. He stood, picked up the tray and stool, and left, unsure if his legs would carry him clear across the room.

JILLIAN

"*M*MMM, BAKED POTATO with sour cream and butter. Oh, and bacon. It's as though they know what I like best," Jillian thought to herself. The tiny bite of steak was done just the way she loved it, her favorite food. She tried to ignore the fingers on her neck, the hand that encircled her throat, the thumb rubbing against her jaw. It was just something she had to endure to get the food. As her belly filled, she realized the sensations of the wandering hand weren't all that unpleasant. Indeed, they were quite soothing.

"Don't be silly," she reprimanded herself. "It's just someone trying to get a little." She concentrated on her food, chewing every last morsel until there was nothing left but the flavor on her tongue. When the hand touched her chin and the glass tipped to her lips, she accepted the liquid, savoring the tart flavor, tracing her lips to garner every last drop. "It might be my last," she reminded herself, but, even as that thought flickered through her mind, she knew it was a lie. Whatever these people had in mind for her, she wasn't in immediate danger. She was sure of that.

When the hand wandered up her arm, she ignored it at first, until the knuckles grazed the outside of her breast. She wasn't sure which disconcerted her more, the hand, or the reaction of her body to the seemingly casual caress. She could feel the tightening of her nipple, the tension in her torso that had nothing to do with indignation. "What the hell was that?" she asked inside her mind. "He's just sneaking a feel," her mind responded. But her body didn't agree and she felt excited and embarrassed in equal amounts.

Suddenly she realized she was alone and she felt a combination of relief and disappointment. "Disappointment?" she asked herself. "What do you have to be disappointed about? You've been lucky so far!" Then her thoughts turned black once again. "So far? What did it all mean?"

As she sat in silken comfort, she went over the last few weeks in her mind.

She remembered the look of pride on Kyle's face as he walked across the platform to accept his degree. The last of her four children to graduate, his graduation marked the end of her tenure as a mommy. His apartment had already been furnished. Most of his clothes, his weights and bench, his trophies and pictures had already been installed there. He had only had a few things to pick up at the house and he was gone.

And they had become empty nesters. The house had gone from being full to bursting to just she and Joe rattling around in it. She had gone from a lifetime of being busier than the proverbial bee to having nothing to do. Joe had been relieved, at first. Finally, he had total control of the remote, but no one to watch the games with. He had regained the garage, but had no projects to work on. He had time on his hands and only her to keep him company.

That was when he had come up with the ludicrous idea of going to a therapist. A *sex* therapist! She not only hadn't wanted to, she had flatly refused, but he'd persisted until she'd finally given in. Reluctantly, she'd sat in that doctor's office, waiting until he'd finished with another patient and trying to get a handle on what kind of person he might be from the objects in the room.

It had been a large, comfortable room with overstuffed chairs and a glass topped table that took the place of a desk. The computer was a Toshiba laptop and sat blinking, waiting for him to open it and enter his newest data. There were drawings on the walls, pastels of children covering almost every bare surface, competing with black lacquer bookshelves for space. Joe hadn't been able to settle down, wandering the room, looking at the titles on the books and examining the pictures.

When Dr. Summers had entered, his wide smile and bright blue eyes welcoming them, she'd wanted to crawl into a hole. He was beautiful! Not just handsome, gorgeous! And Joe wanted to talk about their *sex* life with this Adonis? She hadn't been sure she could speak, much less talk about something so private and intimate with him.

He had put her at ease in minutes, talking about their circumstances, their children and even his own children. When he'd explained that theirs were the faces that graced the many pictures on the walls, lovingly rendered by his grandfather, she'd found herself relaxing, enjoying the talent that had created the portraits as much as the children themselves.

The hour had passed pleasantly, not at all what she had expected, but when she was ready to go, she found that there was more to their initial consultation than just pleasant conversation. Forms in hand, she and Joe had made their way to the laboratory on the second floor where they'd submitted to blood tests and given urine samples. Back up, they were separated, he to one examination room, she to another. None of this had bothered her until she was told to undress and put on one of those atrocious examination gowns that tied in the back. "Why?" she had asked.

"So Dr. Summers can finish his examination," the nurse had replied. "He'll be with you shortly."

Nervously, she had removed her own clothes, folding each piece and making sure she placed her panties and bra under her skirt so no one else could see them. She'd sat on the end of the table, the gown tucked tightly under her thighs, held in place by her hands. When the good-looking doctor had come through the door followed by the nurse, it was all she could do not to bolt. "I thought you were a psychologist," she'd said, somewhat defensively.

"Psychiatrist, yes, I am," he'd answered while donning rubber gloves. "But first I was a gynecologist." He had put his hand on her shoulder, leaning her back. "I went back to school when I discovered that so many of my patients had the same problem you do. Most of the time it's psychological. Sometimes it's a physical problem, though. We're going to make sure your problem isn't a physical one."

After an excruciatingly embarrassing pelvic examination, which included a rectal examination as well, it had been impossible to look the doctor in the face, even when he'd helped her sit up. He'd continued talking to her as though he didn't notice her discomfiture, chatting about Joe and her children, asking questions about her job. It had taken a few minutes before she could meet his eye, but when she did, she found only sympathy and understanding.

She'd ducked her head again, but he'd placed one finger under her chin, lifting. "It's okay," he'd assured her, almost forcing her to meet his eyes. "God made our bodies as they are for a reason. We are the most perfect species on Earth and we are made in God's image. There's absolutely no reason for you to be embarrassed."

"I'll bet when he designed our bodies, this isn't exactly what he had in mind," she'd demurred, her hand indicating her own tall, lithe form. "I'm pretty sure you are more what he was thinking of."

To her surprise he had thrown back his head and let out a big, deep, hearty laugh. "Who knows," he'd chuckled. "Maybe you are exactly what he had in mind." He'd motioned to the nurse, following her to the door. "Go ahead and get dressed," he'd instructed. "I'll see you back in my office in a few minutes. Terry will show you the way."

She and Joe had arrived at the door of the doctor's office at the same time. Knowing just how sensitive she was to anything that had to do with her feminine parts, he'd wrapped her up in a tender, non-sexual hug, allowing her a couple of minutes to gather herself before knocking. They only had to spend a few more minutes there while the doctor went over their tests, assuring them that they were both in top-notch health. "There are no physical reasons for you not to enjoy sex," he had told her.

"I think I already knew that," she had said.

"So now we know just what we need to work on," he'd assured them, arranging a time and date for a second appointment.

Once outside, Joe had suggested they go to a romantic restaurant for dinner. He was the romantic, not she. But then he was the one who always wanted laid. She'd known from the books she'd read and from listening to friends and relatives that something had always been missing from their love life, but had never figured out exactly what it was. And now, having dragged her to a therapist, he wanted to take her out for a *romantic* dinner. It wasn't hard to figure out what he was looking forward to when they got home.

They'd had an expensive meal at the one restaurant in town that still sported tablecloths. There'd been candles on the tables and a nice bottle of champagne to go along with the tender, cooked just right steak and potato. "Steak and potato?" Her mind filed that little tidbit of information away for later scrutiny. It had been after the meal, feeling full and flushed and on their way to the car when the two men had grabbed them. They must have had some kind of knock out medicine. She'd felt a prick in her arm, then nothing. She'd awakened in here, tied to the bed.

She didn't have time for any more reminiscing. The three attendants returned as silently as before, lifting her from the chair and once again leading her into the bathroom. This time they sat her on the edge of a tub, removing the cloth that was still draped around her, lifting her feet and turning her, lowering her legs into the warm soapy water. She could feel the bubbles as she was eased down chin deep into the water where her head rested against some kind of padding and her arms were once again restrained, this time along the sides of the tub. Someone moved her hand until her thumb rested on a rounded knob, pressing with enough force to start the jets of water that spurted from the nozzles of the Jacuzzi. She could control it, turning it off and on whenever she wanted.

She languished in the warm water, turning the Jacuzzi off when the bubbles reached as high as her mouth. She was enjoying the soothing warmth, the fresh scent and, she now realized, the soft music still playing in her ears. When the hands slid down her arms, she wasn't surprised. Rather, she recognized the touch, and had to admit she'd been anticipating it.

Now, with the soap to make her skin slick, the hands wandered first to all the places they already had, her cheek, chin, neck and shoulder. Down her arm and back up, across to the other arm and back the hands traced her outline. When the hand withdrew, she had to admit disappointment, and wasn't at all unhappy when she felt a soapy washrag following the same path. Her breath came in swiftly when the rag slid down off her shoulders, between her breasts to her belly then back up, encircling first one breast then the other.

Down her ribs, over her belly, not even splashing a little as it exited and reentered the water, so subtle was the movement. She quit worrying about the crows' feet at the corners of her eyes, or the wrinkles around her mouth. She forgot about baby stretch marks or extra padding around her middle. Her mind was totally focused on the heat of the washrag as it dragged a line of fire over her body.

Just when she thought it was over, when the washrag no longer moved over her and she was left with nothing more than her ragged breathing, the hands began again, this time at her feet. First one leg then the other was lifted, cleansed and returned to the water. The first leg was lifted again, the washrag slowly teasing each toe, her arch, her heel. Once done with her foot, it moved up to her ankle, on to her calf and behind her knee.

"What a wonderful feeling," she thought as the hands and the washrag circled her thigh, tracing another line of fire up her leg to her . . . ! "Oh, no," she thought, her mind racing. "Here it comes." But it didn't. Over her belly, lifting her and washing her buttocks and back, returning down the inside of her thigh, under her knee, over her shin to her foot. When she thought she could stand no more, it started over again with the other foot.

This time the hands gently pried her thighs apart, spreading her legs so the hands had the freedom to move from the inside of one thigh to the other, gently brushing her labia as they passed. The heat they generated had nothing to do with the warmth of the water and everything to do with something she couldn't name, had no memory of, didn't recognize. She moaned in pleasure. Surely it was sinful for anything to feel this good.

She lay with her knees resting on either side of the tub, open and inviting, when she realized the hands were no longer there. She couldn't suppress the sigh, couldn't comprehend the yearning. Her body was on fire, she wanted . . . what? She didn't know what she wanted, had no recollection of anything that would compare. She only knew something was missing, something more, something she had almost been on the verge of discovering.

JOE

"**I** DON'T THINK I can do this any more," Joe told Dr. Summers when he got back to the control booth.

"Oh, I think you can," the doctor grinned at him, knowing exactly what was going through his mind as well as with other parts of his anatomy. "When I said it was going to hurt, this was exactly what I had in mind."

"I'm so hard, I hurt clear up to my eyeballs," Joe complained.

"And every time you've felt the urge before, she's been there to ease your suffering. Hasn't she?"

"Absolutely," Joe agreed. "She turns me on just sitting still. She doesn't think she's pretty, but I think she's beautiful, Doc. She has the most regal neck it's all I can do not to lick it every time I touch it. And when she moaned in there a few minutes ago, I wanted to get into the tub with her and take her right there and then."

"Don't you get it yet, Joe?" he asked. "That was the first time in both your lives she's had any kind of sexual urge."

"That was a sexual urge?" Joe blurted, astonished.

"To quote you," Dr. Summers chuckled, "absolutely!" He leaned his hip against the desk where the consoles showed Jillian being dried off and returned to the bed. "Has she ever made quite that sound before?"

Joe shook his head. "No, not that I can ever recall. Does that mean she's ready?"

Dr. Summers shook his head. "Not really, not yet. If you don't think you can stand it, you can use the bathroom in there. There are magazines and . . ."

Joe was shaking his head vehemently now. "I've never done that before."

"Because she's always been there to take care of your needs," the doctor said flatly. "When you came to me, you told me that you wanted to give her something to look forward to now that it was just the two of you at home. Still feel that way?"

Joe opened his mouth to say something, closed it, grimaced and answered. "Yes. Yes, I do. She's a wonderful woman, Doc. She takes care of everyone and everything and never complains." He stopped, went on. "You know why she was so excited about the drawings in your office? Because she's a hell of an artist, but she's never had time for her own stuff. She gave up the single most important thing in her life when the kids started coming. And we had four kids in less than four years, Doc. Once they were all in school, she started teaching so I could go back and get my masters' degree. When I was done, she went back for her Bachelor of Fine Arts, then I got my doctorate, then she got her Master of Fine Arts. Obviously, she's had her hands full until a few weeks ago when our baby graduated from college."

"All the more reason for you to continue, isn't it?"

"Yes. Yes it is."

"Good," Dr. Summers once again took Joe by the upper arm, leading him down the hallway. He stopped at the door across from were Joe's wife lay, confined in luxury. "You need your rest," he said, sending the big man through the door. "This will be your room for the duration. Get some sleep, Joe. If you think it's been hard on you today, wait until tomorrow." He winked and closed the door, leaving the bemused man alone.

Joe looked around, his eyes lighting on the clothes hanging in the closet. Not his. Dr. Summers had told him to bring nothing so that nothing he wore would give him away. He sighed, went into the bathroom to take care of necessities, searching the drawers until he found all the necessary items, still in new wrappers. The only things missing were the razor and shaving cream, which he wouldn't be needing for the next month anyway. The other toiletries weren't his usual brands. He shrugged, washed his face, brushed his teeth and returned to sit on the foot of the bed. It didn't even look inviting, although it was every bit as luxurious as that in the room across the hall.

He put his head in his hands and tried once again to decide whether or not he had made the right decision. "I just hope she'll forgive me," he said with a sigh. The last thing he did before crawling under the covers was set the alarm on his watch so he would get up in time to meet with the therapist who was working with him on his hands. He'd been amazed at how stiff his fingers really were compared how they needed to be. Jillian's hands had always been supple and exciting whenever she'd touched him. It had never before occurred to him that his hands had lacked that same agility or that his touch was less than exciting

"I guess I always thought that it was just that she didn't like sex," he admitted to himself. "Maybe they should have classes to teach men how to touch their wives." Then the thought hit him that what he was doing right now was just that, taking a class to teach him how to please his wife. "Huh," he thought. "And I thought it was just to teach her how to enjoy sex." Finally, it occurred to him that Dr. Summers was already aware of the epiphany that he had just had, and he relaxed, assured for the first time that he was doing the right thing.

JILLIAN

THIS TIME WHEN she awoke, Jillian didn't panic as she had before. She had come to the realization that she wasn't going to be harmed. However, now that she wasn't worried about her safety, she concentrated on her husband's. She didn't know what these people wanted with her. She couldn't fathom what they might have done with, or to, Joe. And she was very curious about the man who had rubbed and stroked her in such an intimate way. She was certain it had been the same man each time, but all she knew about him was that he had soft, strong hands.

"And he sure knows how to use them," ran through her mind, immediately causing her to blush, mortified that she could entertain such a thought. But she was nothing if not honest with her self and she had to admit that she had enjoyed the unfamiliar sensations coursing through her body very much.

"If only Joe . . ." she couldn't finish the thought. She began crying again, this time for her husband.

She couldn't imagine what might have happened to him. Her mind wandered then, back to the first time she'd ever seen him. He'd been on the dance floor with one of those cheerleader types, perky, thin, blonde. She hadn't been able to take her eyes off him, but she knew he was the type who would never even look at her.

He'd been the idol of everyone at the small mid-western teachers' college they had attended. He'd played football, of course. Not the quarterback. He'd always said he wasn't coordinated enough to throw the ball accurately or catch it, but he was solid enough to stop any one from getting to the quarterback, and fast enough to catch anyone from the opposing team with the audacity to try to run the ball across the goal line.

She hadn't known any of that until her roommate leaned over and whispered in her ear. All she knew was that he was everything she'd ever dreamed about. He was tall, considerably taller than her own five foot eight. His wavy sable hair begged for someone to run her fingers through it, with red highlights that shone even in the darkened room. His intense brown eyes were framed with long, almost black lashes that lay dark and soft on high cheekbones when he closed his eyes. Only his nose, broken by a baseball bat in a little league game several years before, kept him from being pretty.

She sighed. Until she'd met Dr. Summers, she'd never seen another man who was as handsome as her Joe. And he hadn't changed as she had. Oh, he'd gained a few pounds. Who hadn't? But coaching the different sports at the high school had kept him trim and in shape. And, at fifty, he still had almost all of his hair, albeit with some gray at the temples. Once she had seen him, even before they'd met, she'd known that there would never be another man for her. "God keep him safe," she whispered into the darkness. "Now he'll never know how much I love him," she cried silently inside her mind.

JOE

OE KEPT TRYING to do as the therapist told him, but his fingers wouldn't cooperate. He was used to the 'get a bigger hammer' theory of life. This subtle, intimately delicate manipulation was almost beyond him, but he refused to give up. "Do you really believe I can learn to do that?" he asked, watching the therapist 'walk' a quarter across the backs of her knuckles.

She laughed, nodded. "You'll be surprised what you can do." She took his hands, massaging the fingers, bending them back then curling them under. "Just keep working with your fingers like I'm doing," she instructed. "You'll get the hang of it eventually." She looked at the wall clock. "Oops, you'd better get going. I was supposed to get you back to Dr. Summers by nine." She shooed him out of her office.

He followed what he thought was the hallway to the control room, but realized he was turned around when he came to what looked like a Roman bath house. "Wow!" he said to himself, turning and walking in the other direction. He'd known that the facility was elaborate and luxurious, but his introduction hadn't included a visit to the marble and tile swimming pool.

Finding the proper hallway, he hurried down, knocking at the door to the control room and entering before anyone could answer. "Hi, Doc," he greeted Dr. Summers with his usual cheery attitude, although he wasn't sure if he should feel so cheery, considering the circumstances.

"You're looking pretty chipper," the doctor said, glancing up from the monitor. "And you got here just in time. She just woke up and you're on."

Joe glanced at the monitor. "Hey, she isn't tied up."

"She's still bound, just not spread eagle as she was. It's impossible for someone to get a good night's sleep without being able to turn over once in a while. Her hands and feet are bound to the head and foot of the bed. She still can't reach down far enough to remove her blindfold."

"Will she be able to fight me?" Joe asked, apprehensive at the idea he would have to subdue her.

"If you did your job right yesterday, she won't fight."

"Big if," Joe said as he opened the door, heading down the brief hallway to the room where his wife lay. He hesitated, took a deep breath, opened the door and slipped inside, closing it softly. Crossing the room slowly, he tried to remember everything he'd been instructed to do.

Once again he settled his bulk on the bed, his right hand extended over her belly. As soon as he touched the mattress, she tensed, rolling away from him as far as her bonds permitted. Before she could get all the way over, he rested his hand on her belly, pressing with enough force to arrest her movement, but not enough to harm her. She ended up flat on her back, exactly where he wanted her to be. He untangled the sheet with his other hand, removing it totally from her form. Gently he slid his hand up until it reached the folds of her garment, pushing the material aside enough to be able to rest his hand between her breasts.

He could feel her heart race, could feel the tension in her whole body, and almost stopped. It was all he could do not to run from the room, but he didn't. He knew she'd reacted yesterday, really felt something she'd never felt before, and he knew he could make that happen again. One more quick swallow and he was ready . . . he hoped.

He placed his left hand beside the right, moving both up over her shoulders and back down, pushing more of the satiny material from her as he went. When he brought his hands back down, he ran them lightly over her creamy breasts to her ribcage and back. His hands wandered beneath her breasts, but his thumbs strayed on the bottoms. Again he moved to her sternum. This time his hands traveled directly across her breasts, trapping her nipples and rolling them between thumbs and forefingers.

He heard her gasp, felt the rise of her chest as she involuntarily rose to meet his roving hands, felt the instinctive hardening of the nipples, and he smiled. "I can do this," he assured himself and moved his hands down over her belly, around her waist and under her back. Again and again he repeated the motions, remembering to return occasionally to tweak her nipples, caress her breasts. He watched his own hands hungrily, wishing he could trace the same route with his tongue, something he'd always wanted to do, but had never been permitted.

He was amazed when she began to writhe beneath his ministrations, pushing up against his hands, increasing the pressure. She moaned and he had to suck in his breath to keep himself from going off. He bit his lip, groaned, but kept his hands in motion, each pass over her belly moving lower on her body. When he reached that forbidden spot that he wanted so badly to caress, he moved past, massaging her legs as he had in the tub, finally nudging her knees apart and moving up the insides of her thighs.

She moaned, uttering incoherent sounds instead of words, twisting and squirming against the pressure of his hands. And he was in agony. He touched her center lightly, his fingers tracing up the opening, but becoming trapped when she slammed her legs closed, her gasp followed by a whimper. "That's it for now, Joe," the voice in his ear informed him. "Time to leave

He stood, pulling the silken fabric around her, trying to shut out her sobs, knowing exactly how frustrated she was. He pulled the sheet up over her body as he was supposed to, but couldn't resist running his finger over the upper curve of her breast one more time. "Come on, Joe," the voice in his ear insisted, and he turned and walked from the room.

JILLIAN

"*H*E'S BACK." JILLIAN was pulled out of her reverie by the weight on the side of the bed. She did as she thought she should, trying to roll away from him, but found herself trapped on her back by the strong, splayed hand on her belly. She found herself wondering if he would do whatever he had done before that had caused the wonderful sensations. Again she had to be honest. She was hoping he would do just that. She almost sighed with relief when his hands began roving her body, gasping when they strayed over her breasts and again when she felt her nipples being firmly squeezed.

"I'm a slut!" she thought, but that appellation didn't keep her from enjoying the feelings that followed the movement of the phantom hands or the instinctive swelling of her breasts and nipples. "Oh, my God!" she thought, then could think no more as her mind seemed to splinter into fireworks, colors she'd never before seen, music she'd never before heard. Heat she'd never felt before now assailed her body and she moaned with pleasure, moving upwards, into the fire.

Her body turned to putty, melting beneath his hands. She felt boneless, then made of steel, thrusting against his hands to intensify the pressure . . . and the pleasure. She couldn't hear the groans or grunts she made, didn't care at that moment. Her only focus was her burning body, now ablaze with a passion that was as foreign to her as any extraterrestrial could possibly be.

The hands moved to her legs, and, at first, she was unhappy that her breasts and belly were being neglected, but the fire followed the hands and she twisted to get nearer to them. She sighed when the hands returned to her nipples, ran down over her belly, cried out when they squeezed the inside of her upper thighs.

She felt the long fingers slip up against her most private inner being and she reacted as she had on every other occasion in her whole life. She closed her legs tightly together, trapping the fingers for a moment against her, the sensation so intense she thought she would die. She wanted nothing so much as to keep those fingers there, but her first instinct had been to restrict their movement, making them stop.

She waited, now not afraid for her life, only terrified that the man would leave before she had reached . . . what? What was it that she thought would happen? Weren't the sensations she'd been feeling everything everyone had described to her before? Everything she'd read about? Weren't they enough? Then why did she feel so empty when she felt the satiny wrap covering her body and the sheet pulled to her chin?

More confused than she had ever been in her life, she lay still, knowing that he had gone, wanting him to come back. Wanting more! But she knew it was too late and she wept in frustration, her quiet sobs carrying back to the control booth and to her husband.

JOE

*J*OE WAS ALMOST as frustrated as his wife when he returned to the control room. "I thought I had her," he told Dr. Summers.

"You did," he replied. "Up to a point. You've been married what? Twenty-five years? I think she just reacted the way she's been conditioned to for your whole married life. Right now, she's wishing she hadn't done that."

"You think?" Joe asked hopefully.

"Listen," he instructed, turning up the volume so Joe could hear his wife's muffled sobs. "She wanted what you were offering, Joe. But she wasn't quite ready for entry. That's going to take a little longer."

Joe listened to his wife crying, tearing up himself. "She sounds so sad," he said.

"She is," Dr. Summers assured him. "She almost grasped that one thing that's been absent from her marriage for the last twenty-five years, and she missed. Not because you did anything wrong, but because of her own preconceptions. She's coming to realize that her perceptions were wrong, but instinct took over. Believe me, the next time, she'll let you touch the untouchable."

"I sure hope you're right," Joe sighed.

"Trust me," Dr. Summers said. "I do have a pretty good idea what I'm talking about."

"Yeah, so far, you've been right about everything." He paused, looked at the hands clasped between his knees then up into the doctor's eyes. "Tell me, Doc. How the hell did you end up doing this?"

"Doing what, exactly?" the doctor chuckled. "You're doing all the work."

"Yeah? But if you weren't coaching me, I wouldn't have a clue what I'm supposed to be doing in there. Not to mention having Cheryl teach me how to make my hands more flexible." He grinned. "Can you do that?"

"What?"

"Walk a coin across the back of your fingers like some magician."

"You mean like this?" the doctor produced a quarter, seemingly from midair and proceeded to roll it back and forth over his knuckles a few times. Suddenly, the quarter wasn't there. He hadn't put it in his pocket, of that Joe was certain.

"Where'd it go?" he asked.

Dr. Summers held out his hand, the quarter in the middle of his palm. "It's a habit of mine," he admitted. "I always have one going when I'm by myself. Keeps my hands limber and my wife happy."

Joe let out a whoop. "And that's the whole secret?"

"Not hardly," Dr. Summers said. "Not even close. But it is helpful."

"Okay. I agree." He looked over at the monitor where the bed appeared, but not his wife. "Where is she?"

"She's being bathed. Not like the bath you gave her, though, and I'll bet she's wishing it were." He looked at his watch. "You'll have just enough time to feed her breakfast before your appointment with Janet."

"Janet? What's this one for?"

"Body wax."

"What?! Why?"

"You don't want your wife to catch on that it's you, do you? At least not yet. You're fairly hirsute and that's a real tip off. It'll be sure to confuse her if you don't have any body hair."

"But couldn't I just shave?"

"Daily? Stubble would give you away as much as if you hadn't done anything."

"It's gonna hurt, isn't it?"

Dr. Summers nodded. "Absolutely," he said, a wide smile following the pronouncement.

JILLIAN

SHE FELT CLEAN, shiny almost, but she wasn't sure she really was. How clean could she be when she could think of nothing but a man touching her? And a man who wasn't her husband, at that. She should feel guilty. She should feel dirty. She should be ashamed of the way she'd reacted to his touch. But she wasn't. She wasn't any of those things. She felt exalted, exhilarated. His touch set her on fire, enthralled her, made her body long for something she'd never known existed.

The only time she felt guilty was when she thought of her husband, darling, irresistible Joe. Her very own teddy bear and the love of her life. In every other way, she loved him with every fiber of her being. She couldn't think of anything else that she lacked for, or anything he wouldn't do for her. Enduring sex had been a small price to pay for the life they'd had together. "If only I'd known," she said to herself. "Our time together has been wonderful, but I could have made it so much better for both of us if I'd only known." Then she thought it out a little further. "If only he'd known, I should say. If he had made me feel like this, it would have been so much better."

Again she felt a pang of guilt. "Poor Joe," she thought. "What if they hurt him when they kidnapped me? What if I never see him again?" She couldn't imagine a life without him, didn't want to. "I'd give up any of these sensations for just one more look at him," she sighed.

She didn't have time for more thought. Seated once again in the wide comfortable chair, she felt the man touch her, stroking her throat, teasing her lips. A small bite of French toast slipped between her lips, and she chased a drop of syrup with her tongue. A few bites, and the hands once again roamed her body. No amount of guilt could stop the shudders that rippled through her, the heat rising deep within her. She lost any appetite for food and had to be coaxed into taking the next bite, reluctant for his hands to do anything but explore her body.

This time, he eased aside the garment, capturing her breasts, hefting them in his hands, teasing them with his thumbs. She almost cried when he stopped in order to offer her another bite of food. It seemed to take forever for her to eat. She was torn between trying to finish quickly so his hands would be free, and wanting to eat very slowly to keep him there in front of her.

One last sip of orange juice, once more licking her lips, she gasped when he gripped her knees, spreading them so that his legs were both between hers. She felt the cloth of his trousers against her thighs. "Linen," she thought. "Not Joe. He never wears anything but jeans . . . or sweats." Then she couldn't think as his hands ran up inside the drapery that covered her, sweeping it aside. Again he pressed against her abdomen, his thumbs moving in circles, his hands holding her transfixed. Then a single thumb caressed the opening, widening her, teasing her.

"Oh, Lord," she said aloud. "Please!" She was crying, pushing against his thumb, her hips thrusting toward him, inhibited from moving further by his knees. She felt his thumb inside her, circling, searching and, "Oh, my God!", finding. Deeper inside, a finger reached the very center of her being, flexed within her and she exploded. She couldn't have talked if she'd wanted to. Her guttural sounds resembled no known language. The continuous "na . . . na . . . na . . ." emitting from her turned into a deep cry of fulfillment, of completion. Too low to be a scream, too sustained to be anything else, the sound was torn from her. She was transfixed on the electric probing of his finger, on the insistent circling of his thumb. Every fiber of her being tensed, every cell in her body went rigid with the most exquisite, wonderful, indescribable feeling possible.

She collapsed against the back of the chair, unable to move, totally boneless, gasping for breath, a secret smile forming on her full red lips.

JOE

BREAKFAST WAS AGAIN one of her favorite foods, already cut into bite-sized pieces so he could concentrate on seducing her while he was feeding her. Joe didn't know which to do first, so he took her throat in his left hand, his thumb on one side of her jaw, his fingers on the other. He caressed her, wishing he could kiss where his hands traced. He touched her lips, offering her the bite of French toast before touching her anywhere else, sucking in a breath when she delicately licked a drop of syrup off her lip.

Between bites, he set down the fork, his hands reaching inside the folds of her garment to take her luscious, full breasts in his hands, running his thumbs across her nipples, teasing them into erection, her breasts becoming fuller as he held them. The next bite and he moved around her ribs, tickling the sides of her breasts with his knuckles, moving farther down her sides. And so it went, after each bite another touch, another groan, another shudder, but now she wasn't the only one who groaned.

Finished with her breakfast, he moved his chair until he was directly in front of her, scooting forward as he pressed her knees apart, his own knees within inches of the very center of his life's companion. He grasped her hips, pulling her gently toward him, his hand low on her abdomen as he worked his thumb down into her very essence. That she didn't try to keep him away surprised him. That she was moist and ready astounded him.

He found the tiny nub that he'd been told about and circled it with his thumb, watching her face transform from lovely to ethereal as she climbed heights she'd never before dreamed of. He was heady with success, knowing that, finally, he had found how to give her some small part of the pleasure that she had always given him. Slick with her liquid response, his right finger slipped deep inside, touching her core, tipping her over the edge, her whole body rigid with her climax.

"Shit!" he swore, trying and failing to hold back the fiery spurt of his own fulfillment, his own body as rigid as that of his wife before him.

She collapsed against the back of the chair, panting heavily, totally unaware of the man who struggled to rise from between her legs and flee the room. He closed the bedroom door and leaned against it, gasping for air. When at last he managed to get himself under control, he hurried across the hall to his own room, into the bathroom to cleanse himself, disgusted with himself yet elated with what he had been able to bring to her.

He was just pulling up a clean pair of trousers when he heard the knock, zipping his pants as the door opened and Dr. Summers leaned around. "Mind if I come in?" he asked mildly, but the twinkle of amusement in his eyes told Joe that he was very aware of his humiliation. "Don't worry about it, Joe," the doctor said. "It does happen from time to time."

"Not to me," Joe shook his head, turning to pull his belt from his soiled trousers and thread it through the loops of the new ones. "I'm a teacher, Doc. What do you think would happen if I went off like a rocket every time one of my lovely students rubbed against me?"

"I suspect they don't even give you a hard on," Dr. Summers told him.

Joe jerked his head around, his wide brown eyes growing even wider, then squinting at the man before him. "How'd you know?" he asked.

"When a man is as devoted to one woman as you are to Jillian, he usually only has eyes, and erections, for her."

Joe chuckled. "You're right," he admitted. "And I can't be around her without wanting to be inside her. Sounds pretty crude, doesn't it."

"Not really. She's obviously what turns you on." He sat on the arm of the chair, crossing his arms. "How'd you meet?" he asked.

Joe sat on the corner of the bed before answering. "I saw her at a dance, but we didn't get to talk," he said. "I was with another girl and she was with a group of friends. It was all I could do not to leave my date standing in the middle of the dance floor and grab her. She was the most beautiful thing I'd ever seen." He looked the doctor in the eye and added, "She was so tall and graceful, and she had that long elegant neck, not to mention that she had great boobs. Anyway, the next day I asked around and found out that she ran every morning, so I staked out the track, waited until she passed then ran up behind her.

"I wasn't sure what she'd say, so I just jogged beside her. Ten times around the track! I could barely breathe and she was barely panting. She smiled at me, asked me if I wanted to sprint and took off like a deer." He grinned. "I'm fast, Doc. That's why I got a football scholarship. But I couldn't catch her. Wasn't even close. She waited until I dragged myself back to the starting point, handed me a piece of paper with her phone number and name and ran off toward the dorms."

"Most men would be put off by a woman who could beat them like that," Dr. Summers pointed out.

"Nah," Joe replied. "I was totally in awe of her, and not just her speed. We started running together every morning and I just got better and better on the field. And we studied together nights. She was good for me, really good. Poor thing. All I could think of was how to get into her pants."

"So you married her?"

"She was just a sophomore then. I was a junior. She wanted to finish college, and so did I, so we waited until after we'd both graduated. Instead, I bought a case of condoms and had a high old time, but I don't think she ever had an orgasm. No, I know she didn't. She allowed me to have my way with her because she loved me, but she never enjoyed it.

Not once. At the time, I didn't give a damn. Now, I want her to enjoy it as much as I do."

"I think you've just given her the first taste of what sex can really be like," Dr. Summers told him.

"It sure would've been better if I'd known how twenty-five years ago," Joe admitted. "Now if I can only get myself under control."

"We'll address that problem when you come back. Right now you have an appointment to keep." He stood, opened the door and waited for Joe to pass through, followed. "It should take you a couple of hours," he said. "I'll meet you back here around twelve-thirty. You can feed her lunch. How's that sound?"

Joe thought back to breakfast and his heart rate accelerated. "Do you think I can get a repeat performance from her?"

"I would certainly hope so. Right now, she's probably thinking of nothing else."

JILLIAN

"**W**HAT THE HELL happened just now?" Jillian asked herself when her mind cleared enough for thought to squeeze in. "How wonderful! How perfectly obscene!" Her mind was in a frenzy of thought. "What would my children say if they had any idea?" she asked herself, then laughed. "They'd probably say 'way to go, Mom'." But she couldn't help the guilt that crowded in among her other thoughts. "What about Joe?" she asked herself.

"There's nothing you can do about Joe right now," she told herself. "Whatever has happened, you can't do anything about it. You can't even go to the bathroom by yourself!"

"But you don't have to enjoy yourself so much," her alter ego insisted.

"Why the hell not," she said to herself angrily. "If I have to be here, trussed up like a pig, I might as well enjoy whatever they have to offer. The food's great, I don't have anything that has to be done. All I have to do is lie here and wait for a man to give me pleasure. Just how hard is that?"

"Yeah," she argued with herself. "But what's going to happen when he fucks you?" And that scared her, terrified her. What was going to happen when the man lay on her all sweaty and heavy? What would she do when he spread her legs and thrust into her, groaning and grunting? She was sure it wouldn't be as pleasant as his hands had been. Couldn't be. Nothing could be that wonderful. Nothing in her life had made her feel that fantastic.

"Oh, yeah? What about the kids?" she argued with herself.

"They're brilliant! Great! I love them with my whole heart, just as I love Joe." But nothing, no one, had ever made her feel like fireworks were going off inside her. She was still stunned from the tremendous surge of electricity that had shaken her to her core.

She fought with herself until she could think of nothing else to say. The only thing that ran through her mind like a broken record was, "please. Please. Come back and make me feel like that one more time."

JOE

*H*E SAT GINGERLY on the sofa, waiting until Janet called him into her office. He had to admit he wasn't looking forward to what awaited him in there. He'd heard about wax jobs: bikini waxes, eyebrow waxes. Jillian had had both, several times. It certainly couldn't be as tough as he anticipated. Could it?

By the time Janet called him in, he was fine with the whole idea and sure he could endure whatever she came up with. On the other hand, she took one look at him and laughed. "I think we're going to need help," she said. She went to the door, called to the woman across the hall. "Joan can you help me with my next appointment," she said. "And could you ask Mary or Tracey to come in with you. As a matter of fact, bring them both."

While Joan gathered the other two, Janet led Joe into the treatment room, telling him to strip down to his skivvies. "I'd give you a gown to put on, but we'd just have to take it off. As it is, you'll have to

59

lose the underwear at some point, but you can keep them for now."

Joe didn't know exactly how he was supposed to react to that news. He didn't feel comfortable surrounded by three, no four, women when he was wearing nothing but his underwear. However, he kept reminding himself that he was doing this for Jillian, so he did as directed, hopping up on the table and lying on his back, waiting.

He didn't have long to wait. The four women descended on him en masse, giggling like schoolgirls when they saw his six foot four inch bulk covered in coarse dark hair. "This is going to be fun," one of them said. Warm wax was spread swiftly over his chest by one of the women while another slathered it on his right leg and still another worked on his left.

"That's hot," he complained, squirming.

"It'll cool soon enough," Janet assured him. "Is this your first time?"

"Yeah," he answered. "Usually it's my wife who gets your kind of treatment." He watched the fourth woman hand pieces of what looked like cheesecloth to each of the other three. "What's that for?" he asked.

They broke into gales of laughter as they smoothed the cloth over, and into, the hot wax. "As the wax cools, the fibers become embedded on this side, your hair on the other. When we pull the cloth up, everything else comes with it."

"I get it," he said.

"Not yet," she replied. "But you will." She looked at the other two and said, "On the count of three." When they nodded she started counting. "One, two, three." And all three of them ripped up the cloth, wax and body hair at once."

Joe's breath sucked in with a whoosh, came out with a yelp that could be heard on the next floor. "What the hell?"

But he was talking to himself as the four women repeated the performance, applying a second, heavy layer of wax over another portion of his anatomy. "Hold still, please," Janet cautioned him.

"I'm trying to," he growled through gritted teeth.

This time they didn't wait for each other, each one pulling up the cloth as the wax cooled, moving with practiced ease. And he watched, held his breath, panted, cried, cursed and wriggled away from each application of hot wax. When he thought he could take no more, Janet lowered his underwear, leaving him only with the hair immediately around his genitals.

"Turn over," she told him, a smirk on her face at his discomfiture.

"You're loving every minute of this, aren't you?" he asked as he rolled to his now denuded stomach.

"Oh, yes," she answered, not pausing in the application of wax.

"Why?"

"Why what?"

"Why are you enjoying causing me pain? Ouch!"

"You said your wife gets a bikini wax, didn't you?"

"Yes. Ouch! Damn!"

"Did you ever think about how hard it was on her when she was going through all of that just to look pretty for you?"

"Ouch!" Panting, he swore, not bothering to try to keep it under his breath any more. "No, you're right. Ouch! Oh! Shit! It never occurred to me . . . Ow!"

"Next time you'll think about it, and maybe you'll appreciate it more."

"If I tell you that the only reason I'm doing this . . . Ow! . . . is for her . . . Ouch! . . . would you go easier on me? Shit!!!!!!"

"There's no way to make this any easier."

"There isn't?"

"Nope. The only thing we can do is go as fast as we can and get it over with as soon as we can."

Joe gritted his teeth, trying to keep quiet, trying to be 'manly' and not cry out again, but he gave up. In the end he educated them in the use of words none of the women had ever heard before. "Sorry," he apologized for the umpteenth time.

"No need to be sorry," Janet assured him. "We've all had waxes before. We know how it feels. We just haven't had to have it all over our bodies like this." She lowered his briefs and two of them began applying the wax across his buttocks. "Hang on," she told him, yanking without giving him time to do as she instructed.

By the time the four women were done with him, he felt as though he had third degree burns all over his body, his skin was screaming and his ego was in the gutter. The cream they applied wasn't nearly enough to assuage the pain. And they weren't through with him yet. Each of them took a different quadrant, poring over him with magnifying glasses, plucking wayward hairs that had managed to stay rooted through the entire process.

"All done," Janet told him, pulling his briefs back over his sore ass and patting them in place. "Dr. Summers is waiting for you. You'd better hurry and get dressed." She and the others giggled their way out of the room while he pried his reluctant body off the table and began the slow process of putting his clothes back on.

"That was the most painful, most demeaning thing I've ever had to endure," he told the doctor when he returned to the control room.

"I have no doubt that, for you, that's true. But I assure you it isn't nearly as painful or as embarrassing as what a woman goes through to bring a new life into the world. Especially a woman as shy about her body as your wife." His grin didn't lessen the impact of what he was saying. "Teaching her to enjoy sex is just a small part of it. Teaching her not to be shy about her body is going to take much more time."

"I don't think there's ever going to be enough time for that," Joe said, shaking his head. "She's always thought something was wrong with the way she looked and nothing I've ever said has been able to make her think different."

"What doesn't she like about the way she looks?"

"She thinks she's too tall, too gangly. She doesn't like her hair, hates that she has to wear contacts, although she says they're better than glasses." He sighed, lowered himself into a chair, rubbed his face. "I think she's beautiful, Doc. I love her neck. It's like that statue of Nefertiti, long and slender and regal. And I love that she's so tall. I don't have to lean over so far when we dance."

Dr. Summers chuckled. "I have an uncle who is six three. His wife is almost five feet tall, if she stands on her toes. He's always said he doesn't dance because he gets a crick in his neck bending over so far."

Joe laughed along with the doctor, forgetting, for the moment, about the torture he had endured a short time before. Forgetting the other things his wife didn't like about herself. Things that he loved. He glanced at the screen. "What's she doing?" he asked.

"We put her on a treadmill for thirty minutes. She just finished and they're bringing her back to the room. She should be ready for lunch in a couple of minutes."

"She's gonna smell that lotion those women put all over me," Joe said, wondering if he should take a shower before going into the bedroom.

"Not really," Dr. Summers told him. "They applied something quite similar after her bath, so she won't know what she's smelling."

"You guys really think of everything, don't you?"

"We've had a little practice. Every patient teaches us something, too." He stood, retrieved the tray beside the door and thrust into Joe's hands."

JILLIAN

*O*NCE AGAIN JILLIAN found herself pulled to her feet and led from the chair, still blindfolded and shackled, still unable to hear anything but the music piped through the earbuds. Traveling much farther this time, she was stopped, undressed and led forward, her foot nudged to step upwards. Recognizing the treaded belt of the treadmill, she automatically began walking even as her wrists restraints were attached to the bars. While she was mortified to think that she was being forced to use the exercise machine in the nude, she tried not to dwell on it, realizing she had absolutely no control over the circumstances. "I need the exercise," she told herself, but couldn't help but pray that her attendants were all female.

As she walked, she found her feet keeping time with the music streaming in her ears and it became mechanical, an action that required little or no thought on her part. The heat from lights she couldn't see, made her realize they might be sun lamps and that, for the first time in her life she was going to have an even, all over tan.

Her mind wandered over all that had happened since she'd awakened, bound hand and foot and naked as the day she was born. "Why?" was the question that resounded through her mind, followed closely by "Who?"

She couldn't fathom a reason for her captivity beyond that of white slavery, but everything she'd ever heard or read about the black market selling of women had talked about young women, most only in their early teens. She'd never heard of a woman her age being abducted to become someone's sex slave. Even the term made her blush, but, again, she had to be honest with herself. That was exactly what this man was training her to be . . . a slave to his sexual urges. And if she were brutally honest with herself, she had to admit that she liked what this man had done to her. She looked forward to his touch, wanted, no, craved it. She couldn't believe she had become so wanton, and in such a short time.

"What's the matter with me?" she asked herself. "How could I have changed so much so rapidly?" The answer was simple. There was nothing the matter with her. She was enjoying something that she should have been able to enjoy for the last twenty-five years. "Make that twenty-eight," she thought, for she had been with Joe for three years before they were married.

Her mind took a branch in the path, turning now to her husband. He'd been gentle, loving, kind. There had never been a day she hadn't adored him from the first time she'd seen him. "But," she thought. But he'd never done to her what this man was doing, never wrenched the sounds from her that she was sure she was making although she'd not been able to hear them. He'd never set her on fire and made her want to burn. Why not?

"Because he doesn't know how," she admitted, finally. "Poor Joe. What would he do if he knew how my body reacts to this man?" This was the single question to which she was sure she knew the answer. He'd be furious. And why wouldn't he? She'd never responded to him as she did to this man, a man she'd never seen or heard, a man she'd never touched, had no idea what he looked like. And he'd have every right to be angry, she admitted to herself.

"Why?" her alter ego demanded. "When he can't make me beg for his touch, what right does he have to resent someone who can?"

"Oh, my God," she sighed. "I'm finding excuses for my total lack of propriety."

"Propriety my ass," she countered to herself. "I've been imprisoned, locked up, tied up. I can't see, can't hear. I'm walking a treadmill naked. Hell, I can't even wipe my own ass. What choice do I have but to accept what this man demands from me?"

"You don't have to like it," she told herself, but even as the thought zipped through her mind she rejected it. She couldn't stop this man, but, since she had to endure his ministrations, she was damn well going to enjoy them.

Once she allowed herself to accept that premise, she returned once again to the question of why, but try as she might, she could come up with no answer. She was still pondering the question when the machine slowed and stopped. She felt the soft fabric once again covering her body and her arms lowered. She was turned around and led away, but not to the bed.

Instead, she found herself straddling a low padded bench, her arms and legs fettered by some kind of line that ran beneath it, allowing her some restricted movement, albeit limited. She found she could raise her hands almost to the level of her waist and leaned to see if she could reach the blindfold, but was stopped by a hand cupping her chin.

"It's him!" she exulted, waiting expectantly, breathless with anticipation. The hand raised her head until she was erect, stroking her jaw as it released her. She held herself rigid, the suspense building, her body eagerly awaiting his touch. When it came, it was his finger on her lip, tracing her mouth, signaling her to open her mouth. She wasn't hungry! She wanted him to touch her. Didn't he know that? But she dutifully opened her mouth, surprised when the finger slid between her parted lips, past her teeth, teasing her tongue. "Oh!" she said aloud, although she wasn't aware of the sound. She sucked on the proffered digit, gently circling it with her tongue.

Never before, in her whole existence had she considered something like that to be erotic, but she could feel her nipples hardening and her breath coming in short gasps. She felt like crying when he pulled away, returning only with a spoonful of tasty cream of broccoli soup. She didn't care about the soup, didn't want to be fed. She wanted him to pet her, caress her, touch her. Instead she took the soup, sucked it from the spoon, licked her lips for the last drop.

Much as she wanted his touch, what she got was lunch until the very last morsel had been consumed. As the minutes passed with no more food, no touching, nothing, she began to mourn his absence, weeping silently, head bent. Her relief had no bounds when she felt the slight shift in the balance of the bench, felt his breath on the back of her neck, his hands resting lightly on her arms. Even more slowly than before, he moved his hands over her arms, his fingertips drawing lines of fire and ice from shoulder to elbow, from elbow to wrist.

She realized that he also straddled the bench when he pulled her shoulders back, her arms almost behind her, and placed her hands palms down on his thighs. It was the first time he had allowed her to touch him, and, even though it was through the rough cloth of his pants, it gave her a thrill of discovery to feel the heavy muscles of his leg, tense and hard beneath her hand.

As she tentatively explored the tops of his thighs, she was gratified to feel his hands sliding inside her loose garment, and she arched her back presenting her swollen breasts for his caress. She found herself lying against his chest, her garment falling from her body as his hands explored her chest and abdomen, caressed her belly. She groaned, sighed, pushed her belly against his hands, ground her groin against them.

It took a few minutes before she realized his lips were moving down her neck, across her shoulders, returning to just beneath her ear, his coarse whiskers tickling her. How wonderful, she thought, giving herself to this new sensation. She could feel the tip of his tongue scoring a fiery trail down her neck, and his teeth nipping gently on the ridge of her shoulder. She shuddered, raised her shoulder to give him better access, moaned with pleasure.

There were so many wonderful sensations, she couldn't keep track of them all, and so lost herself, not thinking, not worrying, allowing her body to respond when her mind was unable to do so. When he pulled her back against him, electricity surged through her and she gripped his thighs ferociously, then curled her hands, balling the fabric of his pants in her tight fists. She could feel his big body through the material of his shirt, could feel his belt dig into her back, could feel his stiffened penis against her buttocks. She knew she should've been disgusted, wasn't, didn't care. She reached as far back as her bonds allowed, just able to caress him through his linen pants, her fingers tracing the length of his erection.

She wasn't aware of the effect her own hands had on the man behind her, only that his hands were sending her heavenward, her heart racing, her breath coming in great gasps. When he leaned toward her, pushing her forward, her fingers lost contact, but she was unaware because her mind had turned to mush. When he grasped her thighs, he forced them even farther apart than they had been, kneading the inside of her legs, bending her forward until he could reach her knees, running his hands up until they were one over the other at her apex. He tightened his hold, his wonderful hands hard upon her, his fingers teasing her into a frenzy.

She was lost again, pushed beyond thought, beyond caring. Her hips bucked against his hand. With no idea of what she did, she opened her legs even further, inviting him inside, wanting him, begging him. And then he was there, his fingers widening her, entering her, holding her in the throes of ecstasy until she could barely breathe. Her body stiffened beyond endurance, the muscles contracting inside, drawing him in farther, holding him captive, rigid and tense.

And, finally, boneless, she collapsed against him, panting and weeping, unable to articulate the wonder she felt, the rapture that engulfed her. She barely realized what was happening when he slid from behind her, laying her gently full length on the bench, covering her once again. By the time her mind would focus, was able to formulate a thought, she realized he was gone.

JOE

*J*OE BARELY GOT into the room in time to stop Jillian from getting her hands on her blindfold, almost spilling the tray in his rush. But as soon as his hand cupped her chin it was obvious that she had been waiting for him. There was no resistance when he raised her head, bringing her back straight and presenting her breasts in the most appealing way.

He touched her voluptuous lower lip, intent only on having her open her mouth so he could feed her lunch, but he succumbed to temptation, tracing the delectable bow of her upper lip, returning where he'd started only to find she had opened her mouth. Without thinking, he slipped his finger into her mouth, touching her teeth, teasing her tongue. His surprise was matched only by his excitement when she took the digit further, sucking on it and licking it with abandon. It was all he could do to follow the instructions in his earpiece and simply feed her without any more foreplay.

He nodded to the camera, acknowledging that he'd understood and would behave, but it took all his will power to do what Dr. Summers was telling him. He managed to get himself under control enough to finish feeding Jillian her lunch, but every time she licked her lips or leaned forward, mouth half open in anticipation, he grew more and more excited, until he needed to leave the room, visit the bathroom and relieve himself before he could finish the session.

"This just isn't right," he said aloud, knowing Dr. Summers would hear what he said. Thinking of the seductive woman waiting for him across the hall, he elaborated, "She's ready, willing and able, and here I am whacking off."

"She's not ready yet, Joe," came the answer. "Remember. We add one little thing at a time. This time it will be using a little oral stimulation on her neck and shoulders. Next time you'll take that a little farther. Once she's accepted that, she'll be ready to accept you. Give her more time."

Joe reluctantly nodded in agreement, walking back across the hall and slipping inside. He didn't touch her until he was seated astraddle behind her, but he could see that she sensed he was there. He blew gently on the back of her neck not only stirring her hair, but making the tiny hairs on the nape of her neck stand up. He could feel her tensing,

He did as he'd been instructed, rubbing her arms, tickling them with his fingertips. He pulled her shoulders back so he could bring her hands down on top of his thighs, groaning in his own torment when she kneaded his muscles in return. Smoothing aside her garment, allowing it to fall wherever, he did something he'd always wanted to, he licked her magnificent neck, nipping her shoulder, his hands working her over, stroking, patting, kneading, caressing, pinching.

He was going through his own kind of hell while he seduced his lovely wife, because, although he'd already taken care of himself, he found he was hard once more, even harder than he had been before. When Jillian grabbed the muscles of his thigh, then bunched his pants in her fists, he thought he would lose it all over again, and he almost did when her strong, slender fingers reached back and found him. He leaned forward, forcing her to bend away from him, her hand losing contact and, with a sigh of relief, he began to stroke her from her knees up, sometimes tickling with fingertips, sometimes tightening his large hands around her thighs, finally putting his left hand over his right at the threshold of her very being. He tightened his hold, rocking her against him, maintaining pressure until she was begging him for more.

When he finally took her, entering her, impaling her on his long, thick finger, she was pleading with him, groaning and crying. Her hips ground against his hands, her chest heaved, her breath coming in great gasps and he could only hold onto her, keeping her from knocking them both from the bench. The rigidity of her orgasm was matched by her vaginal spasms as those muscles sucked at his finger, holding him within until she reached total fulfillment.

When she collapsed against him, he did the unthinkable for the second time. His own orgasm was not nearly as satisfying as hers, but was every bit as uncontrolled. Once her breathing seemed to settle and her heart rate slowed, he eased himself from under her, lowering her to the bench and returning to his own room.

Dr. Summers was again waiting for him when he came out of the bathroom. "We're going to have to buy you some more clothes," he joked. "At this rate you're going to use up all we have in a day or two."

"Damn it, Doc. It isn't funny! I've never gone off in my pants before. At least not since I was a kid. I can't believe I don't have more control than this."

"It's really very normal, Joe," Dr. Summers assured him.

"Not for me!"

"We've already discussed this, you know," the doctor told him. "For whatever it's worth, you need to understand what's happening. This is as good a time as any to discuss it. Get some clothes on and meet me in the control room." He flicked a wave, closing the door silently behind him.

It was a good ten minutes before Joe was able to calm down enough to follow the doctor to the control room, knocking politely before entering. He sat heavily, his elbows on his knees, chin on his knuckles. "I'm sorry, Doc," Joe said. "I know what you're going to say. I'm just very disgusted with myself."

"I'll bet this hasn't happened since you were fifteen," Dr. Summers said.

"Thirteen," Joe admitted. "After that I found out that it was much more satisfying with a partner."

"Do you understand why it's happening now?"

"Of course I do," Joe answered. "She's always turned me on. Always had me hard and ready to go in one second flat. Now that she's ready to go to, I'm having trouble because it's that much more exciting. Jesus, Doc. She's a keg of dynamite and when she blows . . . well, she takes everything nearby with her."

Dr. Summers chuckled. "Very apt," he said. "I couldn't have said it better myself. I'm glad you understand."

"Isn't there anything I can do to slow it down? How about a cock ring?"

"That'll help you maintain an erection, but won't stop you from ejaculation," the doctor advised. "You don't really need that kind of help. And the things they use for premature ejaculation aren't really called for here. Actually, it's just as well you go right on as you are. Maybe we'll add some Trojans though, so you don't soil the rest of your trousers."

Joe's look of utter dismay made the doctor laugh once again. "It's not as bad as it sounds," he assured him.

"I know what it's like, Doc," he said. "I just haven't had to use them for a long time." He shrugged. "Oh, well," he said. Taking a deep breath, he brightened. "Did you watch her?" he asked.

Nodding slowly, the doctor replied. "And you. You have trouble following directions, don't you?"

"Not usually," he answered. "It's just that she's so . . . sexy. No, it's more than that. It's . . ."

"I *do* understand," Dr. Summers assured him. "But you don't want to foil the whole thing by moving too fast, do you?"

"No, of course not."

"Then, when I tell you to do something, you really should do just what I tell you." He said it with a smile, his head tilted to one side, friendly, calm, but Joe got the message loud and clear.

"Yessir," he agreed with a sheepish grin and a nod. He almost saluted, but decided that would be too playful and he wanted the doctor to know that he was really taking everything seriously.

"One of the things you are going to have to work on, even after this is all over and you and Jillian are on your own, is to slow down. Be patient. Take your time, because that's how you're going to be able to keep her wanting what you have to offer."

"You mean I'll have to keep up everything I'm doing right now?" Joe asked, sure he'd heard wrong.

"Absolutely," Dr. Summers told him. "It's not that she doesn't like sex, Joe. That should be obvious already. It's that you've never taken the time to excite her to the point that she really wants it."

"So it's all my fault?" Joe exploded, at once dismayed and overcome by feelings of guilt that he couldn't accept.

"There's no fault here," Dr. Summers said, trying to calm the man.

"But you just said . . ."

"I said that she's a very sexy lady who needs lot of foreplay."

"Oh." Joe thought about it long and hard before asking his next question. "But we could have had a lot more satisfying sex life if I'd been more patient?"

The doctor nodded, trying to help Joe reach all the right conclusions for himself.

"And what I've been doing is all part of that?"

Another nod.

"And not being able to control myself is a part of it, too, isn't it?"

Instead of answering directly, Dr. Summers asked another question. "When you do make love, what, exactly do you do?"

"What'd you mean?"

"Do you caress her? Touch her? Warm her up?"

"Uh . . . no, not usually."

"Then, what?"

"I ask, she says okay and we have sex." Joe's answer was an eye opener for himself. He thought about it for a minute and came up with the answer for himself. "Shit," he said. "I don't have any control because I've never needed it. And she's never had an orgasm because I've never given her time to. Right?"

"You've already answered your own questions, haven't you?"

"And this whole charade," he spread his arms to include the monitors and the whole control room. "This isn't for her, is it?"

"On the contrary," Dr. Summers disagreed. "It's for both of you. You're both conditioned to what you've been doing for the last twenty-five years. This is the easiest way to break those habits. Aren't you enjoying yourself? Isn't it satisfying for you to be able to bring her to orgasm? Don't you want to be able to do that when this month is over?"

"Yes, yes and yes," Joe nodded. "I can't say I've ever enjoyed anything quite as much. It's every bit as exciting for me as it is for her and I do want to be able to keep it up once we're home." He was quiet for a few minutes while he watched the monitors, keeping an eye on his lovely wife as she was once again put into bed. He finally reached the conclusion that the doctor had hoped for. "Okay. So how do I go about teaching myself to have more control?"

"It's not quite that easy to explain," the doctor said. "It's really a matter of mind over matter. Meditation would certainly help. And you have to concentrate on it while, at the same time, you have to continue exciting your wife. Sometimes it's a matter of concentrating on something else, something that will turn you off. It's pretty much something that no one can help you with, except make you aware of it."

"You mean there's no easy way, like a pill or something?" Joe asked with a throaty chuckle.

"Sorry," Dr. Summers said with a wry smile. "I can give you some exercises to do that will help, but that's about it."

"I'm a coach, Doc. I do exercises every day."

"I'm sure you do," Dr. Summers said agreeably. "But you might want to try some new ones. We'll work on meditating, it's not that difficult. And you can join me in the gym tomorrow morning. We'll go over some that might help."

"Sure, Doc. What time?"

"I'll be at your room about 5:45."

"Whew, that's pretty early," Joe said.

"Well, I have to get in my exercises before I start my rounds, so they're usually pretty early. There are a few others who do them with me and most of them start the day pretty early, too, so we meet at 6:00 AM."

"I'll be ready," Joe told him. "Now, what about the rest of the today? When do I get to go back in there?" He nodded toward the monitors.

"Not until dinner time," Dr. Winters told him. "Meantime, there are a few other people you need to meet."

"Can't be worse than the body wax," Joe laughed.

"Well . . ."

"Don't tell me," Joe laughed. "I don't want to know.

JILLIAN

*J*ILLIAN LAY, STRETCHED out on the bench, trying desperately to catch her breath, unable to draw in enough air in a single gasp to fill her lungs, panting. "Lord," she thought to herself. "I don't think I'll ever be able to close my legs again. I'm not sure I want to! What a wonderful, glorious sensation!" For the first time, she understood what her girlfriends had been trying to tell her. For the first time, she understood why they looked forward to sex with such eagerness. And she really hadn't had sex yet, had she?

Her mind flew in several different directions at once, but the undercurrent of sexual fulfillment was always there, just beneath the surface. Suddenly, a thought occurred to her that had escaped her notice while she'd been being so thoroughly seduced. It had to be Joe! She couldn't have explained why she thought that. The clothes were different, his hands soft and supple, even the smell was different, but she was sure in her heart that it had been her Joe.

"Don't be silly," her alter ego reprimanded her. "He wouldn't have a clue how to do what this man is doing to you."

But very few men were as big as Joe. And, when she'd leaned against his chest, she'd known that this man was every bit as large, his arms as long, his hands as huge. But the hair that had brushed her cheek when he'd leaned over her had been short and spiky, not long and soft like Joe's, and Joe had never had a mustache.

"So what? He could've cut his hair," she argued with herself. "And he could've had a manicure. And the only reason he doesn't have a beard is because he shaves, sometimes twice a day." She tried to convince herself that this man and the man she had slept with for the last twenty-five years were one and the same. But finally, when she could breathe again and her heart rate had returned to normal, she gave up pretending that the man who had so successfully seduced her in so short a time was the same man she had cherished for so long.

"If it were my Joe, he wouldn't need this elaborate hoax. All he'd have to do is make love to me like this man has been doing," she told herself. But honesty was one of her strongest qualities and she had to admit that even that wouldn't have worked. "I'd wonder what he'd been doing and who he'd been sleeping with," she thought. "He couldn't change that radically overnight."

With that final thought, she sighed and sat up, intent on trying once again to reach the blindfold with her bound hands. But, as though rising had been a signal to her handlers, her hands were gripped, her legs released and she was lifted from the bench and returned to the bed.

JOE

*I*T HAD BEEN a long night for Joe, even though he'd gone to bed early. He hadn't been able to fall asleep immediately and had given up and turned on the bedside lamp. He retrieved the thick manual that Dr. Summers had given him and turned to the page he'd earmarked earlier. "Does he really expect me to remember all of this?" he asked himself, going over again the things he had been supposed to do the first two days. He was relieved to see that he hadn't forgotten to do any of those things and turned to those for day three. He smiled when he saw that he would be expected to introduce much more oral stimulation, but found the descriptions way beyond what he had foreseen or even imagined.

He fell asleep sitting against the headboard with the manual open in his lap and he barely moved all night except to scoot to a prone position. He was startled by the repeated beeps of his watch alarm, alerting him to the start of another day. He dragged himself into the bathroom, took care of his morning duties and dressed in sweats for the morning exercise session. He'd just finished when Dr. Summers knocked on his door.

"Ready?" Dr. Summers' smile was firmly in place, although Joe wasn't certain whether he was smiling at him or laughing at him.

"Guess so," Joe agreed, following the doctor down a maze of hallways and into a full size gymnasium where more than a hundred other people waited. "Holy shit," Joe said, looking around at the men and women who leaned and stretched, limbering up for their daily routine. "I didn't realize there would be this many others," he said.

"Much as I would love to tell you that this is just for you, it'd be a lie," Dr. Summers chuckled. "We do this every morning."

"Who are all these people?"

"Some are patients just like you. Some are staff members. And some are members of my family." He looked over his shoulder, smiled and excused himself, telling Joe to do whatever stretching exercises he was used to. He hurried to the opposite door where two elderly men had just arrived, greeting them with obvious affection.

Left to himself, Joe began the warm-up exercises he usually used to prepare himself for the calisthenics that he had used for years to toughen the bodies of the young boys he coached both in football and wrestling. He joined the others, aligning himself in the back row, trying to follow the movements of the leader. Within minutes he realized he was way out of his league, but he valiantly tried to keep up, stumbling, losing his balance, unable to accomplish the twists, turns and kicks that the leader . . . and most of the other people . . . seemed to do with ease.

After what seemed an eternity, the hour was up and the session ended. Red in the face, out of breath and totally embarrassed, Joe stood, bent over, hands on his thighs, hoping his heart would slow down enough that he wouldn't pass out while most of the others filed out of the gym. He didn't even notice Dr. Summers standing in front of him until he'd said his name for the third time.

"You okay?" Dr. Summers asked, not nearly as concerned as Joe thought he should be.

Without enough air to speak, Joe nodded, then thought better of it and shook his head.

"Let's set him over here," another voice spoke, one even deeper than the doctor's. Then hands were gripping his arms and he was helped to a bench in the back of the room. He sat heavily, leaned his head against the wall and struggled for breath, unaware of the stethoscope that probed his chest or the hand holding his wrist, taking his pulse.

"I'm all right," Joe finally managed to say. "I just need a minute."

"I was watching him," another voice said. "That's a lot to ask of a fifty year old man without working him up to it slowly. He tried to keep up the whole time."

"Yeah, I know," Dr. Summers answered, hanging the stethoscope around his neck. "I was keeping an eye on him."

"Maybe you should have stopped him, Case," the voice said, scolding the younger man.

"No, no," Joe tried to argue, panted instead. "I should have been able . . . to keep up."

"No, you shouldn't," Dr. Summers said. "I figured you'd give it a try and give up after a while. I have to give you credit for sticking to it, but you should take it a little slower at first."

"Lots of those people were older than me," Joe wheezed.

"Most of them have been doing it for a lot longer. It gets easier after a while."

"I'm sure it does," Joe chuckled, now feeling much better. "Now I know how my football players feel the first day of practice when they're all sprawled all over the field, gasping for air. *Them* I can keep up with."

The three men laughed with him, helping him to his feet. "Joe, these are both of my grandfathers. Pedro "Pete" Valenzuela and John Summers."

While he shook hands with the two older men, Joe got a good look for the first time. "I saw you in front of me," he said to John. "You didn't seem to be having any trouble keeping up. And you're quite a bit older than I am, aren't you?"

"I'm eighty-seven," John nodded, his wide smile having lost none of its charm over the years. Sandy gray hair and heavily freckled face with many laugh lines said he was considerably older than Joe, but he would never have guessed he was that old. "I've been doing the morning drill like this since I was three. So has Pete, here."

Joe turned to the other man, realizing at once that here was where his doctor had gotten his good looks. With regal bearing and a full head of steel gray hair, he, too looked much younger than anything Joe would have guessed. "You have to take it easy at first," the octogenarian assured him. "After a while, you'll be able to do the whole hour without too much effort."

"We need to get going," John said, giving his grandson a hug and pat on the shoulder and leaning to shake hands once more with Joe. Another hug and another handshake and the two men strode across the floor toward the door. Just before they left, John turned, calling out to Dr. Summers. "Hey, Case. Don't forget you're supposed to be out at the ranch for dinner Sunday."

Dr. Summers waved and nodded then turned back to Joe. "How're you doing?" he asked.

"I'm fine," Joe lied, still having trouble catching his breath.

"Do you always have this much trouble breathing?" the doctor asked, his hand on the older man's wrist, counting.

Joe pointed to his nose. "Only since I took a baseball bat in the face when I was twelve," he laughed. "I snore pretty loud, too."

"Ever thought about having that fixed?"

Joe just shook his head. "Always seemed to be too many other things going on," he explained. "Jill and I talked about doing something this summer vacation, but I thought this was more important." He glanced past the doctor, then took a step toward the main floor of the gym. "What're they doing?" he asked, changing the subject while watching the twenty or so young people who were donning different types of protective garb.

"Some of them are going to practice fencing and some are going to do some martial arts. Those four over there are stick fighting . . . well that's not the technical term, but that's what we call it. Most of the kids you see there are family and we take our morning drill pretty seriously."

"Serious as a heart attack," Joe commented. "That's not an exercise, that's a life commitment," he added.

"Exactly," Dr. Summers said with a grin.

"And that's what you're trying to tell me, isn't it? And not just about the exercises."

"Yep. You know, you're pretty smart for an old guy."

"Old!? Who're you calling old?"

"Well, you're older than I am," Dr. Summers said, gathering up the towels from the bench and pulling his t-shirt back over his head. "Ready?"

"Yeah, I'm ready." He followed his doctor back through the halls. "So your name is Casey?" he asked, wiping his face once again with the tail of his t-shirt.

"No, it's Case. No y at the end."

"Unusual," Joe commented.

"You have no idea," was the enigmatic reply.

"Do you mind if I call you Case? I mean, it sure seems we should be close enough for first names. After all you're the one who's watching my wife and me on TV. In all our glory, I might add."

"I don't mind at all. Go ahead and get your shower. I'll meet you in the control room in half an hour."

"Slave driver," Joe grumbled, pushing open the door to his room. "See you."

JILLIAN

THERE WAS NO way to tell what time of day it was, or even what day. Jillian had no idea how long she'd been confined in this single room. There was no way to tell the passing of time except for the regularity of meals and her need to use the facilities.

Sensing the presence of someone, her heart raced, but it was only those she had come to call her 'handlers'. Whoever they were, they were very adept at moving her from the bed to the bathroom and on to the treadmill, keeping her bound but able to walk without stumbling between them. Again, her feet moved easily to the rhythm of the machine and to the music in her earpieces. She had become accustomed to the white noise, but was relieved when it changed to the soothing melodies she always enjoyed.

She pondered the fact that they always seemed to play the appropriate music for her. Usually when she ran, she listened to something lively on her iPod, keeping her feet moving in time to the music.

When she was working around the house, she often listened to something softer, more romantic. Those days she wasn't at work she seldom had the television on, but almost always had some kind of background music, and her captors played the same kind of music for her that she would have chosen herself. Someone who knew her well had to have told them about her usual selections, someone like Joe.

Joe. What had happened to him? Was he even alive? Was he her mysterious lover? Her thoughts sped in circles as she tried to convince herself that it had to be Joe, then had to concede that it couldn't possibly be him. But if it was Joe, why? And if it wasn't, who was it? Who was the man who was playing her body as though it were a fine musical instrument and he a world-class musician? And why was he doing whatever it was that he was doing? Not that she had any complaints on that score. Her body longed for his hands, for his touch. Just what kind of person was she?

She was sweating profusely by the time they stopped the exercise machine, her breathing heavy. She wasn't panting or out of breath, but she knew that she had been at it for at least an hour and felt that she had run her usual six miles although she had never gone faster than a brisk walk. Once again she was bathed and draped in a silken wrap, but wasn't returned to the bed or to a chair. Instead, she found herself standing with her arms spread, waiting . . . for what? Or, better, for whom?

She didn't have long to wait. She could feel the subtle breath on the back of her neck, the long fingers sliding down her throat. She shuddered in anticipation, hating herself for wanting whatever he had to offer. She felt the cloth slip from her body, wished she could move her arms to cover herself, blushed in embarrassment. Then she forgot to be self-conscious, forgot her self-loathing, forgot everything she had ever known before.

The hands wandered over her shoulders, down her back, under her arms. She gasped as they caressed her breasts, teasing her nipples into hardness, lightly pinching, gently kneading. Now she could feel the man behind her, his bare chest against her back as he reached around her, his arms embracing her ribs, his wonderful hands pulling her against him as they slid down over her belly. Her body was quick to respond to his touch, aching for the release that left her boneless and breathless. She squirmed to keep contact, moving up onto her toes to hasten his hands to where she wanted them to be, but he slowed, stopped and she wanted to cry.

Then he touched her again, but he was no longer behind her. Instead, he embraced her, his smooth chest brushing her breasts, his hands again at her throat. She shuddered when she felt his tongue drawing a line down her neck, tracing her collarbones, his teeth nipping softly on her shoulders. "He's licking me!" she thought. "Oh, my God!" At first repulsed by the idea, she quickly found that the sensations were even more erotic than the hands had been as his tongue slid down between her breasts.

She whimpered when she felt him cup her breasts, taking her nipple into his mouth and sucking gently, his teeth worrying the nipple into such an intense state of rigidity she wanted to swoon. Licking and biting, he transferred his attention to the other breast, repeating the seduction of that nipple as well. When she thought she could stand no more, his tongue traced a line of molten lava down her belly, his hands holding her captive at the waist, then sliding down over her buttocks.

"No!" She knew she had said it aloud, demanding that he stop, wanting him to go on, hungering for whatever he offered. When his arms encircled her thighs, spreading them wide, opening her to his seductive invasion, she resisted feebly, understanding that she shouldn't want what he offered, totally beyond caring.

His tongue touched her center, licked her, thrust into her and she cried out, begging him to stop, then not to stop. She was screaming her frustration that she couldn't reach him, couldn't guide him, when he found that tiny part of her that had become the focus of her life. She went up on her toes once more, widening her stance, giving herself to him, thrusting her pelvis toward him, demanding with her body what her mind and mouth rejected.

While his tongue continued it's invasion, his hands held her waist, then her hips, moving around to her inner thighs and up, his thumbs spreading the liquid response that flowed from her into a slippery avenue for entry, sliding into her, widening her even further. Now his tongue thrust deep inside and she forgot to be disgusted, forgot her protests or even how to protest. She couldn't think, couldn't talk, could only feel. And what she was feeling was beyond description, beyond imagination, beyond her wildest dreams.

The sounds that came from deep within her had nothing to do with speech. Low, guttural groans, they grew in volume when his fingers followed his tongue, thrusting into her, receding, returning. She pulled against her bonds, arching her back, her whole body becoming rigid, muscles turning to steel. Her climax shot through her like electricity, white hot, continuous, every cell on fire.

The intensity had barely eased when she felt the probing tongue begin again, the long supple fingers of one hand invading her while those of the other hand slid down her buttocks, finding the crevasse between cheeks, pressing against her anus. She was too far gone to register this newest invasion, couldn't separate the sensations coursing through her when one pinkie finger entered, forcing her sensitive flesh against the frontal assault that continued without pause.

The intensity of her orgasm made those that had come before seem like child's play. She couldn't inhale, her groans becoming a low throaty growl that increased in volume and timbre until she had no breath left. Her hands fisted, pulling mightily against her restraints, the muscles of her arms tightening until they felt as though they were being pulled from their sockets. Her abdominal muscles contracted repeatedly and her legs shook with the effort of trying to hold herself open to him.

Finally the hurricane passed and she slumped, unable to hold herself upright. His strong arms enfolded her, holding her gently against him, giving her the support she needed until her rubbery legs could once again hold her upright. Of all the sensations to which she'd been introduced, this one was the only one that seemed familiar. This simple, non-sexual embrace required nothing of her, allowed her to regain her equilibrium and gave her time to get her breathing under control.

And then it . . . and he . . . was gone.

JOE

*J*OE HAD READ the manual, knew what to expect, but the sight of his lovely wife with arms spread and tied at the wrists almost broke his heart. He hadn't really expected this, even though that was what he'd read. "She must be at her wits' end," he thought. "I don't know if I can do this to her." But he did as he'd been instructed, approaching her from behind, caressing her, removing her garment and pressing her against his chest. Her response was nothing like his expectations.

"She's waiting for me," he said to himself with a kind of wonder. "She's got to be driving herself nuts, wanting this and knowing that it's something she's been disgusted by all her life." Nevertheless, he continued smoothing his hands over her body, stroking her with his fingertips, weighing her pendulous breasts in his hands, pinching the nipples to arousal. When she moaned, he allowed his hands to slide down off her delicious body, walking around to face her.

He peered closely, realizing that Dr. Summers had been right. She wanted him, or, rather, she wanted this, whether she would or could admit it to herself. He gathered her against his body, her breasts teasing his own until his nipples were as hard as the rest of him. Finally, he was able to do something he had wanted for as long as he'd known her and he leaned into her, outlining the delicate length of her throat with his tongue, tracing her collarbones, ending at the shoulder, tasting that delicacy with his teeth.

Instead of protesting, she seemed eager, enjoying the sensations. His surprise was exceeded only by his own excitement, his thoughts in turmoil. Being allowed to suck at those delightful breasts, feeling the nipples harden to thick, hard buds inside his mouth was something he'd been dreaming of since he'd met Jillian. Licking her in her most intimate areas, toying with her, touching her, and, finally, thrusting his tongue deeply into her secret crevice . . . these were all dreams that he'd never expected to fulfill. Having her not only allow these liberties, but enjoy them was something he'd never, ever anticipated.

Hearing her groans, seeing her writhe in anticipation, feeling the tightening of her muscles when she reached the summit, he felt a euphoria that sexual release had never given him. His thoughts were fragmented, torn between doing as he'd been instructed, and giving her even more of what she so obviously wanted.

He renewed his efforts, again using tongue and hand to stimulate her, to bring her up to the point of climax a second time. Using his left hand, he sought and found her anus, circling it until he could coax her to accept his pinkie inside. He manipulated her from both sides, increasing the strength of her ultimate orgasm, goaded on by the guttural moans that spoke volumes of her pleasure. He barely heard the voice in his ear, instructing him to stop.

When her muscles finally relaxed, she hung limply from her bonds and she had never looked lovelier to him, exhausted, disheveled, fulfilled. He stood and took her in his arms, holding her gently, kissing her forehead, her ears, her mouth.

"Joe," he heard repeated in his earpiece and he knew he needed to leave. He nodded to the two women who had entered and would return her to the bed and he left, shrugging on his shirt as he walked down the short hallway to the control room to face the possible wrath of Dr. Summers.

"Sorry, Doc," he said before the doctor could even open his mouth. "I know I should have left as soon as she made it. I just couldn't. She was so ready."

"Yes," Dr. Summers agreed. "She was very ready for most of what you did, but she might have second thoughts about some of it when she really thinks about it. And she might have a sore behind that could be a real turn off for your next session."

Joe hung his head, knowing it was altogether possible that he had blown the whole thing. "You're right, of course," he granted. "But . . ."

"Joe, there really are no 'buts' in this case. Once you get back home you can do whatever you and she decide, but she should have that choice, don't you think?"

"She doesn't have any choice in anything we're doing," he argued.

"Yes and no," Dr. Summers reasoned. "I'm sure she's enjoying sex for the first time in her life and there are very few taboos here in the clinic, but anal sex is one of them. Too many women have too many problems in that area. Especially women who have had children and have trouble with varicose veins or hemorrhoids. The tissue is too fragile, not muscular like vaginal tissue. As a doctor I would never recommend anal sex. As a gynecologist I would never condone any kind of anal penetration beyond a yearly examination. If this is what you want to do, it's up to you, but not here and not now."

"Oh," Joe didn't know what to say and so, wisely, kept quiet. He glanced at the monitors and saw the two women tending to his wife. "What are they doing?" he asked, seeing her on her stomach.

"They are putting an ointment on her to make sure she doesn't have any problems. She's sure to be sore without it and, if she's sore there, she'll fight any other sexual overtures."

"I guess that never occurred to me," Joe's quiet voice spoke volumes. "I thought it would excite her. I didn't think it would hurt her."

"Yes, it did excite her, for the moment," Dr. Winters told him. "But what will it do to her when she has a moment to think about it? Especially if it hurts." He took a deep breath, let it out slowly as though trying to gain control of himself and Joe could see that he was very angry. "And why do you think we insist on having you wear an earpiece? It's so you'll know when you're going too far, or doing something wrong. If you're going to ignore me when I speak to you, you might as well not bother.

And, if you're not going to bother paying attention to our instructions you might as well not be here."

Joe sat heavily on the chair, his face reflecting the gloomy feelings that threatened to overwhelm him. "I'm really sorry, Doc," he said with a sigh. "I seem to be saying that a lot around you, don't I?"

"Yes, you do," Dr. Summers said softly, taking pity on the devastated man. "And, I suspect, it's not something you do, or even have to do, very often. Right?"

"You have no idea how right you are," Joe answered. "I've always tried to do what everyone expected of me so there wouldn't be anything to apologize about. But this," he waved his hand toward the monitors. "This is so far outside my experience that I don't seem to be able to control myself."

"And control is one of the things we've already talked about," Dr. Summers prodded.

"I guess I thought you were just talking about my . . . um . . ."

"Guess not," Dr. Summers chuckled, now no longer angry, but still concerned. "Hereafter, if you still plan to stay in the program, you will follow my instructions implicitly. Right?"

"Yes, I will," Joe answered, obviously relieved. "That means we can stay?"

"If you promise to follow the manual and instructions to the letter."

"I promise," Joe agreed readily. "This is the first time in her life she's understood what everyone else is talking about, Doc. I don't want to blow it for her."

"I can't guarantee you haven't already done just that," Dr. Summers cautioned. "But we'll give it another try." His smile widened. "It's just starting to get good."

"It can't be better," Joe's statement was really a question.

"Didn't read ahead in the manual?"

"No, I didn't. I was trying to memorize everything I had to do for each session. I didn't want to confuse the issue."

Dr. Summers chuckled. "We've gotten her to the point where she's begging for sex. That's as good as you thought it could get. Now let's see if she likes it well enough to take care of some of your needs as well."

"She's always taken care of my needs," Joe argued.

"Yes, she has. But there are other things she can learn to do that will increase your pleasure, too."

"There are?" Joe asked, amazed.

"Oh, yes. If she can be coaxed into learning some new techniques, it'll make you into a new man. Promise." He paused, then added, "Provided you haven't broken her trust so far she can't get beyond it."

"I sure hope I haven't," Joe admitted.

"I hope you haven't either," Dr. Summers told him. "No matter what, I can almost guarantee you're going to have to start at the beginning, or at least partway."

"You think so?"

"Absolutely," the doctor assured him. "For now, we're going to give her a break."

"What do you mean?"

"We're going to let her loose, no restraints, no ear pods, no blindfold. She can't go far, but it might ease some of her anxieties to be able to see where she is."

"I sure hope so," Joe grumbled mournfully.

"Me too," his therapist murmured.

JILLIAN

*E*XHAUSTED, JILLIAN LAY still, allowing her handlers to minister to her, only half aware of what they were doing. "How could he?" she asked herself for the hundredth time. "How could I?" she asked herself over and over again. Not only was it appalling that he had touched her in her most untouchable place, it was inexcusable that she had enjoyed it! To have him poke his finger up her butt was beyond revolting. It was filthy, foul, nauseating . . . incredible.

She was disgusted with herself, but even more so with him. He had betrayed her trust, had gone beyond the usual boundaries into a realm that wasn't even remotely acceptable. The more she thought about it the more confused she became. How could something so unspeakable have felt so fantastic? What was the matter with her? Were there no bounds? Why couldn't he have settled for doing what he had been doing before? What else was he planning to do to her? For those questions and for all the other endless uncertainties she had no answers.

She started whimpering when she felt the soothing ointment being smoothed into her behind, not because it hurt physically, but because she was so heartsick. Not only had he gone where no man had ever gone, these people knew what had happened. How else would they have known to put some kind of salve there? Her embarrassment was multiplied tenfold, knowing that there were others who were aware of every move she . . . and her unknown lover . . . made.

She was still ruminating the treachery of the man who had so successfully seduced her when she became aware that her attendants had gone. She sighed, tried to move and discovered that she had no bounds on her wrists. Sitting up, she checked her ankles and found that they, too, were free. She reached up, slid the blindfold off her face, probed for the tiny earphones and removed them as well. Not exactly free, she was, nevertheless, liberated from her confining fetters.

She pushed aside the coverlet, moving around the darkened room with her arms in front of her, trying to find some kind of light switch. Before she could make contact with anything, a dim glow arose, revealing her surroundings. Without considering her environment, she became aware of her nakedness, crossing her breasts with her arm, her hand covering her lower regions. Frantically she searched the room, her eyes lighting on a soft, sheer robe draped over the back of the single overstuffed chair.

As she donned the delicate, shimmering dressing gown, she gazed around the room, taking in the luxurious, if few, appointments. She admired the lovely hues of blue and lavender in the down-filled comforter, echoed in the lush blue of the armchair and the few scattered pillows. The deeper sapphire blue of the plush carpet was repeated on the walls in the jacquard pattern of the wallpaper, and in the painted woodwork. The whole was soothing, comfortable and totally luxurious.

She blushed, remembering everything that had taken place on the king-sized bed and in the big, comfortable chair, but no matter how hard she looked, she was unable to detect any kind of clasp or anchor for the restraints that had held her in place.

Curiosity consumed her, dragging her feet toward each doorway in the large, comfortable room. The first was locked, giving her no information except the refusal to open. The next gave on a wide, well-appointed bathroom, complete with separate shower and Jacuzzi tub. The marble floor was covered by jewel toned rugs that glowed in the muted lighting. The mirrored walls reflected her rumpled image and suddenly all she wanted to do was take a shower and wash her hair.

Searching the drawers of the cabinet, she quickly found everything she would need and she turned on the water until it ran hot and hard, stepping under the stream, unconsciously hoping to wash away the confusion that ran riot in her mind. She stood in the shower until her skin glowed red and she began to prune, reluctantly finishing when her hair and body were squeaky clean, her mind still as muddled as before.

She was delighted to find her own brand of makeup, her own kind of creams and lotions and she took great care in applying all. She tried to tell herself that it wasn't so she would be attractive to her mysterious lover, but she knew that would be a lie. She tried to convince herself that she didn't want him to return, but she knew that was a lie as well. She pretended what he had done to her didn't make any difference, but that was the biggest falsehood of all. Her emotions seesawed, her brain spun, her wits roiled in unaccustomed turmoil.

Finished in the bathroom, she again slipped into the silky kimono-style robe and wandered around the bed to the last door. She was surprised to find it opened on a small exercise room with the treadmill, a stair-stepper and a stationary bicycle. To one side was a long cushioned bench on which she was sure she had sat before, but she tried to ignore it. Instead she concentrated on the treadmill. "Hmmm," she thought. "Should have found these before I took a bath." She turned the switch on the treadmill, adjusting it to a quick jog, and began to run. Within minutes she knew the floor length robe was in the way and she discarded it without missing a step, ignoring her nakedness as she had when blindfolded.

She turned up the speed, running swiftly, head up, arms pumping, and kept at it until she was exhausted, surprised to find she had been running for over an hour. The whole time she ran, she tried to come to some kind of decision: would she keep allowing this man to bring her so much pleasure? Or would she fight him off, stop responding, turn away? When she turned the machine off, she still hadn't come to any kind of conclusion.

Sweaty, she hated to put the rich robe back on, so hurried back to the bathroom, taking a second shower and reapplying her makeup. This time she made use of the hair dryer that hung on the wall like one of those in a nice hotel. Surveying herself in the mirror, she had to admit that she didn't look any worse for the wear. The subtle blue of the robe brought out the startling azure of her eyes, the low collar showed off her long elegant neck. Without pins, bands or hairspray, her thick golden hair fell around her shoulders in a lustrous, silky, sexy cloud.

Returning to the bedroom, she looked around for a television set or a radio or even some magazines, but there was nothing there for her to use to take her mind off the single question that returned time and time again to the forefront of her mind. Now that she was free, what would be her response to her mystery man when he returned? She had no doubt he would return, but couldn't have said exactly why she was so sure.

She was still considering the question when the dim lights winked out, leaving her in darkness. Backing into a corner, she waited, sure that he would come to her, still unsure how she would react. When his hands touched her shoulders, no thought prompted her response. She reacted as she would have had some stranger on the street grabbed her. Her knee came up, hard, smashing his testicles up into his body, she pushed on his shoulders with all her might, shoving him even more off balance as he folded over, her other knee following, catching him in the face. Before she could think, she stepped over his inert body, fleeing for the one door that had remained locked in her search. She backed against the wall beside the door, waiting until someone came, sure they would, hoping she could slip past them in the darkness.

She heard the click of the door latch, holding her breath, hoping whoever came through would run over to the injured man who groaned and writhed in pain on the floor. The heavy door banged against the opposite wall, but, instead of hurrying across the room, the man who rushed through spun toward her, his arm catching her around the waist, pinning her arms against her body, whirling her around until her back was wedged against him. Her struggles were completely useless against his strength, her arms worthless. She felt a prick in her arm, then felt nothing at all.

JOE

*J*OE RETURNED FROM his afternoon session with the therapist frustrated with his lack of coordination, still unable to 'walk' a coin over his knuckles. He didn't return empty handed, however. She had given him something called worry balls, ivory spheres that clicked against each other as he manipulated them over each other in his hand. He had the control room to himself for a while. Not sure what he was supposed to be doing, he played with the worry balls while he watched his wife move unfettered around the large bedroom. He tried to imagine what was going through her mind, but couldn't. He knew that she was deep in thought, however. He had seen that look on her face a million times.

Dr. Summers arrived just as she finished applying her makeup for the second time. "How's she doing?" he asked, taking his place beside Joe at the console.

"She's thinking," Joe answered, explaining the look of deep concentration on her face. "That look was on her face the whole hour she was running, too."

"She ran for a whole hour?"

"Yeah. Actually, a little more than an hour. She's used to that. She has a couple of routes she runs most of the time and they both take her just over an hour."

"Do you still run with her?"

"When I can," Joe answered, turning his body and his attention toward the doctor. "In the late summer and in the fall I have to be at practice, so she runs alone. It didn't used to bother me, but, with everything that happens these days, I'd rather she didn't."

"Ever try to get her to take one of those self-defense courses?"

"Oh, sure. Both she and our daughters, Jolyn and Kate, have taken them. It makes me feel a little better, but not a lot."

"You'd be surprised how effective a woman can be, even if all she does is keep a man from getting his hands on her until she can run away."

Joe laughed. "Yeah, that's the idea. There aren't very many men who could catch her if she managed to run. And Jolyn is almost as fast."

Dr. Summers watched the lithe woman in question exit the bathroom, her eyes searching the bedroom for something. "You ready?" he asked Joe.

"Now? When she's free? She'll see it's me."

"Not if I turn out the lights." He smiled, winked. "Go ahead," he said. "I'll turn them off when you get to the door."

Joe all but ran down the short hallway, paused just outside the door, took a deep breath and cracked it open. His only thoughts were that he hoped against hope that she would not be so angry that she wouldn't accept his ministrations. He slipped inside, standing for a moment with the door against his back. He had a good idea where she was and moved in that direction, his hand against the wall to guide him.

When he judged he was just in front of her, he reached out, his hands coming to rest on her shoulders. With a smile, he clasped them, sliding his hands down her arms. Suddenly, without warning, her knee crushed into his balls, the force of the blow and the delicate region where it was concentrated combined to double him over, his whole being focused on the intense shards of pain radiating out and up from his crotch. He barely felt her hands on his shoulders, pushing him down, but the second knee smashed into his already broken nose as he curled around his manhood, and pain exploded red and hot in his brain. He fell heavily to the floor, curled protectively around his injured testicles, his twice-broken nose now throbbing and bleeding profusely.

He wasn't aware of her stepping over him or of the slight scuffle at the doorway. He was barely conscious when Dr. Summers knelt beside him, holding a rough pad of tissue against his nose, hooking an arm through his to help him to his feet.

"Unhh . . . no. Don't," he cried, unable to get his feet under him, his legs refusing to close near his wounded cajones.

"C'mon, Joe," Dr. Summers urged. "Let's get you out of here."

Joe tried to shake his head, his hand taking hold of the heavy pad that was growing darker by the minute. "Shit!" he groaned, struggling to his knees. He leaned heavily on the doctor until he got his feet under him, finally able to straighten up and walk, awkwardly, to the door.

"Still worried about her running when you're not around?" Dr. Summers asked with a grin as he helped Joe lower himself onto the bed in his own room.

Joe had to chuckle, even though he hurt all over. Shaking his head, he muttered through the bloody wad of tissue. "Heaven help the poor S.O.B. who tries to grab her." He tried to laugh, but it came out with a spurt of fresh blood.

Dr. Summers handed him the hand towel from the bathroom, taking the soggy mass he had in his hands. He turned when the door opened and one of the nurses handed him a bowl of ice. "Here," he said, wrapping some in a towel and holding it to Joe's face. "Both your eyes are already turning a nice shade of purple." He chuckled, turning Joe's face to examine him from both sides. "Let's see if we can't get the bleeding stopped and clean you up. Then we'll take you down to talk to my cousin."

"You're cousin? Why?"

"He's a plastic surgeon. Specializes in noses. Maybe he can help you with yours. I was going to recommend you to him anyway, considering the trouble you have breathing. Now it seems the question has been taken out of your hands."

"What about Jillian?" Joe asked.

"She's sleeping peacefully," was the answer. "But the most refreshing thing that's happened in the past three days is having you ask about her when she just messed you up really good." He laughed, all the while holding the ice in place, surreptitiously taking his patient's pulse, counting his respirations. After a while, he pulled the towels away. "Looks better," he pronounced. "Get cleaned up while I make a phone call. I'll be back in a few minutes."

JOLYN

JOLYN CAUGHT UP with Dr. Summers just before he left the gym. She had tried to keep to one side more or less out of sight since her father had started coming in to do morning drill with the whole group, but she hadn't seen him for the last couple of days and she was worried.

"Excuse me, Dr. Summers," she touched him tentatively on the arm.

He turned, greeted her with a wide smile. "Wait a minute," he held up one finger, turned back to his companion and excused himself. Turning back to her, he grinned, already knowing what her question would be.

"I thought my dad was going to be doing morning exercises with us," she said. "But I haven't seen him. Is he all right?"

"More or less," Case chuckled, his arm around her shoulders guiding her out of the gym. "Your mother took him out, but he's recovering pretty well."

The shock on her face was echoed in her voice. "She took him out? What happened?"

He quickly described what had happened in the darkened room. "It wasn't nearly as bad as it sounds, but I sent him down to Alex to see if he couldn't fix his nose for good. Wait until you see him. I think it's actually going to be straight."

She giggled. "That'll be a first." She knew she shouldn't ask, but couldn't help it. "Is Mom all right?"

"Jolyn, when your father asked to be included in our clinic, you and I talked, didn't we?"

"Yes, sir," she nodded, eyes downcast. "I know I'm not supposed to discuss them with you. I'm sure they'll tell me if they want me to know anything. I'm just really worried . . . about both of them."

"I understand," he nodded. "But I can't discuss their therapy. It not only wouldn't be ethical, it would be breaking a promise I made your father. When you suggested he come talk with me, he made that a stipulation. He didn't want his daughter knowing exactly what they would be doing. That's the main reason I'm the one who's monitoring them instead of you or Tom."

"Oh, I know," she nodded. "I'm sorry I asked."

He smiled again, understanding. "I know. It's hard, isn't it?" When she nodded, he went on. "If it would make you feel better, you could go visit your dad while he's recovering. I think he'd like that."

She brightened considerably. "Could I?"

"Sure," he answered. "Go ahead. He's back in his own room."

"Thank you," she said, almost running down the hall. She turned before she got to the hallway. "Thanks," she called again with a wave.

Even though he'd told her about her father's injuries, she was shocked when she saw him. His voice had been low when she'd knocked on the door, and he managed a half smile when she slipped inside, but it wasn't his usual quirky grin. The bandages across his nose didn't bother her nearly as much as the two black eyes, bruises that rose into his eyebrows and traveled across his cheeks. "Oh, Dad," she said, approaching slowly, her hand reaching out.

He shied away from her touch, reaching out his hand to capture hers. "Hi, Kitten," he said, his grin lopsided on his face. "Glad you could take the time to come see me."

"I asked Dr. Summers where you were this morning and he told me what had happened. You look awful," she said.

"Gee, thanks," he chuckled. "I'm okay, Kitten. Dr. Valenzuela says I'll even be able to breathe through my nose. I haven't been able to do that since I was twelve."

"Maybe it'll turn out to be a good thing. But what an awful way to have it happen."

"Not so awful," he disagreed. "Now I know I don't have to worry about you two running in the dark. She was just doing what you guys have been trained to do."

"I didn't know it would look like that!" she told him. "Anyway," she paused. "How's the therapy going?"

"You know I'm not going to answer that," he scowled. "We agreed, remember?"

"Yeah, I know. I didn't know how hard it would be on me for the two of you to be here and not to be able to talk to either one of you. I . . . we all miss you."

"It's only been a week," he cajoled. "How much can you miss me in a week?"

"Little Joe keeps asking for you," she answered. "He toddles around the house going 'Gwanpa, Gwanpa'."

"Maybe you could sneak him in to see me for a few minutes," he suggested hopefully. "I miss him, too."

"I won't sneak him in, but I will ask Dr. Summers if it would be okay. He was the one who suggested I come see you. I don't think he'd mind. Maybe tomorrow when Tom is on duty and I'm off."

"Off? Does that mean you're in class?"

"I don't go to class, anymore, Dad. I just have to meet with my advisor now and then while I'm working on my dissertation."

"And how's the dissertation coming?"

"It's getting there," she said. "I still need a few more examples, but the information I've been able to collect here just from observing has been invaluable. When Dr. Summers suggested writing my doctorial thesis on sexual dysfunction, I wasn't really that enthusiastic, but the more I see, the more I want to be able to help."

"Like your mother and me?" he asked.

She looked at her hands, not wanting to answer, but knowing she owed it to her father to be honest.

"It's okay, honey. I know." He patted her hand, smiling up into eyes that were an exact copy of her mother's. "And I'm learning. I always thought it was just her. It's been an eye opener to realize that she responds when I do the right things."

"Is she really responding?" Jolyn asked eagerly.

His slow smile grew as he thought about the last few days, but he just nodded, not really wanting to share his wife's newly discovered sensuality with anyone, especially not with his daughter.

She took the hint, looking at her watch. "Gotta go. You're not the only couple in the clinic, you know."

He looked pensive for just a moment, then asked, "Do you always use the same scenario? You know, kidnapping etc."

"Oh, no. There are a lot of different things. That was just the one that seemed to be the most likely to work for Mom."

"And you and Tom are the ones in the control room for these other couples, right?"

She nodded, knowing it was preying on his mind. "But neither one of us are allowed in the control room when Dr. Summers is observing you and Mom. There is an alternate room for monitoring other suites, so we stay in there most of the time. When you decided to give this a try, he discussed it with us." Seeing the look on her father's face, she held up a hand, stopping him. "Only that it wouldn't be proper for either your daughter or your son-in-law to be the ones to monitor you. He let us know in no uncertain terms that we were forbidden to see your tapes and weren't to ask about your treatment."

When Joe relaxed, she looked at her watch again. Leaning over to give him a kiss on the forehead, she once again told him how horrible he looked. "It's okay, Dad," she said with a snicker. "I still love you."

She barely got the door closed before the tears started, and she hurried to the control room, into the arms of her husband who was monitoring another couple in the throes of ecstasy.

"Hey," he said, holding her gently, his hands soothing her back. "What's the matter?"

"I just saw Dad," she sobbed. "Both his eyes are coal black. Mom kneed him in the balls, then caught him in the face. Broke his nose again."

"What?! Wait." He turned to the monitor, made sure everything was going as planned, sat in his chair and pulled his wife into his lap. "Now, what happened?"

When she explained, he started laughing.

"It's not funny," she said, batting at him.

"Yes it is," he chuckled. "He's always been worried about you two running like you do. He's the one who insisted you take those self defense courses. And he's the one who got the proof they work." He dried her tears with his thumb. "Maybe I'll go pay him a visit this afternoon. I'll ask Case if he thinks it'd be all right, but I'm pretty sure it will. But I don't think you should bring Little Joe in. Seeing his grandpa all torn up like that might be a little more than he could take."

"Oh, shit," she said. "I all but promised to bring him in. But you're right; it might not be a good idea for him to see Dad like that."

"I'll explain it to your dad. Maybe you could give him a call and let Joey talk to him. How would that be?"

"Good idea."

"Good." He got to his feet, pushing her down into the chair he vacated. "You're turn," he said, pointing to the monitor. "They should be good for the next couple of hours. They almost always sleep afterwards."

"Why are they still here?" she asked, turning to observe the couple who were lying, panting, next to each other on the wide bed.

"They signed up for the whole month. Guess they want their money's worth." He gave her a sweet promising kiss, touched her gently on the cheek and turned to go. Before he could get to the door, it opened and Dr. Summers stepped in.

"Hey, just the people I wanted to see," he said, catching Tom by the arm before he could escape. When he groaned, Case laughed, turning to Jolyn. "Since your dad is out of commission and your mom is loose in her rooms with a couple of good books, I don't have much to do. Thought I'd give you both time off until your dad is able to resume therapy."

"Really?" Tom asked, brightening. "And I thought being your junior partner was going to be all drudgery."

"Admit it," Case urged. "You're loving every minute of it."

"Not exactly," Tom laughed. "Watching these couples is nothing like those porn flicks we had at my bachelor party."

With a hearty laugh, he ushered them out of the control room, sitting in the still warm chair and going over Tom's notes.

"Is your dad okay?" Tom asked Jolyn on their way to the day care center to pick up their toddler.

"I think so," she answered. "Tom, you're Case's resident. Couldn't you ask him about their case?"

"Nope," he said. "Wouldn't be ethical." He leaned across the seat, slipped his arm around her and squeezed her shoulders. "No matter what happens your parents aren't going to want us to know everything that goes on here. And I intend to keep my word to your father."

"You're right. I know. I just worry about them. You didn't see what she did to him."

"I'll go see him tomorrow, honey. Just relax. It'll be okay. As long as she never finds out that it was your idea in the first place. Or that your brothers and sister know what's going on." He paused. "Did you get a hold of Jack?"

"No, not yet. Either he never listens to his voice mail or he's out of cell phone range. I just hope I can get to him before they get home. He needs to know what's going on so he won't ask any embarrassing questions about where they were."

Even though they both laughed, both realized that it was a very real concern.

JILLIAN

*J*ILLIAN SAT CURLED up with her legs under her, totally absorbed in the book in her lap. She had already read two of the books that had been left for her, both the newest offerings of her favorite authors. She'd never heard of the author of this particular book, but had been intrigued by the cover picture, a sword lying on top of various artists' paraphernalia. So far, the book had lived up to the cover, even though there had been a few sex scenes which were usually a turn off for her. She had read those swiftly, but had returned to peruse them more carefully, realizing that she could now associate with their content, something she had never been able to do before.

She wasn't sure how long it had been since she'd last had human contact, but the books had appeared on the floor beside the chair while she had been on the treadmill, just as her meals appeared while she was either in the bathroom or the exercise room. Obviously her handlers were being careful to avoid coming into contact with her, but she wasn't sure if that was because the lights were always on and they didn't want to be seen, or if they were afraid of her because of the way she had handled the man.

She sighed, marked her place and closed the book. It was very good, a good story, well written, but she had to think and she couldn't do that while reading. Thinking wouldn't do any good, either, she had to admit. She'd been over and over what had been happening to her and still hadn't reached any conclusions. More than anything, she wanted to be free, but she accepted that being allowed the freedom of these three rooms was the best she could hope for. She vacillated between being smug about having been able to take down the big man who had spent what? Three? maybe four? days seducing her, and feeling remorse for having harmed someone who had given her so much pleasure.

She wasn't sure how much damage she'd done, but she was sure that she would be made to pay, in one way or another, for her actions. What she couldn't understand was why she was still here, alone. Her needs had been met since she'd awakened unfettered and alone a few days ago, but the man hadn't returned and she'd seen no one else. "Well, what'd you expect?" she asked herself. "He sure isn't going to be interested in me now."

And she had to ask herself the ultimate question: did she really want him to be interested? No matter how hard she tried to convince herself that she did not, she always came to the same conclusion: yes. If she couldn't have her Joe, she would take this stranger with the exciting hands and electrifying tongue. If she couldn't have her old life, she would settle for the thrilling sensations he brought to her, the sensual awakening of her body, the slow seduction of her mind.

"Well, you've pretty much squashed any ideas he might have had about spending more time with you," she told herself. "It's been at least three days. At least, I'm pretty sure it has. I think I've had nine or ten meals since I woke up." She opened the book again, but, before she could concentrate on the written words, the lights dimmed. They didn't wink out as they had before, but there was barely enough light for her to see across the room. Almost too low to be heard came the melodious sounds of Il Divo, one of her favorite singing groups. She wasn't surprised when the doors to the bathroom and the exercise room swung shut, the locks closing with a soft click. It had happened several times over the past three days. She should be used to it, but she wasn't.

She couldn't decide whether she was scared or not, but she was sure that the mood lighting and the soft music heralded some kind of change. "Maybe he's going to come back," she thought, then chided herself for yearning for just that to happen. She didn't realize she was holding her breath until the lights came up once more. She exhaled with a sigh, wanting to cry, but for what she couldn't have said. Setting her book aside, she rose, going to each of the doors to make sure they were locked. She looked around, trying to find something that might be different, but there was nothing. Finally, she settled on the bed, curling into a ball, the tears she had held back before now flowing steadily.

She didn't notice when the lights went out entirely. Her eyes were tightly closed against the overwhelming tears of grief that wouldn't stop. She didn't hear the door open or the man walk across the floor. The first time she was aware of him was when he sat beside her on the bed, rolling her over and up into his arms. She couldn't help herself. She wrapped her arms around him, her wet cheeks against his chest and she sobbed heartbrokenly into his shirt.

She could feel his heartbeat, felt comfortable and safe in his arms, snuggled closer. She couldn't help herself, couldn't push him away. Over and over she said the same words: "I'm sorry. I'm so sorry." After a few minutes, he laid her back against the pillows, his hands running through her hair and across her cheek. She sniffled, allowing the caress, wanting more. She cried out when she felt the weight lift from the bed, heard him walk across the room and heard the door open and close.

Her sobs increased in volume, her tears came in torrents. Once again the lights came on but she curled into the fetal position and cried herself to sleep.

JOE

*I*T HAD BEEN a rough few days for Joe. The surgery
to correct both recent and previous problems
with his nose had gone off without a hitch, but he'd
still been groggy for a couple of days. He'd spent
most of the time in bed, rereading the manual,
sleeping and wondering what was going on in the
room across the hall. Seeing first Jolyn and then Tom
and talking to Little Joe on the phone had been the
only thing that had helped keep his sanity. It wasn't
until the third day that Dr. Case Summers and his
cousin, Dr. AlejandroValenzuela, allowed him to get
up and get dressed.

Now he followed Case into the control room,
asking again about his wife before he could see her
for himself. "Is she happy?" was his final question.

"Probably not exactly happy," the doctor told
him. "Not even content. More accepting than
anything. She's a voracious reader, though. It takes
me a lot longer to read a Stephen King novel than it
takes her."

"She speed reads for the most part. When she finds something she really enjoys, she'll go back and really read every word." While he was talking he was looking over the doctor's shoulder at the monitors which showed his wife snuggled into the cushions of the big overstuffed chair. As he watched, she put down the book and a faraway look came over her.

"Wonder what she's thinking about now?" he asked aloud.

"I'm not sure," the doctor answered, turning to the monitor. "But she's done that several times over the last three days. I suppose she's trying to decide whether or not she wants you back."

"As Joe, or as the mystery man?" Joe asked.

"I'm sure she wants Joe back," Case laughed. "She calls out your name in her sleep." He turned back to his patient. "I think she's trying to decide whether or not she wants the mystery man back."

"She sure had a funny way of greeting me the last time," Joe said, his hand gently touching the bandages on his face. "I'm not sure what I'll be able to do the next time. I sure can't get close enough to touch her with my tongue."

"We have an array of goodies for you to use," the doctor assured him. "Speaking of your injuries, besides the black eyes and your nose, how's the rest of you?"

"I don't think I'll have to worry about not having any control for a while, if ever. I'm black and blue half way to my belly button." He snorted, but even that hurt and his hands flew to his face, covering but not touching, just as he'd been instructed.

Sympathetically, Dr. Summers patted him on the shoulder. "It'll be better soon," he promised. "And Dr. Connors assured me that there weren't any permanent injuries to your genitals."

"Dr. Connors?"

"He's our resident urologist. At my request, he checked you out while Alex had you on the table. Seemed like a good idea at the time." He manipulated the rheostat on the console, dimming the lights in Jillian's room. He inserted a CD, setting the volume almost as low as it would go.

"Thanks, I think," Joe said, watching what the doctor was doing. Again his attention focused on the monitor. "Why'd you do that?"

"To get her used to reacting to the lack of lights without panic," Dr. Summers said. "We've been doing it periodically over the last few days. We also close and lock the doors."

"And is she getting used to it?"

"Sort of. Watch when the lights come back on. If she does as before, she'll check the locks." Even as he spoke, he turned the rheostat back up and they were quiet, watching her reactions. When she curled up on the bed, Joe felt as though his heart would break.

"Ah, shit," he groaned. "She's crying."

"Again," Case told him. "She does do that occasionally, too. Can't say I blame her. She managed to attack the only person she's come into contact with for the last week. Now she's lonely, frightened and confused." He turned again to Joe. "Want to go down and console her for a minute?"

"Could I?" Joe asked, smiling for the first time in a long while.

"Sure," Case nodded. "Just make sure you don't do anything but hold her, pat her back maybe, then get the hell out of there. No more than a few minutes." He handed the earpiece to Joe. "And if I say leave, do it," he instructed.

"I will," Joe agreed, happy just to get to hold his wife for a few minutes.

He hurried down the hallway once again, wedging the little listening device in his ear as he went. He waited until the lights went off before silently opening the door. This time he was sure where his wife was and went straight to the bed, lowering himself gingerly beside her. He reached out, gathered her into his arms and held her with a longing that he couldn't have described.

He had held her like this before in their lives. When her father had been diagnosed with cancer she had been a brick for everyone else, but alone in their room she had cried until there were no tears left. Other times and other events had occurred that had tried their patience and their strength and she had always faced them with understanding and courage, saving tears, sorrow and sadness for the warm refuge of his arms.

Now she pleaded forgiveness to someone she was sure didn't know, indeed, had done her best to put out of commission. In his usual understanding manner, he soothed her, knowing that there was a lot more to her misery than simply an anonymous man who turned her on.

He followed Dr. Summer's instructions to the letter, laying her on the pillows and leaving when he heard the voice in his earpiece telling him to. What he wanted to do was turn on the lights, take his wife in his arms and just hold her, letting her know that it had been him all along. It had become much more complicated than just learning how to make love to his wife so that she would enjoy it as well. It had become a beginning of a whole new way of life for them both and he intended to make sure it was the best life it could possibly be.

JILLIAN

*J*ILLIAN WASN'T SURE how long she'd been asleep, but there was a tray of food for her when she awoke. On its own legs, it contained a sandwich with a thick slice of ham, cheese and lettuce on rye, her very favorite. "Must be lunch," she thought, sitting on the edge of the bed and pulling the tray in front of her. She munched the chips, sipped the lemonade, not really paying attention to what she was eating. Her mind was in a whirl, but, for the first time she wasn't confused. She knew without a doubt that her mystery man was her very own Joe.

Nothing had changed, really. She was still being held captive in a luxurious room with all the facilities she could want. And she had never yet seen the man who had become her sole companion. The short hair, soft, supple hands, and smell of his cologne were all different, as was the bare chest which had always been covered with dense, curly hair, but she knew it was Joe. She didn't know how or why, she didn't have any answers at all, except the certainty that her strange and exciting new lover was her own, cherished husband, the man she had chosen to spend her life with.

A sly smile curled her lips at the corners, unaffected by the sandwich that she chewed automatically. Never, not in her whole life would she ever feel as comfortable or as comforted as she felt in Joe's arms. And the man who had held her while she sobbed her heartache that morning was the same man who had held her on those rare occasions when she had broken down before. She knew it in her heart.

"Now, what do I do about it?" she asked herself. "And what have I done to him?" She wasn't sure about the answers to her questions. She did hope that she hadn't hurt him, although her self-defense instructor had assured her that a knee to the groin followed by one to the face were the absolute best weapons an unarmed woman could use on a man. "What if I did permanent damage?" she asked herself. "How ironic it would be for him to make sure I enjoyed sex only to find himself unable to perform."

That thought stopped her cold, her smile vanishing, the rest of the sandwich lying forgotten on the plate. Did she really hurt him? How could she be so stupid? Why hadn't she figured it all out before? That answer was easy: because he was so different. Why had he changed? Her mind whirled, going over and over the same questions. And, of course, she began to doubt. He was different, very different, too different to be the same man. It just couldn't be Joe.

She was sure it was late afternoon or evening when the lights dimmed again. This time only the door to the exercise room closed and locked while the bathroom door remained open. She took the hint. It was obvious that she was supposed to get ready for bed and she obediently began preparations, washing her face, brushing her teeth and all the other things she usually did before bedtime. There were no pajamas, no underwear, just another beautiful, sheer robe and she didn't really want to wear it to bed, but she needed to be clothed somehow. It made her feel a little more normal.

She'd no sooner made herself comfortable among the plump feather pillows when the lights went off altogether. "Guess they don't want me to read in bed," she thought to herself as she snuggled down beneath the soft satiny comforter. She was almost asleep when she felt the mattress sag under his weight and she turned toward him with anticipation, her hands reaching for him. She felt his strong hands close around her wrists, and found herself pinned with her arms over her head.

Her first instinct was to fight when she felt imprisoned, but he held her firmly, keeping her calm by moving one hand up her arms and back down, almost petting her while the other hand easily held her captive. She gave up, relaxed a bit, until she felt the restraints close around her wrists. "No, please," she whimpered, pleading with him, pulling against her bonds, rolling away only to be caught and turned back around.

She felt him change positions, felt his leg along her side, his hands moving over her neck and shoulders, up and down her arms, tickling her armpits, the robe pushed aside. He shifted again, his hands sliding over her, capturing first one breast then the other, worrying her nipples, caressing her middle, around her waist, up her side. He slid the comforter to her waist, his hands never stopping, following her jaw line, caressing her throat, wandering over her shoulders and down her sides, returning to her breasts time and again, torturing her with an agony of desire.

She wanted him, wanted what he'd done to her before, wanted his hands to move lower, but when they did, they bypassed her essence, moving lower still, pushing the blanket off completely, kneading her thighs, teasing her behind her knee, rubbing down her calf to her ankles. Now she pleaded with him, twisting beneath his hands, writhing with anticipation. Unashamed, she begged him for release, but he continued the slow torture, ignoring the one place that would give her what she wanted.

She would have embraced him, but her arms were tightly held, her hands curled into fists, pulling against her restraints. Her legs, however, were free to move and he bent them, working over them, caressing her up the inside of her thighs and down again. When she thought she could take no more, when she was almost consumed with frustration, when her whimpers sounded pathetic in her own ears, he smoothed her legs apart, moving her right leg up and around until it was resting in his lap and she was completely open to him.

His fingers teased her, gathering her own fluids to slick his way, sliding a little way inside just briefly, then back out, driving her wild with frustration. Again she felt something enter, but she froze, realizing it wasn't his finger, nor was it any other part of his anatomy. "What?" she couldn't fathom, but the constant movement of his hands eventually made her forget her question and she not only allowed the strange penetration, but welcomed it.

Gently, a little at a time, she felt herself invaded, the sensations driving her over the edge, her whole body tight as a drum while a searing climax took her, the strange intruder held still within her while the mystery man's fingers played her like a many stringed harp. Unbelievably wonderful convulsions raked over her time and again until she collapsed, panting, exhausted. Even as she lay, nerveless and bone weary, his hands never ceased roving her body, caressing her breasts, gently soothing and calming her.

Once her breath returned, she felt the invasion begin again, a little at a time, sliding inside and withdrawing, the depth increasing with each gentle thrust until she was filled to capacity. "Oh . . . my . . . God!" she screamed, her body responding recklessly, frantically trying to reposition herself to allow better access. She widened her legs even further, thrust her pelvis up, driving herself against the hands that held her, deepening the penetration and the intense friction that drove her up toward Nirvana once again. Her second orgasm erupted through her, stronger than the first, a volcano that engulfed her, its fiery heat consuming her.

She couldn't stop her reactions, couldn't keep her hips from pushing against whatever it was that held her transfixed, impaled. Even as one orgasm passed, she bucked against his hands, her legs thrashing for purchase, striving for yet another. Without her ear pods, she could hear his heavy breathing, knew what he was doing to her was also exciting him, but there was a new sound that took her a moment to comprehend. Although she'd never owned a dildo, she understood that this was what she was hearing, could feel the intense response deep inside her body to its shape and the power of its vibrations.

She no longer cared who the man was or what he held inside her. Her mind had long since conceded any control, her thoughts totally concentrated on the intensity of her body's response, the 'little death' of orgasm, the electricity that coursed through her, the heat of her center. "Please," she begged, straining against her bonds, holding her legs even wider to give him better access.

She could feel the tension mounting, the fire consuming her, the repeated shock of the gathering storm. "Yes . . . Yes . . . unh," she repeated, beseeching, insistent. "More . . . deeper . . . harder." Her voice was a hoarse whisper that grew into continued groans, deep moans, guttural grunts that rose in volume with the increasing pressure inside her. She had no conscious thought as she begged, pleaded and cajoled for more and more. Her world had coalesced, concentrated on the unspeakable pleasure she hadn't known existed until a few days ago. She whimpered and writhed, grunted and ground against him until she exploded, a star burst deep within her very being, and she screamed her wordless ecstasy to the darkness.

Slick with sweat, wrung out, exhausted, she wasn't even aware of the comforter sliding back over her or the lessening of the pressure on her wrists when the restraint was released. She couldn't have moved, didn't even try. She wasn't sure whether she passed out or fell asleep. All she knew was that when she woke up, the dim lights were on and he was gone.

JOE

*H*E HELD THE two instruments in his hand as though they were snakes as he hurried to the room. He was pretty sure he could get her tied up, but wasn't so sure he could use the 'toy' that Dr. Summers had handed him. He'd never even considered something like the soft rubbery dildo that looked very much like his own penis, albeit somewhat smaller. And he'd almost choked when Case had shown him how to turn it on and felt the vibrations against the back of his hand, but his tongue was out of commission for the time being, so he'd agreed to try it.

He wasn't sure how he felt when she reached for him. It was hard to be jealous of himself, but she didn't know it was him, so that was the emotion that came to the surface for just a second before he could capture her wrists and secure her arms over her head. It didn't take him long to get into the rhythm of stroking her, touching all the forbidden spots that he'd had to forgo for the last twenty-eight years, caressing her long, elegant neck, weighing each plump breast in his hands and then pinching her nipples into erection.

He took his time, enjoying teasing her, loving when she twisted and turned, reveling in the frantic gyrations of her body when he touched her. Her lovely legs were slender and long, still tight from all her years of running and he gave them special attention, manipulating the muscles of her calf, running his fingernails behind her knees and across her instep. He ignored her pleas, driving her relentlessly, his hands clenching on the inside muscles of her thighs.

He shifted until his torso was out of the way, lifting her leg over him to rest in his lap, giving him access to that part of her where he, and she, most wanted him to be. The unremitting darkness didn't deter him. He knew her anatomy by heart and he played with her until he could stand her piteous cries no more.

He groped in the darkness for the little plaything, blowing on it a bit to warm it up, using her own moisture to lubricate it. He was slightly hesitant to introduce it, especially when he could sense her tension as soon as she felt the difference, but it didn't last long and he slid it in and out slowly, a little at a time. Her reaction was more than he could have believed, far beyond any expectations he might have had and, when she came for the second time, he decided he might as well turn it on and see if she would respond again.

He smiled at the frenzy with which she sought to climb the heights once again, her whole being focused on the little buzzing device that was inciting such an intense reaction. He continued his manipulations, almost laughing at the gyrations that all but dislodged the dildo, smiling when she achieved a third orgasm.

Deciding on his own that she had had enough, he rose, reached across her for the corner of the comforter and pulled it across her. Reaching up, he released her wrists before turning and walking from the room, the little gizmo tucked firmly in his pocket. He was all smiles when he returned to the control room to find a laughing doctor waiting for him.

"That was wonderful!" he exclaimed as soon as he walked into the control room. "I never thought these things were all that good, but . . . well, you saw her! She was totally out of control."

Dr. Summers chuckled while his patient ranted about the efficacy of the small sex toy that he had had to convince him to use. "They're pretty good in a pinch," he agreed.

"In a pinch?" Joe whooped. "Are you kidding? She'll probably never want to have sex with me again. She'll want one of these."

"And you two can have a good time finding them, once she gets past the idea," Case assured him. "It's one thing for her to accept what one of them can do when she has no choice. It might be quite another for her to opt to use one when she is in a position to say no. On the other hand, maybe you can bring her to the point where she no longer finds things like this to be taboo."

"And just how do I go about changing her mindset?" Joe asked. "Do you think she'll just do a complete turnaround when this is all over?"

"Maybe, but probably not," the doctor agreed with his assessment. "However, she may learn that it's fun to be a little naughty once in a while."

"Let's hope you're right," Joe laughed until his nose hurt. "And you were right about something else," he finally said. "Even black and blue, everything still works . . . no permanent damage."

"Good thing," Case answered, chuckling. "'Cause you're going to need it tomorrow."

"Tomorrow?" Joe's head snapped up, his jaw falling open. "But I thought that didn't come for a few days yet."

"Normally it wouldn't," the doctor replied. "But, with certain other anatomical problems, you're going to have to skip ahead a couple of chapters in the manual. I would suggest chapter eight."

"What's in chapter eight?" Joe asked.

"You can read it tonight and we'll discuss any questions you might have tomorrow morning."

JILLIAN

"*M*Y GOD," JILLIAN said aloud to no one in particular. "What was that all about?" She rolled to her side, curling around one of the many pillows on the wide bed, hugging it to her, careful not to let it touch her tender and still sensitized nether regions. She couldn't believe he had invaded her with a dildo . . . *a dildo!* And, even more unbelievable, she'd responded. "Responded, hell!" she thought. She'd relished it, no loved it . . . adored it. Was that what she was supposed to have been feeling for the last twenty-eight years? Or was that only possible with some kind of sex toy? She didn't know, but she was damned well going to find out.

"Oh, sure," she giggled to herself. "And how do you propose to do that? You can't just tell this man that you want him to fuck you so you can find out if the real thing is as good as the gadget, you know." And she giggled again. "I can't believe I even thought that word," she said to herself. Oh, what was the matter with her? She was being held captive, didn't know what had happened to her husband, was being sexually assaulted in the most perverse manner and what was she thinking about? How soon she could have sex again with some mystery man.

She lay for a long time trying to sort everything out, but finally fell asleep without having come to any conclusions.

Morning found her on the treadmill once again, sprinting for a while then settling into her usual quick trot. And, as usual, her mind had nothing else to do but ponder her predicament. No matter which way she looked at it, she couldn't come to any conclusions other than that she definitely wanted more. She had finally gotten past being disgusted by some of the things this unknown man was doing. It felt too good. And, as always, she was honest enough with herself to realize that she might have been more open to some of the things her husband had wanted to try if she had been able to get past that initial revulsion before.

She smiled to herself when she imagined her Joe, armed with a vibrator. He would never be able to bring himself to buy one, of that she was sure. And she had to admit that the intensity of her orgasm had been augmented by the finger this man had inserted in her behind, although she wasn't sure *that* was worth repeating. What was a revelation to her was how her body was responding to being manipulated by him. The question was: what would happen when he actually decided he wanted to have sex? Would it be more of the same thing that she and

Joe had done all their lives? Or would it be more of the same thing that this man had been doing to her? Or, rather, what he was doing *for* her?

A sudden thought popped unbidden into her mind, bringing her to a standstill, causing her to slide off the treadmill, barely catching her balance as this new idea overwhelmed her. Was he doing it *for* her? Who would want to do something like this *for* her? A sex therapist, maybe? What if this man was their new sex therapist? What if this was his idea of therapy?

"Oh, please, no," she moaned, tears spurting at the idea. She shook her head, rejecting the idea even while the possibilities assaulted her brain. The short hair, the hairless chest, the different aftershave, the supple hands. And he was every bit as tall as Joe, although he was leaner, not nearly as massive as her husband. The idea wouldn't go away, no matter how much she tried to refute it. Joe had insisted they go to see Dr. Summers. Maybe he'd arranged all of this.

"No, he wouldn't," she argued with herself. "He wouldn't allow another man to touch me." But this man hadn't had sex with her. He'd introduced her to the joys of sexual fulfillment without actually having intercourse with her. But she was still confined. That meant there was more to come, didn't it? What was the next step?

The more she thought about it, the more agitated she became and she worked herself into a frenzy, pacing around the room, into the bedroom and back over and over again, ignoring the fact that she was still stark naked. "What difference does it make if it's the doctor?" she asked herself and immediately came up with the answer. If it were Dr. Summers, that would mean that Joe had arranged everything and would know what was going on. It was no longer an anonymous man teaching her about the sensuality of her body, but her doctor . . . her very good-looking doctor. And, worst of all, was Joe watching?

When the lights went out, she screamed, repeating "no" over and over again until the lights came back on. She crouched against the wall, hands over her eyes, tears trickling through her fingers, shudders wracking her body. It took a while for her to regain a modicum of the control that usually served her so well, but finally she slid upright against the wall, sniffling, wiping her nose with the back of her hand. She straightened, remembered that she was still naked and hurried back into the exercise room for her robe.

Belting the silky fabric securely around her waist, she sat on the arm of the chair, trying to remember everything she could about the man who had so successfully seduced her. The hands could easily be those of the doctor, as could the mouth and tongue. The hair was definitely cut the same way. But what about his chest? Twice he'd held her back against his naked chest, the hard muscular chest of an athlete. Could that have been Dr. Summers? She couldn't remember for sure, didn't know enough what he would look like without his shirt.

And then she smiled. It couldn't be Dr. Summers. The man who had held her while she cried her heart out was much broader than the slender doctor. Her arms had barely circled him, but he definitely wasn't a fat man, just big and very solid. And that brought her full circle, back to Joe. He was a very large man, tall, with broad shoulders and massive chest. And he had never gone to fat the way so many athletes did. But why would Joe be doing all of this?

She added all the facts she had together and came to the same conclusion she had so many times before. She just didn't know. The only thing she was sure of was that she wanted more of whatever this man had to offer.

JOE

"*H*OW'RE YOU DOING?" Dr. Summers asked Joe when he came into the control room. "You don't look quite as gray as you did when you left the gym."

"I'm fine," Joe assured him. "It may take me a while, but I really want to learn all the exercises you do every morning. I may look like death warmed over right now, but it seems to be worth it."

"I think you'll find you have a lot more energy once you really get the swing of it," Dr. Summers told him, then changed the subject. "Did you go down to talk to Alex?"

"Yeah, I did. I walked with him to his office from the gym. He took the packing out of my nose."

"Breathing better?"

"You have no idea," Joe said smiling. "This morning was the first time I can remember that I was able to gargle without gagging. And I can take a deep breath with my mouth closed."

"You'll find the exercises much less painful now that you can breathe properly."

"And I won't sound like I'm panting when I make love to my wife," Joe pointed out, turning to the monitors. "What's she doing?" he asked.

"When I got here she was already on the treadmill," Case told him. "She seemed to be in a real pensive mood and then she just stopped. Damn near fell off the treadmill. Now she's pacing back and forth." He adjusted something on the console and the lights went out, although they could still see her image with the infra red camera. Neither one of them was prepared for her screams, nor the way she crouched down against the wall with her hands over her face.

"What the hell?" Joe demanded, leaning closer to the monitor.

"I'm not sure," Case answered, turning the lights back on. "But I am sure it has to do with whatever she was thinking of when she stumbled off the treadmill."

They both sat, tensely waiting to see what she might do next. It was apparent she was having an intense thinking match with herself. The conflicting emotions that passed through her mind were reflected in the animation of her lovely face.

"I sure would like to get inside her mind right now," Joe whispered as though she could hear them while they were watching her.

"I'm not sure you'd like that," Dr. Summers chuckled. "What if she's deciding whether she wants you back or would rather keep her new lover?"

Joe shrugged. "Doesn't matter," he said. "I still win." He stood back, leaned against the console on the opposite wall. "What if she decides she doesn't want either one of us?" he asked.

"I doubt you'll have to worry about that. She's always loved you, no matter what. That'll be the deciding factor, you know."

"I sure hope you're right." He peered more closely at the image on the screen. "She seems to have made up her mind," he said, nodding in that direction. "Do you think she's ready for chapter eight?"

Dr. Summers nodded. "Looks like it. Question is, are you?"

"As ready as I'll ever be," Joe answered, a slow smile replacing the worried expression of a few minutes earlier. "At least I'm sure all the plumbing works. I think I can keep it all under control. I hope I can."

"Most of what happens in the next couple of hours is going to depend on you doing just that," the doctor cautioned. "Remember, go slowly, very slowly. You have all the time in the world to get there, but only one shot at it. If you can't bring her to orgasm using nothing but yourself and your little friend there, she might just decide she wants to use toys instead."

"What d'you mean little?" Joe asked with a fake scowl, breaking into a hearty laugh. He sobered instantly, though and admitted that he understood what he needed to accomplish and how important it could be for their future. "I've been practicing what you told me," he admitted. "When I think I can't hold back, I concentrate on something else."

"What did you come up with that works?"

"Snakes."

"Snakes? Why snakes?"

"'Cause I'm terrified of the little buggers," Joe answered.

"Really? Why?"

"Never trust anything that doesn't have shoulders," was Joe's reply.

JILLIAN

THE SECOND TIME the lights went off, Jillian didn't panic as she had before. She settled into the big easy chair and waited to see what would happen. It wasn't long before she sensed someone nearby. She could hear his breathing in the still air and suddenly she wasn't sure that she had surmised correctly. Joe had always had trouble breathing, indeed, usually breathed through his mouth. This man seemed to have none of those problems, his breath coming in softly as in most normal people

She wasn't prepared to feel his arm circle her shoulders, the other under her knees. She felt herself lifted from the chair and before she could really react, she was deposited gently in the center of the bed, her head propped up on the fluffy feather pillows. She reached up, trying to touch him, but he had moved away from her. Before she could roll to the side, she felt his hands at her waist. Again she reached for him, but this time he caught her wrists and pulled her arms above her head.

"No, please, don't," she begged. "I'll be good," she promised.

He didn't speak, didn't reply, but he also didn't cover her wrists with the restraints. Instead, his hands slid down her arms, smoothed her robe off her shoulders and stripped it away from the rest of her body, the belt sliding apart with a deft movement. He began the slow seduction that he had used before, his hands setting her body on fire as he kneaded her shoulders, weighed each delectable breast, teased her nipples and smoothed the flat muscles of her belly.

She wasn't sure how much time had passed before he reached the fine curly hair at the base of her abdomen. It could've been only minutes, but it seemed like hours. By the time he moved to her thighs, she was in an agony of desire, writhing against his hands, pushing against them, whimpering and begging. The slow seduction of her legs continued unabated, no matter how much she pleaded, no matter that she was panting with need.

When he rolled her to her side away from him, she was almost sobbing with frustration, but it didn't seem to have any affect on him. His hands smoothed the muscles of her back, over her hip, reaching over her to fondle her breasts once more. When his hand smoothed down over her belly, her conscious mind fled, all her senses concentrated on the fingers that toyed over her. She barely noticed when he lay down beside her, his legs covering hers, trapping them. She didn't care. Her body was totally beyond her own control.

When he slid his right arm beneath her, circling to meet the left as it pressed into her, she finally became aware of his naked body against her back, his legs wrapped around hers, his erection hard and tight against her buttocks. "Oh, no," the thought slid through that small part of her mind that was still capable of thought, but it wasn't strong enough to stick and she quickly forgot all about it, especially when his fingers parted her, slid inside, took her up through the cosmos, a shooting star in the dark of night.

She could hear her own grunting moans and tried to contain them, not caring when she failed. She was almost in tears when he moved, pulling his arm from beneath her, releasing her legs. "Not yet," she begged. "Please don't leave yet." She felt him shift on the bed, held her breath, waiting. He grasped her by the hips, turning her all the way over to her stomach. She wasn't sure what to expect, but prayed for more and more. She felt him holding her hips, lifting her to her knees, spreading her legs apart and kneeling between them. The bed rocked beneath his weight as he slowly adjusted his position until she was forced to open wide to him. His hands began again, this time from behind her, caressing her back, down her ribcage, reaching around to knead her breasts, sliding down, down, down.

She didn't fight, didn't move away although she might have. She didn't try to stop him, didn't want to, couldn't. Indeed, she leaned back against him, pushing herself onto his lap, her legs shaking from the effort to get closer, her arms straining against the mattress. When he spread her apart, opening her to him, she didn't object, wanted what he had to give, humiliated herself begging for it.

She felt his penis between her legs and reached for it, her fingernails grazing his testicles, her hand guiding him to her entry. As soon as she felt the tip slide into her, she pushed herself hard against him, impaling herself on his rigid shaft. Her breath left her in a single gasp as she was stretched, filled, expanded until she thought she would tear apart. And his hands were never still, his fingers teasing her, his hands pressing her against the hard staff embedded within her.

When he didn't move, she wriggled against him, leaning forward, pushing back, her own hand searching him out, finding him, tickling him. After a few agonizing moments, he began to move inside her, retreating and thrusting in an ever quickening rhythm, his hands now holding her hips against him so that she had to move in rhythm with him.

She felt his arms encircle her, his hands pressing low, then lower on her belly, until his finger slid just inside and he stroked the tiny nub with his finger as he drove deeply into her. The sensations swelled, growing as a tsunami inside her, cresting at heights she'd never dreamed of. She came as she had never come before, great waves of fire engulfing her, her whole being centered deep within her as every muscle became rigid with an ecstasy that went to her very soul.

When she thought it was over, when she wanted to fall forward and lay gasping for breath, when she knew nothing could ever be so wonderful or so enervating, she felt him measure himself within her, felt his hands beginning their sensuous movement again, felt them slide up to her breasts and felt him lean over her, his chest against her back, his legs forcing her onto her stomach. Connected by his throbbing erection, she was pulled over onto her side, her whole body measured against his, her left leg was pulled backwards over his hip holding her open to him.

She didn't know how much she wanted him until he began again, stroking inside her, caressing her, pulling her against him, driving into her. Her body responded in wanton abandon, grinding against him, arching into him, rocking her pelvis to his rhythm, moving faster and faster until she and he climaxed together in earth shattering unison.

JOE

*H*E HESITATED AT the door and took a deep breath before twisting the knob and sliding inside. He knew she was on the chair, so turned in that direction, his hand on the wall to guide him. Slipping his arm around her shoulders, making sure to capture her arms as he did, he slid the other under her knees, lifting her against his chest, cradling her to him, crossing the floor until his knees bumped against the bed where he gently settled her into the pillows. When he felt her hands on his arm, he captured her wrists, not wanting to tie her again, but prepared to if she persisted. When she promised to be good, he slid his hands down her arms, tickling and caressing, hoping she would keep her word.

He found it especially arousing to slide the silky robe from her shoulders, untying it and smoothing it from her body. He settled beside her and began the seduction that they both had come to take such pleasure in. He especially enjoyed tormenting her, driving her higher with each stroke, each caress, ignoring the curly entry that beckoned, seducing her thighs, knees and calves instead. It took him almost an hour before he felt secure and in control enough to roll her away from him, quickly stripping off his clothing then lying behind her, his legs over hers, his erection nestled in the cleft of her buttocks.

He sighed in contentment when she didn't fight, increasing the pressure and intensity of his caresses, finally sliding his finger into her, maintaining the pressure until she became stiff against him, her orgasm almost setting him off. "Snakes," he thought, conjuring up a writhing mass of hissing vipers. Sweat poured off his forehead, slicked his body, but he managed to contain himself, holding his rigid wife against him until he felt her tension ease, her muscles relax.

He rolled her to her stomach, shifted and came to his knees. Bracing himself with legs spread wide apart, he grasped her hips, raising her up onto her knees, spreading them farther apart with his own legs until they were both in perfect position. Again he stroked her, stoking the embers, igniting wild fires inside her. Again he had to envision scaly reptiles to contain himself, taking deep breaths until he was sure he was under control.

He smiled when she began to beg him for release and he scooted forward until his penis slipped between her legs, throbbing against her, ready for penetration. He held his breath, praying she wouldn't fight or try to get away and was rewarded by her firm little bottom rubbing against him, her fingers skimming along his erection, tickling his balls. He was so hard he was sure he wouldn't be able to hold off when he introduced just the tip of his shaft into her innermost sanctuary, sucking in his breath when she responded by pushing against him, forcing him deeper.

Her moans incited him and her fingers ignited him as he rocked back and forth inside her, clenching his jaws in concentration, trying to contain himself. His hands slid down her sweat slickened body, slipping into her, strumming her as he thrust deeper, tormenting her until she exploded in a violent eruption that gripped him tightly, the strength of her contractions pulling him deeper inside, her behind grinding against him. "Snakes," he thought. "Snakes, pythons, vipers, asps, rattlers," and so on. He recited a whole litany of synonyms for the shoulderless reptiles, his blackened eyes squeezed tightly shut as he fought for control. When he could feel the storm passing, he breathed a sigh of relief, sure that he could retain his erection for the rest of the time . . . as long as it wasn't too much longer.

Wrapping his arms around her, his chest against her back, he forced her face down on the bed then rolled them to their sides, pulling her leg up over his hip to give him better access. Again he impelled her to the heights, driving into her, his hands never ceasing, his fingers joining his penis at her apex, setting her on fire, burning him with her until theirs was a single violent eruption that consumed them both.

JOLYN

"*H*EY, DAD," JOLYN called out, trying to get Joe's attention before he could leave the gym. Hurrying across the room, she had time to take him in, unable to believe that this was the same big, furry teddy bear of a father who'd thrown her into the air when she'd been a little girl, his big hearty laughter a harmonious counterpart to her squeals of delight. The area around his eyes was still a sickening shade of dark green tinged with yellow, and he still had a bandage across his nose, but the rest of him looked like someone else.

"Hi," she ran into his arms, the feel of his embrace the same, the warmth unchanged and she breathed a sigh of relief. "Wow," she said, leaning away from him to give him a slow perusal. "What've you been doing to yourself?"

"Just these exercises," he said, then shook his head, admitting, "and working out with Carl, and doing my own workout. There isn't much else to do when I'm not with your mother or at the house, working on the den."

"Has she seen the new you?" she asked.

"Not yet," he said. "I think it's scheduled for today, but I'll be wearing a mask, so she won't see my face."

"Won't matter. She'll be so busy checking out those abs she won't have time to look at your face. And the beard and mustache make you look real mysterious," she said, tweaking the short whiskers on his jaw line. "You look really sexy!"

He blushed from his neck to his hairline. "You're my daughter," he said. "You're not supposed to notice things like that."

She patted his chest. "Hard not to when you don't have a shirt on."

"None of the other men do," he said defensively, brushing her hand away.

"I'm not criticizing, Dad," she told him. "I think it's great. Has Tom had a chance to check you out yet?"

"I don't think so," Joe replied. "I saw him yesterday morning, but didn't get a chance to talk to him." He paused, went on. "When you and Tom told me about all of this, I really had no idea what it was going to be like. I'm not sure who is going through the greater change, your mother or me. I still do most of my own exercises, but I think this morning drill is even better and Dr. Summers says I can keep coming in the mornings even after we're done."

"Maybe Mom will do it with you," she suggested.

His face brightened. "Do you think she would? It'd interfere with her running."

"It doesn't interfere with mine. I just don't run as far anymore. I don't think I need to."

He glanced at the clock on the far wall. "Oops, I'm gonna be late."

"Where you headed," she asked, falling into step beside him as he hurried from the gym.

"I'm gonna get one of those spray-on tans," he chuckled. "Can you imagine that? Guess I'm supposed to be tan all over."

She whooped, laughing at the idea of her father allowing the cosmetic treatments to his hair, skin, hands and, she realized, feet. Pointing, she asked, "A pedicure, Dad?"

"Not my idea," he grumbled. "Case said my feet were a dead giveaway."

"And you're supposed to be barefoot today, right?"

"You already know the drill, don't you?"

"Not really, Dad," she answered. "Every case is different. Each patient's needs are unique. It's just that some of them require the guy to be barefoot."

"I'll be glad when this is all over," he admitted. "I'll be more than happy to keep up all the things I'm supposed to do to, and for, your mother. But some of the rest of this is really weird for me. They've even got me walking differently!"

"Dad, have you looked in the mirror lately? Or noticed the looks all the women give you when you walk into the gym? You're far and away the most attractive man in there . . . well, maybe Dr. Summers has a little on you, but only because he's younger. He's not nearly as big, his muscles aren't nearly as well defined and he doesn't have that sexy beard and mustache." She started laughing once again when she saw the dark red blush creep once again to his hair line. "Go ahead," she said. "Get your tan on. Mom won't have to see your face to think you're sexy, Dad. She'll take one look at your body and go ape!"

JILLIAN

*U*NSURE OF THE time of day, or, even, the day, Jillian came awake with a smile and a feline stretch, reveling in the feel of her own body, smiling like the proverbial cat who had eaten the canary. "Sex! Oh, yes. Sex!" she thought to herself, her alter ego agreeing completely. Over the last several days she had been penetrated, seduced, hell, let's be honest . . . *fucked* into insensibility and she gloried in it. Her body felt reborn, sensitive in places she hadn't known existed, alive!

It no longer mattered who it was or why. All she could think of was the next time he would come to her, would touch her, caress her, screw her mindless. She no longer cared that she might be considered wanton, that it might be wrong, that he wasn't her husband. She had no other worries to consider, nothing to take her mind off the things he did to her body, the feelings he induced, the sensations that coursed through her.

The single dark thought that kept her from being totally satisfied was that she still didn't know what had happened to Joe. Not that she was in any position to do anything about it, but she would have liked to know that he was all right.

She rose, stretched and walked into the exercise room, surprised to see a large package in the corner where nothing had been the night before. Curiosity overcame her and she knelt beside the box, prying it open. Lifting out the wrapped present inside, she opened the little address card, finding only her own name. She tore open the paper and gasped with pleasure. Inside was a double layered box of pastels in a large assortment of colors. She dove back into the box, pulling out tablets and a drawing board, pencils, charcoals and erasers. Now she had something to do with the times when HE wasn't around. She lifted her head, smiled and said a loud thank you to the cameras that she was now certain were located around the room.

As she jogged on the treadmill, she pondered which she would use first, what she wanted most to draw, how to compose her first picture. She was pleased to see how rapidly the time passed and stepped from the machine after an hour and a half, heading to the bathroom and a hot shower. No water flowed when she turned the dials, though, no matter how she twisted and turned them. She leaned over the tub, turned on the water there and decided to take a long soak, since she couldn't shower.

She poured the bubble bath, set out the shampoo and soap, slid down into the oversized Jacuzzi tub and relaxed with her head against the pad, closing her eyes and luxuriating in the sensuous feel of warm water rippling over her. The jets burbled, increasing the bubbles, filling the tub to the top, and she slid down until her nose was just above the water level. Dreamily she floated, both mind and body, eyes closed, drifting. She wasn't sure what caught her attention, but she sat up suddenly, her eyes popping open.

HE was there in the dim light, tall, muscular, bare feet crossed as he lounged languidly against the door jam. With a black mask covering his face from just above his thick, luxurious mustache, she was unable to tell exactly what his face looked like, but the rest of him left nothing to be desired. He was incredible. His unbuttoned shirt exposed a heavily muscled bare chest. His pants rode low on his lean hips, displaying a perfect set of abs, everything tanned and glistening. She wanted to touch him everywhere and began to rise from the water, but stopped when he shook his head.

It was then that she noticed the two delicate stemmed glasses in his left hand and the wine bottle in his right. She understood his gesture, sank back down and waited for him to come to her, smiling when he stepped toward her, his big body exuding confidence and sensuality. "No wonder he excites me," she thought, admiring the physique of her mystery man. "He's absolutely exquisite." She waited while he set the glasses on the wide rim of the tub, pouring a little wine into each, giving the bottle just the right twist to avoid losing that last drop.

"My very own phantom," she thought, taking in the black mask. "I've never seen eyes that blue," went through her mind, reminding her that this man was different, wasn't her Joe, her husband, but she squashed the thought down, tucking it into another compartment of her mind for later.

When he extended her glass to her, she reached from under the bubbles, but he withdrew it, making her reach farther, running his hand down her extended arm.

Shudders started with his touch, her hand shook as she took the glass, especially when he grazed her hand with the back of his fingers as he released the stem to her care. She watched with jealousy when he lifted the other glass to his lips, realizing for the first time that the one thing they had not done was kiss, wondering what it would be like to actually meet his full lips, surrounded as they were by silky mustache and the short beard that lined his jaw and climbed his chin.

She didn't have time to ponder anything else. Her eyes grew large as she watched him skim out of his shirt, slowly unzipping his pants and allowing them to drop to the floor. "Magnificent," was the word that ripped through her mind, unsure if she was describing his body or the engorged shaft that sprang proudly from the mass of curly black hair just below his firm belly. Watching him step over the edge of the tub, lifting her enough to slide down behind her, settling her in his lap, she was hypnotized by him, realized she would have done anything he asked of her at that moment. Her eyes closed and a slow smile lit her face as his hands began their slow seductive dance, enhanced by the slick, soapy water and the feel of his erection sliding gently against her.

Sloshing over the side unheeded, the soapy water puddled on the marble floor while the bubbles popped and melted away. She didn't even notice. Her whole mind and body were concentrated on the incredible sensations coursing through her. When he lifted her just enough to allow him entry, her hands were on him, guiding him, goading him. When he seemed to stop, she wriggled and thrashed, creating unbearable friction, tipping herself over the summit. No sooner did she gain her breath than he started over again, driving her to a second climax in minutes.

When she could take no more, he turned her sideways, cuddling her against his chest, his hands never still, soothing her back, her arms, her legs. And then he gathered her in his arms, curled his legs under him and stood, water sloshing, slipping and sliding sensuously over them. He set her down on the wide ledge surrounding the tub, turned and retrieved the glasses, pouring a little more wine into each. As she put her glass to her mouth, he tipped his, dribbling wine down her chest, over her breast and belly.

Unconsciously, she held her breath, watching in amazement as he lapped the wine from her, pausing to give extra attention to her breast, suckling and nipping. Twice more he dripped wine over her breasts, twice more his tongue and lips ignited her fires anew. And then he poured a small amount of wine lower down, allowing it to run down her belly into the damp, golden curls between her thighs. Again he licked the juice from her, following the flow. Easing her legs apart he licked and sucked, his tongue finding her once again, thrusting, licking, probing. Climax followed climax, a continuous eruption gripping her, until there was no air left with which to scream and every nerve ending was on fire.

Holding her gently until her breath returned, he waited patiently, caressing her, soothing her. When he judged her ready, he stood, took her glass and spilled a little down his own chest, offering himself to her. She barely hesitated, leaning toward him, licking the tight, firm muscles, her hands holding his hips, unknowingly pulling him toward her. More wine flowed down his belly, and she followed it with her tongue, greedily lapping at him, nipping and biting his belly as he had hers.

She looked up, took the glass from his hand and spilled a little over his erection, giving him a shy, but knowing, smile. Hesitantly, she tasted him, found him delicious and devoured him, her mouth slathering over him, gobbling him, her tongue sliding around the shaft, over the tip, giving as good as she had ever gotten. Her hands kneaded his thighs, slid over his balls, grasped his buttocks, trapping him, spreading him and, finally, sliding a single finger inside.

She wasn't prepared for the force of his ejaculation, or the salty taste of semen that flooded her mouth. Neither was she prepared for the involuntary thrusting that forced him deeper into her mouth, gagging her. She pushed against him, trying to dislodge him, panicked, close to vomiting. Thankfully, he withdrew, going down on his knees before her, his head resting between her breasts, his arms around her. "Sorry," she whispered. "I've never . . . I didn't . . . I'm sorry."

"Shhh," came the first sound she could remember him making. "Shhh."

Her hands in his short hair, she kissed the top of his head, leaned to kiss his forehead. "You've given me so much," she whispered in his ear. "I want to be able to give back to you. Teach me."

She waited, held her breath, almost wept with relief when he nodded. She reached for him, but he stopped her, taking one of the wide bathing towels from the rack and wrapping her in it. He took another for himself as he stepped out of the tub, turning to take her hand, making sure she didn't slide on the slippery floor. He retrieved his clothes, slid them back on, then helped her into the sheer robe.

Leading her into the exercise room, he handed her one of the tablets and a pencil, then walked to the other end of the room. Sitting languidly in a sexy sprawl on the long padded bench, left arm propped on his bent left leg, right leg extended, he nodded, letting her know that he would pose for her.

She was ecstatic! This was something she had always wanted to do, but never had the chance. She loved drawing people, but, mostly, she loved the play of light on a superbly fit body, the subtle angles, the deep shadows. It only took her minutes to set up. She started small, with pencil and twelve by eighteen paper, but it didn't take her long to graduate to a much bigger size, using charcoal pencils with broader lines, smearing shadows, erasing highlights.

She could have continued for hours, but when she finished the third drawing, he stood, blew her a kiss and left. By the time she got to the door of the bedroom, the outer door was closed and he was gone.

She was elated and disappointed at the same time. She had done something she would never have dreamed of doing and then been allowed to do something she had always dreamed of doing. Maybe, if she learned to please him better, he would pose nude for her, she thought, dreamily wandering into the bathroom to finish her morning ablutions.

JOE

"*Y*OU'VE MADE SOME great progress for only being here a couple of weeks," Dr. Summers complimented Joe when he arrived for his morning session with his wife. "I don't think we've ever had anyone who has responded as well as you and your lady."

"We're pretty motivated," Joe answered with a smile. "She wants out of here and I want to please her."

"I don't even know if she really wants out of here any more," Case replied. "She seems pretty satisfied, especially with the sex."

"Oh, she wants out," Joe assured him. "But, I think, she seems to like the sex, too."

"Absolutely," Case agreed. "But I was thinking more of you."

"Huh?"

"You've gone along with every change we've made in your appearance. Nothing seems to bother you, not the beard or mustache or the short hair. Sally said you even stood still for the spray on tan without a single argument. You didn't complain about the body wax or the manicure. And Cheryl said you managed to 'walk' a quarter all the way across the back of your hand twice this morning. Carl said you were already in great shape, so it didn't take much to define the muscles that were already there and you've worked very hard to improve your posture. You've learned to meditate and keep up with our exercises, and you still do your own afterwards. I don't think there's much more we could ask of you. But, if we did, you'd do it, wouldn't you?"

"If it would help Jillian, I would," Joe replied truthfully.

"Okay, then," he held up a black mask, the kind that courtesans had worn in the days of Louis XIV, stiff and unbending.

"What's that?"

"Most of you is different and I'm sure she wouldn't recognize you in broad daylight. But, your eyes and face, even with the nose repair, those she'd know in a minute. So, you get to wear this. It'll not only hide your face, it'll protect your nose." He handed over the mask. "And these." He handed Joe a small contact case.

"Why those?" Joe asked, taking both. "I can't see didly squat without my own prescription contacts."

"These are made to your own prescription, but they're a very dark blue. They have to be to camouflage the dark brown of your own eyes." He produced a mirror, but Joe shook his head.

"Thanks, but I've worn them for so long, I don't need that," he said, popping out the left contact and replacing it with the blue. "Pretty good," he said. "It just darkens stuff a little, but I guess it won't be too bad." He changed the other then pulled the mask over his face. "Oh, Doc. Did you give her the box?"

"She found it this morning," the doctor answered with a nod.

"And?"

"She seemed to be delighted," he said. "I think it's a great idea, by the way. Especially if you let her draw you."

"That was the plan," Joe said. "She's very visual. Likes to be able to see whatever it is that she's drawing."

"Well, let's see if chapter fifteen does the trick. She's in the tub, relaxing. Good luck," the doctor said, handing him a bottle of wine and two flutes.

"Yeah," Joe said, taking a deep breath. "I don't think this is going to work."

"You never know," Case told him. "You didn't think she'd ever touch you and you didn't even have to show her. Now she does it with regularity. I think she's growing to like it."

Heading for Jillian's room, Joe realized he'd gotten used to the loose linen trousers and silky unbuttoned shirt, even though they weren't quite his usual style. And he'd never gone without underwear until he'd come here, but he had to admit it made undressing a lot easier. He'd decided that he would do whatever it took when he'd made the arrangements to do all of this, though, and he would change whatever was necessary to get her to enjoy sex.

He slipped inside the bedroom, peeping around the corner of the bathroom to make sure she wasn't looking then stepped inside, leaning against the door jam, trying to appear at ease when he felt anything but. Once in place, he gently clinked the glasses together to get her attention.

"Snakes," he said to himself. Over the last week or so, he'd taught his wayward appendage to ease up whenever he thought of reptiles. Now all he had to do was think the word and he found himself under control. And it took all that control to stroll nonchalantly across the bathroom, pour some wine, caress her and then strip slowly. Once in the water, control wasn't so difficult and he was able to relax and enjoy petting her, stroking her, stoking her fires. By the time she was ready, she was easily wet enough for him to slip into her, working her into a frenzy, taking his pleasure from her satisfaction.

"Snakes," he thought as he felt her tension, trying desperately to keep her from taking him with her. He almost went over the brink, did everything he could think of to keep from losing control, almost contained himself when she wriggled, rubbing her fine behind against him, pushing herself onto him. He set his jaw, tensed every muscle he could think of, lost it anyway.

He wasn't as unhappy as he might have been. He'd found that he was ever ready when it came to pleasing Jillian. Even when he came, he was often ready again within a few minutes, her excitement fueling his own. He allowed her to rest for a few minutes, cuddled against him in the cooling water, then gathered his legs beneath him before he could lose his courage and stood up, setting her gently on the wide surround of the tub.

He reached for the wine and the glasses, saying a silent prayer as he did. He chased the first dribble with his tongue, licking her delicious body as he'd always wanted to. By the time he got to her breast he was hard all over again and he could tell that she was almost ready, too. Twice more he poured wine over her and lapped it up, always taking the time to savor her breasts, always moving his hands over her. The wine that disappeared into the hair nestled between her thighs drew a sigh from her. He wanted desperately for her to enjoy this for two reasons: to please her, and to get her to return the favor.

Her hands on his head pulled him into her, her thighs closed against the mask, almost unseating it, but he spread her legs again with his hands as he nipped and probed, licked and thrust, finally sliding two fingers inside, grinning when her internal muscles gripped them and pulled him deeper. Her back arched, her hands tore at his hair, her legs curled around his shoulders, heels digging into his back. He had set her aflame and she burned in his mouth.

Now comes the ultimate test, Joe thought, holding her until her breath returned, soothing her, calming her. There was no one to calm him, though, and his heart skipped beats, hurrying toward the final test. When he could, he stood, taking her glass of wine and dribbling a little down his own chest, inviting her to return the favor. He was almost faint with relief when her tongue reached out to him, lapping up the wine, tentatively sipping the small runnel. Another tiny rivulet of wine found its way down his belly and she happily licked that as well, her sharp little teeth nipping and biting, her tongue leaving a blazing trail on his belly, her hands burning against his hips.

He couldn't believe it when she took the glass from him. The shy, sexy look she gave him turned his already hardened penis to stone. The wine did nothing to calm the flames that scorched him, her mouth and tongue incinerating his will power. When he felt her finger slip into his anus, he could contain nothing any longer. He could barely stand. His legs threatened to collapse beneath him. The flood spurted, a liquid jet that gushed from him, taking his mind and all conscious thought with it. Spasms shook him, his hips pumped into her, his hands tightened on either side of her face.

Her frantic gyrations as she tried to get away from him brought his senses back in an instant. He released her head, withdrew, held her while she gagged and choked, knelt in front of her to rest his head on her chest. He could have cried when *she* apologized to *him*, wanting nothing more than to apologize to her. He finally nodded, rising to help them both from the tub, still stunned by both his own lack of control and her contrition.

He knew he needed to be far away from her for a while, mostly because he wanted so badly to gather her in his arms and tell her that she didn't need to apologize to him, that it was his fault. Leading her into the exercise room, he pointed to her drawing materials then went to the other side of the room. He pretended indifference, lolling languidly on the bench, but his stomach was churning. She'd completed the third drawing when he decided he needed to leave, blowing her a kiss and hurrying out the door.

He stood against the closed door, squeezing back tears when Dr. Summers came out of the control room. "She thought she did something wrong!" he blurted out. "She apologized to me! But it was all my fault. I lost control."

"Hey, calm down," Dr. Summers took him by the arm, leading him across the hallway into his own room.

"I wasn't supposed to do that," he said. "I wasn't supposed to come in her mouth. I didn't mean to."

"Well, she had her finger up your butt," Dr. Summers laughed. "I don't think I'd be able to control myself if someone did that to me. Now you know how she felt when you did that to her."

"Holy shit," Joe exclaimed. "That's my fault, too, isn't it? If I hadn't done that to her, she never would've thought to do it to me."

"Exactly," the doctor agreed. He removed Joe's mask, surreptitiously checking the older man's pulse. "She obviously enjoyed it when you did it. She thought it would make it better for you."

"It did! But . . ."

"But it made you lose control."

"Yeah," Joe rested his head on his fists, aware that he had probably blown his chances of ever getting another blow job. "If I were her, I wouldn't do it again," he said.

"But you're not her. She thinks she did something wrong by gagging like that. I really don't think you have anything to worry about. See what happens tomorrow."

"But we already finished the manual," Joe said, unsure what was expected of him now.

"Yes, you did. Now you're on your own. You have almost a whole week before we turn her loose. What do you think you should do in the next couple of days?"

"Well, for starters, I think I'll pose for her. Maybe let her decide what she wants to do."

"Very good. Excellent. I think you've given her the very best avenue she could have to allow her to explore what she's learned." He paused, smiled. "Feeling better?"

"Yeah, I'm fine," Joe answered. "I think guilt was the primary emotion there. I mean . . ."

"I do understand, Joe," Dr. Summers told him. "Let's see what happens tomorrow."

JILLIAN

WHEN SHE CAME out of the shower, Jillian realized she was disappointed that he hadn't come yet. She'd half expected him to join her under the hot spray, had even stood there longer than usual to give him time. She was used to the routine now, knew that there would be a silky robe lying across the already made bed, but she remained in the bathroom, smoothing on body creams and face lotions, putting on her makeup and doing her hair. A month ago, she wouldn't have considered doing any of that without getting her clothes on first, but now she stood naked before the mirror, completely oblivious to her nudity.

When she finally strode into the bedroom, she was surprised to find an oversized button-down white shirt, a pair of jeans, creamy, lacey panties and matching bra lying on the bed. For some reason, seeing something so normal in this anything-but normal place caused her to break down, sitting on the bed with the shirt wadded in her hands and sobbing her heart out. She wasn't sure why she was crying. She'd never been harmed, indeed had always been treated like royalty even when she'd been bound.

The thought slammed into her, overwhelmed her, took her breath away. She had spent most of her time this last week waiting for her mystery man to come to her and take her to the moon. She'd almost forgotten that she was being held prisoner, had barely thought about her husband for more than a fleeting moment. Guilt rode her, tore at her, until she could barely breathe. And another emotion smote her: Anger. Where was Joe? How could he have left her like this? Why hadn't he come to rescue her? Why hadn't *he* set her on fire? "Oh, God," she chastised herself. "How can you be angry with poor Joe?" What if he'd been injured when these people had taken her? What if he'd been killed? And here she was . . . *Fucking*! And not just fucking, but loving every minute of it.

The same arguments that she'd wrestled with over the course of the last three weeks all came back in full force, causing her tears to become a flood, great sobs wracking her body. She curled up on the bed, the white shirt clutched to her breast, crying until she had no more tears left. After a while, her sobs slowed, her tears dried and she sat up, shaking her head at the thoughts that sped through her mind.

It was only then that she realized she was still stark naked. She gave a half-hearted laugh, realizing that, for the first time in her life, she didn't care, didn't give half a damn whether she had clothes on or not. "Well, that should make Joe happy," she thought. "He's always said I shouldn't be so shy about my body." Then, "Joe, oh Joe. Where are you? Are you all right? Did they hurt you?"

She went over every argument she'd used to talk herself into, and out of, believing her mystery lover was Joe. He was the same size, but this guy was in much better shape. He was hairy, her lover was not. Joe slouched, but not this guy. He had beautiful posture, head erect, shoulders back, hips sexily thrust forward. Even when he sprawled on the bench for her to draw him, he didn't slouch, didn't hunch over. And his hands and feet were soft and smooth, unlike those of her husband. "He could've changed all of that," she thought. "And grown a beard and mustache and cut his hair."

Finally she came to the single thing that convinced her that her lover couldn't be Joe. Blue eyes. Her lover had blue eyes. Joe's were a rich dark shade of brown with little flecks of gold. She loved his eyes, she realized. They were warm and expressive, full of laughter and full of love.

Love. She loved Joe. She had loved him from the first moment she'd seen him. Did she love her mystery man? Her phantom? "No," she admitted. "I'm not in love with him. I'm in love with the things he's awakened in my body, with the feel of him inside me, with what he does with his hands and tongue. But not with the man, himself."

And she was lonely. She missed her kids. She missed Jolyn's little boy, Joe and Kate's little girl, Megan. Had Jolyn finished her dissertation? Had Jack gotten that promotion he was hoping for? What about Kyle? Had he settled into his apartment? Had

Kate and Jeff gotten moved into their new house? So many questions ran through her mind. So many things she was missing out on. And no one to share any of her thoughts with. That was the worst part of all of this. She had no one with which to share her fears, her emotions, her love. She missed her Joe.

"No sense crying over something you can't change," she told herself, getting to her feet and starting to dress. It didn't matter that the shirt was totally rumpled. She didn't care that the bra and panties felt deliciously decadent. She slid the jeans up, zipped and snapped them automatically, not caring how she looked. She buttoned every button on the shirt, wiping her eyes with the shirt tail, leaving a black smear of mascara.

One last sigh and she straightened her shoulders, swiped once more at her eyes and strode purposefully into the exercise room to retrieve the new drawing materials. She carried them into the bedroom, laying them on the floor by the big chair before settling herself onto the cushions. She tore out a few pages, clipped them to the drawing board, wiggled around until she had it comfortably propped against the arm of the chair and began to draw.

She lost all track of time, didn't move anything but her pencils until she heard something in the exercise room. Curious, she set her materials aside, rose and slowly crept toward the doorway, but when she got there, nothing was different, no one there, nothing had been disturbed. It wasn't until she returned to the bedroom that she understood. The sound had been a lure to get her out of the bedroom long enough for him to enter and lie down on the bed, his head propped on his left hand against the plumped pillows.

He didn't smile, made no move at all toward her, simply remained comfortably ensconced in her bed. She didn't know what she was supposed to do, what he expected of her. "Do I have any choice?" she asked herself. "Let's see." She returned to the chair, picked up her tablet, turned to a clean sheet of paper and began to draw. The quick sketch rapidly turned into a beautifully rendered portrait of her mystery man, complete with black mask.

"So far, so good," she thought, changing to another size paper, selecting a charcoal pencil. She motioned to him to turn over and was pleasantly surprised when he did as she indicated. Nodding to him, she began a second drawing, not even considering how uncomfortable the position she'd put him into could be. Again she lost herself in the drawing, again it was a flawless portrait, and, once again it was breathtaking.

"Too bad I don't have an easel," she said aloud. "I'd love to do you in color." She didn't expect a reaction and was surprised when he rose to his feet and left the room. "Damn," she complained. "Just when I was getting into the groove. Putting the finishing touches on the second picture, she decided to give it up for a while, putting everything aside. She went into the bathroom, automatically closing the door behind her. When she returned he was once again sprawled across the bed, barefoot, shirt open, relaxed.

"Um . . ." she didn't know if he would do what she said, but it seemed to have worked so far. "Could you take off your shirt?" she asked. He rolled toward her but made no move to undress, merely sat quietly, waiting. She put out her hand, pulled at the collar, tugging it across his shoulder. He made no move to stop her, but his hand caressed her arm while she pushed the fabric from him. She whimpered, wanting that caress, wanting him to touch her, but also wanting him to pose for her.

She tried to ignore his hands while she pulled his shirt the rest of the way from him. Hesitantly she pushed at him until he leaned away from her and she could reach his zipper. Trying not to think about what she was doing, she unzipped his trousers, hitching a hand on either side of his waistband to pull them down. He cooperated fully, lifting himself from the bed enough for his pants to slide off his hips and over his thighs. She gasped, seeing the full tumescence of his erection.

She couldn't help herself, but reached down tentatively, petting him, her fingernails just grazing him, the tip of her tongue moistening her lower lip. "Oh, what the hell," she sighed aloud, sliding down to her knees in front of him and taking him in her mouth. Slowly she licked and sucked his swollen member, her hands finding first his tight abdomen, then his erect nipples. She pushed his pants the rest of the way to the floor, her hands never still, her caresses turning rough as she kneaded his thighs, played with the curly hair at their apex, grasped his balls.

After a few minutes, he lifted her, pulling her over him like a blanket, then rolling them both over so that he leaned above her, one hand freeing her buttons, the other pulling the snap on her jeans. He skimmed her jeans from her swiftly only to return to lie beside her, his hands beginning their sensuous dance over her body. When she began to writhe in his hands, he turned, his tongue lapping the base of her belly while he presented himself to her mouth.

And she took him, tasted him, savored him while he in turn tasted her. For a brief moment a trickle of fear took hold of her, but it wasn't strong enough to retain its presence and she found herself enjoying giving him the same pleasure he was giving her. She raked her teeth softly along the shaft and over the tip, wrapping her tongue around, over and under, her mouth never still, her hands always in motion. When his tongue thrust into her, she gasped, tensed, tightened her hold on his hips, sucking him deeper into her mouth.

He groaned, pulled away, turned them so that he was kneeling between her legs, his fingers spreading her open to him. He paused, poised above her, and she raised her hips to him, opening herself for him, reaching down to guide him into her very essence. When he thrust into her she met him, ground against him, literally sucked him in. Her hands clutched his buttocks, pulling him even deeper, her legs wrapped around him, holding him in place while her own hips bucked and twisted against him.

She could feel his need just as he had always seemed to feel hers and she slid her hand between them, her fingers just reaching behind the shaft, grasping the tight full sac that slammed against her. She felt him shift until his hand rested just beside hers, his fingers sliding beside his penis, entering her, manipulating her until she went rigid in ecstasy, her own hand closing tightly around him. She could feel the heavy spurt of his climax as he emptied himself into her, an eruption that matched her own, exploding from him, filling her, fulfilling her.

She couldn't believe it when he rolled her so her back was to him, spooning her, his hands gently caressing her breasts, her belly. She felt so comforted and comfortable, so cherished. After a few minutes her breathing returned to normal and she could think again, assessing just what had happened. "He let me do what *I* wanted!" she thought, wriggling contentedly against him. "He let me make the choice."

It was a whole new concept for her. She had become the aggressor, had initiated the encounter. "I did it," she thought. "I wanted him to fuck me, and he did!" The more she thought about it, the better she liked the idea. "I can decide when and where," she thought. And then the ultimate idea hit her. "I *wanted* it." For the first time in her life, she wanted to have sex, wanted that feeling of being totally out of control, of tension, of electricity.

"And what would he do if I said 'no'?" she asked herself.

"Why on earth would you want to?" her new alter ego asked. "No, not alter ego," she thought. "Libido. I have a libido. And it wants to have sex. Lots and lots of sex. And he seems to want to give it to me." Indeed, even as he held her, his hands began again. She rolled within the circle of his arms, her own hands moving seductively along his hips, down his legs, around his thigh, over his buttocks. But when his mouth closed over her nipple, she forgot to move, forgot to breathe.

When he knelt with one leg on either side of her, pinning her arms over her head, again presenting himself to her, she sucked him in, licking and slurping greedily. When he slid down her body until his penis rested between her breasts, her chest rose to meet him. Freed, her hands clasped her breasts on either side, closing them around him, rubbing him gently, teasing him.

She pushed against his shoulders, rolling him to his back, throwing her leg across him. Sliding down farther and farther, she sat astride him, lifted enough to guide him inside and settled down over him until she could accept no more, was filled totally and completely. After a moment, she began to move, her hands against his shoulders, her feet curled over his knees, pinning them to the bed. He held her hips, his hands tightening around her thighs, his thumbs widening her, entering her, goading her.

She could feel the tension mounting deep within her, climbing through her, tearing into her. The chafing of his thumbs, the tightness of her vaginal walls gripping him, drawing him into her, the friction as she ground herself against him all combined into one continuous orgasmic wave that surged through her very being. Her climax was doubly intensified by the sudden repeated jets that burst from him, his hips heaving and rocking, the pulses thickening him, grinding him inside her.

She wasn't sure whether she fainted or just collapsed, but when her eyes opened her cheek rested on his heaving chest. She fought for breath, could feel him doing the same. She didn't have the strength to move, didn't want to and so she lay upon him as the minutes passed and they both recovered. Just when she had decided it was time to leave him, she felt him hardening within her once again.

"I can't," she whispered even as her hips started to wriggle in response. "I can't," she cried as she pushed against his chest, rising once again to impale herself on his thickened organ. "I can't," she said for the last time as she began rhythmically grinding against him, forcing him deeper, increasing the friction, fusing herself to him. He drove her ever higher, thrusting into her with all his might, finally wrapping his arms around her and rolling the two of them over until she was beneath him again, her legs wrapped around his waist, her hands pulling against his hips.

As wave after wave of fire engulfed her, she forgot to breathe, forgot about her family, forgot everything but the incredible, indescribable, unbearable heat that speared through her, ripping through every fabric of her old life and leaving her complete.

"I can't," she thought when he rose from the bed, pulled on his pants and left. "I can't stand this any more. I'm coming apart at the seams. I only feel alive when he's inside me. And I want him inside me all the time, always, ever more. What am I going to do?"

JOE

"*I* KNOW SHE WANTS to draw me," Joe told Case just before he opened the door to her bedroom. "You've seen the pictures she's already done, haven't you?"

"Yes, I have," Dr. Summers answered. "And she's very good. As a matter of fact I showed a couple to an uncle of mine who has a gallery and he says he might be interested in having a show for her if she can get together a couple of dozen or more. He's got a clientele who are very interested in the male form, especially nudes."

Joe blushed. "No, not me," he said. "She does other things."

"Yes, but the only ones we've seen are the ones of you and those are the ones he's got the clients for. See if you can get her to do a few more."

"I'll give her a couple of hours to draw before I do anything else," Joe promised.

"There goes the outer door," Case said. "It's time." He quietly pried open the door, making sure Jillian wasn't in the room, then motioned Joe inside. "Good luck," he said softly as he pulled the door closed.

"I'm gonna need it," Joe thought, quickly crossing the room and crawling across the bed. He plumped up the pillows and had just posed himself against them when she came back into the room. No matter how sexy those silky robes were supposed to be, she had never looked sexier than she did right now, in jeans and an oversized button down shirt. He found himself instantly ready, painfully aroused, hard as a rock. He swallowed, closed his eyes tightly, repeated his litany. "Snakes," he conjured, trying to calm down. He was relieved when she sat down and started to draw, and he soon slipped into a state of reverie, remembering the good times they had shared over the years.

When she motioned him to turn, he tried to get into the position she indicated, finally settling uncomfortably into a contortion that found him peering at her over his shoulder. Before she was halfway done, he was shaking from the effort of keeping still, but he held the position until she finished. When she blurted out that she wanted an easel, he quickly got up and left the room. Just outside the door, he told Dr. Summers what he wanted.

"I'll see what I can do," Case promised. "She's gone into the bathroom," he cautioned.

"Good," Joe answered, popping open the door and slipping inside. Again he went directly to the bed, making himself comfortable.

When she asked him to take his clothes off, it was all he could do not to tear them off, tear hers off as well and take her, ready or not, but that was the old Joe. This one played cool, sitting still and allowing her to make the first move. When she tried to pull his shirt off, he grazed her arm, tenderly caressing her ribs, allowing her to undress him while his hands wandered over her delicious body. The second she touched his zipper he sprang to attention, and was at full staff by the time she lowered his pants to his thighs.

He held his breath, waiting to see what she would do. When she touched him, he almost went off, just barely maintaining his cool. He sighed with both relief and contentment while her mouth tasted him, tested him, tormented him. This was more than he had ever dreamed she would do. For her to take the initiative was way beyond his wildest dreams. And she was a natural, seeming to know just how to skim her teeth over him, how to use tongue and lips to excite him.

When he was within seconds of coming, he drew back, pulling her with him and over him, giving him a few seconds of reprieve while he slowly undressed her. Again he tormented her with tongue and hands, deciding to go for it before he lost his nerve. Lying head down beside her, his erection just inches from her face, he sought her with his tongue, teasing her, licking and lapping, his mind willing her to take him. When he felt her tongue on him, when her mouth closed around him, he had to go through his whole litany of reptiles again and again to stay the explosion that was just below the surface.

Finally, when he knew he wouldn't last more than a second or two more, he moved out of her reach, once again giving him a few moments reprieve. He turned around once again, rolling her to her back, spreading her legs, and kneeling between them, caressing her, giving himself time. When he felt he could hold back, he positioned himself above her, his fingers widening her entry, waiting to see if she would initiate consummation. When she raised her hips to meet him, arching her back, going up on her toes to give herself lift, he gratefully sank into her.

When her unexpected wandering hand closed around his testicles, he knew he was almost at the end of his control. Knowing he could ignite her already simmering body even further, he slid his hand between them, his finger joining his penis within her. It couldn't last, *he* couldn't last. Beginning at the base of his spine, a surge of heat left him with the force of a freight train. The collision pushed her over the threshold, sending her spiraling heavenward in her own fiery completion.

Wanting only to hold her, he turned her from him, spooning her in the single most comforting position he was capable of. Even spent, sated beyond belief, his hands continued to smooth over her body, caressing her breasts, pulling her even closer. Unbelievably, he found himself ready for her once more, but waited, giving her time. When she turned in the circle of his arms and began caressing him in return he was ecstatic. This was what he'd hoped for, prayed for. She wanted more, wanted sex, wanted him!

Licking and nibbling his way down her neck, over her collar bone to her breast, he took that succulent object in his mouth, his whiskers rasping the tender flesh, heightening the sensations, chuckling when her breath left her. Coming up on his knees, he held her trapped between his legs, her arms above her head. He leaned forward just enough to present his swollen shaft, almost weeping with joy when she once again took it in her mouth, laving it with her supple tongue.

"Snakes!" he forced the thought into his mind, staving off another climax, withdrawing from her. Scooting down just a little, he freed her hands while sliding his penis between her breasts. It didn't take much wriggling to impart the idea and he was rewarded when her hands pushed her breasts together around him, creating another crevasse for him to enjoy.

And then she took the initiative, pushed him over on his back and mounted him, guiding him into her, settling down over him until there was no more of him to give. When she began to move, he began to chant the different kinds of snakes over and over in his head, trying to hold on, trying not to disappoint her, wanting it to be as wonderful for her as it always had been for him. He pressed his thumbs into her, finding that secret spot that would set her off, but wasn't prepared for the force with which she gripped him as the final throes of ecstasy spun her in an ever upward spiral, squeezing him, grinding against him, tearing the juices from him. Control was the last thing on his mind as he bucked upward, thrusting into her, holding her in place until his cyclonic release was complete.

When she collapsed onto his chest, groaning, he couldn't move, could barely breathe, but his hands still continued their sensuous dance. When he felt her move, her bare breasts heavy against his chest, he quickened once more, alive as he'd never been before. He barely heard her cries of "I can't". It would have made very little difference. For the final time he drove them both up the mountains of desire, wrapping his arms around her to roll them both over, bracing himself on his arms as her legs wrapped around his waist, cresting on a wave of rapture that seemed to go on forever.

When all he wanted to do was lie beside her, hold her, cuddle her in the aftermath of their frantic lovemaking, he did as he was bidden, rising from the bed, taking only enough time to step into his trousers before leaving the room.

JILLIAN

"*N*o, please, don't go." She didn't say the words, but she wanted to. She needed something more, she realized. The sex was incredible, more than anyone could ever describe, but she wanted more. She wanted what she had at home. She wanted someone to talk with, to laugh with, to share her thoughts and dreams with. In a word, she wanted Joe.

It didn't matter that her body longed for more. Even when she was still panting from one orgasm, she was ready to go for another. It didn't matter that she had never before felt what she was feeling now. What mattered to her had been taken from her. She had lived for forty eight years without enjoying sex and it hadn't prevented her from having a good and fulfilling life. She loved her family, loved her husband. She'd laughed and cried, but mostly, she'd loved!

But, as soon as she thought about those things she was missing, she reminded herself that she had no choice. She was being held against her will, period. She couldn't just walk out. "Or can I?" she thought, going to the door. She wasn't surprised when it didn't open, not even disappointed. She'd known that it would be locked.

With a sigh, she returned to her drawings, trying to remember how his body had looked without clothes. All she could remember was how his body had felt, how he had felt inside her, how his hands had felt on her, his mouth on her breasts. "I'm going crazy," she thought. "I can't think of anything else!"

His shadow on the paper made her jerk her head up, her eyes widening. When she started to set her drawing board aside, he held up a hand, stopping her. Walking over to the bed, he shed his shirt, unbuttoning his pants but not removing them. Again he sat on the bed, leaning back, the muscles in his arms bulging, his belly concave beneath his loosened waistband.

"Oh," she couldn't think beyond that simple word, but she took up her charcoals and began to draw. After half an hour, he stood, leaning against the door jam, legs and arms crossed. Again he nodded, indicating she should draw him in that position. For hours he changed positions, allowing her only twenty or thirty minutes in each pose, each more seductive than the last.

When he shed his pants, allowing her to draw him full frontal, his stance with flaccid penis was like that of Michaelangelo's David and the drawing was dynamic. He turned away, looking over his shoulder, the tight muscles of his back and buttocks casting delectable shadows across his body. Each pose gave her some other part of his anatomy to concentrate on, stressed the strength and power of the whole man.

Sitting Indian style on the bed, chin resting on one fist while the opposite forearm was crossed on his knees in front of him, unmoving, he exuded power, and she was able to capture the feel, the potency, the vigor subdued within this otherwise calm pose.

And, finally he lay across the pillows, one arm extended above his head, the opposite hand resting on his flat, hard belly. As she drew, he came erect, full and throbbing, calling to her without saying a word. She managed to finish the drawing, as magnificent and wrought with sensuality as the man she depicted.

She lay aside her materials, rising, stepping to the bed and crawling up from the foot, kneeling above him, taking him into her mouth while her hands caressed him. She was overjoyed when he reached for her blouse, and she crawled up his body just enough for him to reach her buttons. Her bra followed her shirt onto the floor and with breasts cradled in his hands, she had to follow the gentle tug that drew her upwards. When he popped the snap on her jeans, skimming them down to her knees, taking her panties with them, she twisted to give him greater access.

With a lithe movement he rose to his knees, turning her away from him while he pulled her jeans from her. Taking her by the hips, he pulled her firm little bottom against him, grinding his erection between her legs. She reached down, took him in her hand and guided him into her, sliding her hand on down to capture his balls. Oddly, this time, with very little coaxing on his part, she achieved orgasm within minutes, holding him in place with a firm grip on his testicles.

Rocking back and forth, head thrown back, moaning with completion, she ground into him again and again, tipping her over the edge two then three times, each climax as intense as the first. Held prisoner he could only do as she bid, driving into her, his hands sliding down her belly, his fingers finding her, holding her when her body tensed with the rigidity of yet another climax.

When she finally released him, it was only to give her the freedom to roll beneath him, turning to face him, one leg on either side of his. Again she grasped him, guiding him inside, encircling him with her legs, drawing him deeper and deeper within her. Her hands on his hips determined the rhythm as she pulled him into her, her legs trapping him.

Her back arched, her groans rose to a crescendo, her pelvis thrust against him as she tried for one more climax, but, until his mouth closed over her nipple, turning it into a hard sensitive knot, that ultimate orgasm escaped her. She felt his teeth worry first one nipple, releasing it only to turn to the other, while his hands worked their way down her belly. With the first touch of his finger, she erupted, spewing fiery hot dew over him, squeezing his own burning, liquid response from deep within him.

She lay, limbs entangled with his, gasping for breath, incapable of more than that. When he finally lifted himself to a sitting position, she touched his shoulder, begging him to stay. "Just a few more minutes," she pleaded. "Just don't leave me alone." Gratefully, she leaned into him, snuggling against his chest within the circle of his arms. Much as she would have liked to, she didn't talk to him, sure that he would not respond and even more sure that it would break her heart when he didn't.

When he finally left her, she curled on the bed, once again giving into tears. "Please," she begged. "Please let me see my family. Please let me go home."

JOE

*W*ITH NOTHING ELSE to do, Joe asked Dr. Summers if he could return to Jillian's room and pose for her.

"I don't see why not," was the response. "I think she's just about at her wits end. It might be better for her if she has company today."

"Did you find an easel?" he asked almost as an afterthought.

"Should be here this evening. It'll only give her a few days with it, but it should be enough, don't you think?"

"I think so," Joe agreed.

"I thought she was an art teacher," Case asked. "How come she doesn't do her creations at home?"

"She just never seems to have time," Joe told him. "I thought she'd get everything out and start drawing once everyone left home, but she never got around to it. Maybe she will when this is all over."

"It would be a real shame for her not to exhibit," Case said. "What I've been able to see of her work is really dynamic. There aren't very many people in the world who can really portray movement in people, much less emotion. She seems to be able to do both. Zach was really excited about them when I showed him pictures of them."

"Zach?"

"My uncle. He has a very avant garde art gallery. One of those that set the standards of taste for the rest of them. And he's pretty sure he can find buyers for everything she's done so far."

"What? He have some kind of kinky clientele?"

"No, not at all. There are some in the art world who think the nude body is the purest form of all art. And some of them have a lot of influence, not to mention money. If he shows her work and they like it, it could be the beginning of a whole new career for her."

"Rich and famous, huh?"

"Could be," Dr. Summers agreed.

"Really?"

With a smile he repeated that one word that had come to epitomize Joe's whole metamorphosis. "Absolutely."

Joe chuckled, went to his room to pick up a couple of things, then walked the distance around the unit to the opposite side where the door to the exercise room was hidden. Looking up, he nodded to the camera, heard the snick of the latch and pushed open the door. Silently, he tiptoed across the floor, peering into the bedroom, waiting for just the right moment. Once he was sure she was still concentrating on the drawing in front of her, he strode across the carpet until his shadow fell on her paper. When she looked up, he backed to the bed, shedding his shirt, loosening his pants and leaning back, flexing his biceps, head back, posing.

He changed poses every twenty or thirty minutes, knowing that she would be able to put finishing touches later on any she hadn't finished before he moved. He tried to present a different part of his anatomy for each pose, tried to make it more interesting and more challenging for her. After a couple of hours, he shed his pants, standing naked in a classic pose, knowing she would recognize the single piece of statuary that he mimicked.

When he lay languidly on the bed, one hand over his head, one on his belly, he watched her, gazed at her long lovely neck as she peered over her drawing board, trying to catch the essence of her mystery man. He couldn't help it when his other brain decided to make itself evident, didn't even try to hold back the enormous erection that sprang from the tight curls at the base of his abdomen. He held his breath, waiting to see what she would do, but her response was beyond his wildest expectations.

When she cat-crawled up his body from the foot of the bed, he thought would pop off before she even got near. When her mouth closed over him, he didn't have time to sigh before he had to chant the entire class of snakes in his head, repeating them again and again while she lathed his penis with her nimble tongue. He reached for her, pulling her further up his body until he could reach her buttons, smoothing her shirt from her, unsnapping her bra with one hand and discarding that frilly item as well.

Rising, he turned, sealing her bottom against his groin, allowing her to be the one to decide the next move. He was elated when she guided him to her, but became a little alarmed when she grasped his testicles, holding him where she wanted him to be, *using* him. He thought she would release him when he felt her grow rigid, her orgasm tightening her around him, her grip tightening on his balls, but she began again, groaning, grinding, gripping harder and harder. He didn't have to try for control; the pain in his scrotum was making it hard to retain his erection.

When she finally released him, but before he could escape, she squirmed around, lying on her back, again taking a firm hold of him, pulling him to her, impaling herself on him. Her long legs wrapped around his waist squeezing him, holding his penis hostage, her hands digging into his hips while she ground against him. He sensed her panic, knew her frantic gyrations weren't doing what she needed, and he took pity on her, leaned to suckle her left breast, his hand wandering between their bodies until his fingers found her. With a few deft movements he sent her over the edge, following her into oblivion.

Lying panting, entangled in the bedding and her arms and legs, he knew he needed to leave, but she stopped him with a touch on the arm and a plea, and he couldn't go. He wrapped her in his arms, holding her to him, his big hands soothing her back. Once she seemed calm, he rose, slid on his pants, picked up his shirt and walked back into the exercise room and out the back door.

He all but ran around the unit to the hallway and into the control room. "What's the matter with her?" he almost shouted.

"I'd say she's confused and frustrated," Dr. Summers replied calmly. "It's not that unusual. She's trying to please you, but at the same time, she's trying to gain the same sensations she was getting in the beginning."

"Have I forgotten to do something? What'd I do?" Joe was almost in tears. He'd done everything the manual had said, but now, instead of responding as she had, she was frantically trying to achieve orgasm after orgasm without the joy. That wasn't what he'd hoped to have her learn.

"You haven't done anything, Joe," Dr. Summers said. "Just calm down." He waited for the older man to get a grip on himself. "Sit down for a minute, Joe," he said, turning back to the monitor, turning down the sound.

"She's crying again. Why's she crying now? She was the one who was in control the whole time. I didn't make any moves toward her at all."

"You got a hard on," Dr. Summers explained.

"Wasn't I supposed to?"

"It was a perfectly normal response. But she might have looked at it as an invitation. One she was afraid to refuse. She did what you've trained her to do."

"Oh, no. I didn't train her to get a death grip on my balls. I just wanted her to learn that sex could be fun. At the rate she's going, I'll have a heart attack just trying to keep myself under control until she's satisfied. Or I'll have one 'cause I'm having two or three orgasms in a two hour session. I can't keep that up, doc."

Instead of looking worried, Dr. Summers grinned, giving a deep chuckle before going on. "I have to admit it is unusual for someone your age to climax quite that often. Actually, that's more like the frequency of a horny teenager. You should be satisfied with three or four times a week, I should think. It's a little more reasonable expectation. That's one of the beauties of the dildo. She can get satisfaction without doing you in. What did you think it would be like when you got home?"

"Hell, I don't know," Joe answered. "At first, I thought it would be great to have sex that often. But I'm pretty sure I can't keep it up much longer and, if she wants sex two or three times a day, I'll have to resort to some sort of toy."

"You've already introduced her to a vibrator and she seemed to be pretty accepting. It's just that she's more demanding right now. But I think you'll find once she's in her own home and her normal everyday situations, she'll adapt very well." He took a deep breath, leaned closer, forcing Joe to look him in the eye. "She's one of those people who's used to having something going on in her life every minute of the day. Right now, she only had four things to do, five if you count bathing. She runs, reads, draws and has sex. All four give her a great deal of satisfaction, but none of them give her the interaction she needs."

"I guess having sex isn't interaction, then," Joe asked somewhat sarcastically.

"Joe, you know what I mean," the doctor said, getting a little disgusted with the man's attitude. "When was the last time she had someone to talk to? I mean, she can talk to you when you're there, but you can't talk to her. She needs more than sex. That's why she asked you to stay."

Joe slumped, the winds totally gone from his sails. "You're right. Again. But I can't talk to her; she'll know it's me."

"Right. You have to realize that she's getting to the point where she needs to go home, which is exactly where we want her. She's learned to love sex. She's gotten an extra plus in that she's drawing again. She's even gotten to the point where she'll initiate sex. That's way beyond the response of most of our patients."

"If she initiates any more, I won't be able to keep up," Joe observed.

"Next time, you start it. Don't wait for her. You've done everything we've told you, Joe and done it very well. Very few of our spouses have taken the time or had the patience to do everything you've done. Now, you have to go against the manual. Just because she's willing to make the first move, you don't have to wait for her. And you don't have to give her multiple orgasms unless you just want to. Wait until she's almost there before penetration and you won't have to worry about control, either."

"I'd sure like that," Joe said with a sigh. "I'm running out of names for snakes."

"Takes all the fun out of it, doesn't it?" the doctor asked him.

Joe looked up, realizing once again just how observant the doctor was. "Does it always work that way?" he asked.

"No, not at all. Once she's home, you can discuss it with her. Foreplay doesn't have to be painful, Joe. Obviously, she's gotten to the point where she doesn't need quite as much foreplay as she did at first. Now, she'll be able to tell you when she's ready. One of the reasons she had so many problems today was that she wasn't quite ready. It's just one of those things you'll have to work out together."

"Okay," Joe nodded. "So when do I take her home? And how?"

"I'd say two or three more days. We'll work out the details tomorrow. You might want to talk to your kids and make sure all of you have your stories straight. She won't be quite so understanding if she thinks they are all in on your little escapade."

"Jolyn has warned Kate and Kyle. They're all okay with everything. They were going to pretend we had been on a cruise, but now we've decided to say she was in an art colony. That will explain the drawings, at least. And the tans. Although hers is better than mine. Mine's just paint. We still haven't gotten a hold of Jack. He was trying to get a promotion a month ago and, if he got it, he was going to be in Japan for a couple of months. Anyway, he obviously got it because he's sent a couple of postcards. It's just that no one's gotten to talk to him."

"Okay," he turned back to the monitor where he could see that Jillian had returned to her drawings. "Oh, I forgot. Tom found an easel. It's in your room. I think you should wait until tomorrow before you visit her again, but you might go ahead and put it in the exercise room."

"Good idea," Joe extended his hand to the younger man, wanting him to know just how much he appreciated everything he'd done for them. "I'm sorry to have been so whiney," he said. "I shouldn't complain when she's doing what I was hoping she'd do."

"You weren't whiney. I'd say panicked described you better. Can't say I blame you. Even without being bruised from before, it would be incredibly painful to have someone get a tight grip on your gonads, no matter what the reason."

"Exactly," Joe said, smiling for the first time since he'd left his wife.

JILLIAN

SHE'D GONE TO sleep beside her mystery man, cuddled peacefully against him and as content as she'd been in the last month. The last few days had been wonderful.

He had come into the room, posed for her for a couple of hours then left without demanding anything from her. No sex, nothing. And she hadn't thought about it at first, so engrossed was she in the newest pastel she was working on. He'd let her touch him, move him, indeed, twist him around into any pose she'd wanted, and he'd done everything she'd asked of him without trying to seduce her in the process.

When he'd returned, just as she was finishing the last portrait, he'd come straight to her, taken her chalks from her and taken her into the bathroom, running a tub full of water while holding her gently. He'd removed her clothing slowly, caressing her skin, skimming his knuckles across her cheeks, down her jaw, his long fingers smoothing down her neck and chest, ending at her waistband. Her zipper had succumbed in seconds and he'd placed a hand on each side of her hips, skinning her jeans off her in a single move.

He'd placed her fingers on his buttons, letting her take his clothes off while his hands moved everywhere over her body, tying her into knots that only he could release. He'd stepped into the tub, leading her behind him and she'd gone willingly, wanting to please, wanting what he had to offer, wanting him. He'd set her on his lap facing him, something he'd never done before, scratching her skin gently with his mustache, nipping her shoulder and collarbones, leaning her away from him to lick her neck.

Where the day before she'd been frantic for him, grinding against him to achieve that wonderful sensation that only he had been able to bring to her, now she lay languidly against his hands while his mouth and tongue slowly stroked her neck, her shoulders, her chest. With her breast in his mouth he'd groaned, setting her on fire, making her move against him.

She'd groped in the soapy water, seeking him, finding him and guiding him, raising herself to position him, sliding down over him until he'd filled her. But he'd trapped her hips with his hands, keeping her from moving, slowing her, allowing her time to savor the delicious sensations that had coursed through her. And she'd understood for the first time, realized that all the frantic gyrations of the day before had been unnecessary.

Slowly, slowly, taking his time, a little kiss here, a little nip there, his hands gentle as they coursed over her, keeping her still around him, he'd aroused in her such an intense sensation that she couldn't contain it, couldn't remain still, had to move. After an eternity he had allowed her to rock against him, slowing her when she became frantic, calming her with his hands. Inches at a time he'd slid into her, gently filling her then receding, small movements that incited a riot within her, wanting more, wanting what he was doing, wanting . . . wanting.

Finally, he'd wrapped his hands around her thighs, spreading her, thrusting hard, just once. And she had come and come and come again, unable to stop, one orgasm spilling over into another, so close that she'd had no time to catch her breath, so many, so intense that she thought she would die. When he had surged into her a second time, another wave of continuous orgasms had hit her, each peak a little higher, each climax a little stronger, her body so rigid that she'd feared she might break.

And a third time he had driven into her, holding himself deep inside as they found the heights together, her vaginal muscles squeezing around him, drawing him deeper still until he'd erupted in a volcanic spasm that sent her on a journey through an ultimate burst of flame that had consumed her. When she'd collapsed against him, she'd had nothing left inside except the man who had taken her to the stars, burning her in their heat.

Later he had returned, allowing her once again to position him for more drawings without touching her, not attempting to seduce her, only humoring her in her quest for perfection in her art. And she'd reveled in that freedom, the freedom to draw, to create, to capture his firm, hard body on paper; the freedom to touch him with no sensual tension or sexual overtones.

And still later, tired but replete, she had laid her drawings out, on the floor, on the bed, the chair, against the wall, and she realized she had created more in the last few days than she had been able to do in the last twenty years. And she smiled, knowing in her heart that they were very, very good. "And I owe that to him, too," she had said quietly. Finally, she had stacked them all together and gotten ready for bed.

Coming out of the bathroom, she'd been very surprised to find him lying under the comforter, waiting for her. She'd come to him hesitantly, unsure of his desires, but he'd taken her in his arms, turned her back to him and tucked her against him, holding her gently, lovingly, with no sexual overtones, until she had gone to sleep.

JOLYN

"**A**RE YOU SURE you don't want one of us to wait around until she wakes up," Jolyn asked her father as she helped carry the last of her mother's drawings into the den. "She's sure to be upset," she argued.

"And let her know that you've been in on her whereabouts for the last month?" Joe asked. "Do you really think that's a good idea?"

"No, of course not," she agreed. Then, shrugging her shoulders in defeat, she tried one more time. "I could just stay here, in the living room and then I'd be near if you need me."

"If I did my job right in the first place, neither one of us is going to need you right now," he told her, taking her by the shoulders and turning her to look at him. "We'll be over for dinner for sure," he promised. "Kate and Kyle are going to be there, aren't they?"

"Yes," she nodded. "I'm still not sure that's the best idea though," she argued.

"Hey, if we really had gone on vacation, the first thing she would want to do is see the babies. Right?"

"Right."

"Well, this way the only one who'll be in trouble will be me." His smile finally convinced her and she turned to leave. Taking her keys from her purse, she turned back. "Oh, I forgot. I talked to Jack for about two minutes the other day. He called to say he'll be home in the next week and he's bringing someone with him. I think he's found a girlfriend."

"'Bout damn time," Joe said, shaking his head at his eldest child's behavior. "I was beginning to think he'd never settle down. What'd he say about your mom and me?"

"That's just the thing," she replied. "I still didn't get a chance to tell him. He told me he was coming home soon, that he was bringing someone and would I go over to his apartment and turn on the air. That's it. He hung up before I could say anything more than yes."

"Shit!" Joe's expletive surprised his daughter. She wasn't used to hearing him swear.

"It'll be okay, Dad," she promised. "When he flies in, he'll need someone to pick him up at the airport. He'll call one of us and we'll be able to warn him."

"I sure hope so," he said. Shaking himself mentally, he smiled again. "Go ahead," he told her. "It'll be all right."

She slid into the car, still unsure that she was doing the right thing.

Tom leaned across the console, giving her a quick kiss on the cheek. "It'll be all right," he promised. "Case showed me the last tape. She's really hot, Jolyn. And she's as ready as she'll ever be."

She couldn't believe what she was hearing. "He showed them to you?" she demanded. "He promised he wouldn't."

"No, he promised we wouldn't be the ones to monitor them. For teaching purposes, he can use the tapes if he thinks it's necessary."

"And just what was he teaching you?" she asked sarcastically.

"Technique," he said with a slow smile as he put the car into gear.

"Tom!"

"Well," he glanced at her, gave her a wink. "Your dad has come up with some ideas that we are going to include in the manual. He's a natural, Jolyn. And your mother is as responsive as any woman I've ever seen."

"In the manual? You're going to include my father in the manual?"

"Not by name," he told her. "Besides, that's how we learn and how come we have the success rate we do. Just because they're *your* parents doesn't mean we can't learn from them. Just think about it, sweetheart. How many couples have you already monitored? And every time we see something new that works, we discuss it. And if we think it's truly universal, we include it. We're rewriting it all the time. You know that."

She sighed. "I know. It's just too personal, I guess."

"I suppose tonight wouldn't be the right time to try out some new ideas, huh?"

"You want to do to me what my father is doing to my mother?" she asked, appalled.

"Hell, Jolyn. We've already been doing that. We do have a child, don't we?"

She giggled. "You're incorrigible," she said. "Just don't tell me when you do it. Okay?"

"Absolutely," he chortled. "I have to say something, though."

"What?"

"I'm so glad that you haven't waited until we've been married twenty-five years to learn how much fun sex can be."

"Maybe it's because you already knew some of the things that turn a woman on. My dad didn't. That's why he's been so successful at the clinic. All you had to do was show him what needed to be done, and how."

"And your mom just needed someone who knew what he was doing."

"Wow!" she said. "Wouldn't it be great if they were all so easy?"

"Yeah. That's for sure. Most of the men fight everything every step of the way. Some of them never learn. Remember that one guy, Mr. Pershey? He was just sure that the fault was all hers. Didn't want to change anything. He figured all he had to do was sit back and we'd fix her for him."

"And a month later, she was still as frigid as the day she walked in. Too bad we couldn't introduce her to someone who'd take care of her."

"Whoa," he laughed. "That's not the purpose of the clinic."

"I know it isn't," she said, laughing with him. "But every now and then we see someone who shouldn't even be married. He was one of those. He was so egotistical, you couldn't convince him that he needed to make some effort."

"And your dad is so in love with your mother, he was willing to change every thing about himself to please her."

"Just so he doesn't change too much," Jolyn said. "I kinda liked him the way he was."

"I don't think he's changed much when it comes to his family," Tom said. "I do think he's changed physically in ways that will be of benefit for him for years to come. His breathing has always been labored and now he's not having any trouble at all. He's fine-tuned his body, but he was already in great shape, so it didn't take much. And that beard makes him look like a real rogue."

"Wonder how Mom will react when she knows for sure it's him."

"I think she'll be relieved above all else. It's been harder on her than it has on him simply because she didn't know for sure."

"I think she might have had some idea," Jolyn argued.

"Maybe. Maybe not," Tom said. "Either way, now that she's home, she'll be happier knowing she didn't have sex with some mystery man."

JILLIAN

*E*VEN THE GENTLE stroking on her abdomen didn't keep Jillian from panicking when she awoke, bound and sightless. "Oh, God, no," she cried. "Please, not again." Blindfolded and bound, she became frantic, thrashing, twisting, trying everything she could to get free, but it was not to be. Not since the first week of her imprisonment had she had to undergo this extreme confinement, and it terrified her. After only a few moments, however, she responded to the familiar caresses, calming somewhat, reacting as her body had been taught.

"Please," she begged. "I'll be good. I'll do whatever you say. Just let me go. Please."

It did no good. The hands moved over her body with ever more insistence, and she succumbed to the sensations they brought her, writhing in harmony with them, allowing herself to enjoy the solace of their ministrations. It didn't take long for her to forget her bonds, losing herself in the seduction of the sensuous hands, following their progress from her throat to her breasts and beyond, until they arrived at the curly, golden hair at the base of her belly.

Unable to stop herself, she rolled her pelvis toward the hands, only to find that the confinement of her ankles kept her from achieving her goal. As she struggled against her fetters, they were suddenly loosened, allowing her to bend her legs, spreading them wide for those marvelous hands. She dug in her heels, thrusting herself against him, her body arching off the bed, offering herself to him.

And she thanked him when he responded by slipping his fingers into her offering, teasing her with his thumbs, sliding a single thick finger inside. "Oh, yes! Yes!" she repeated again and again, moaning in her anxiety to acquire the maximum sensations. When his hands moved up her body once more, she cried out in dismay, wanting them to return to her. But they captured her breasts, his mouth feasting on her swollen nipples, and she writhed in response to his tongue as he licked his way from one breast to the other.

She struggled to free her hands, wanting only to hold his head against her chest, and suddenly, she was free. She grasped his shoulders, her hands running down his biceps, clasping his arms, pushing them lower and lower until his hands were once again where she wanted, no needed, them to be. "Please," she pleaded.

Still he teased her, sliding his hands down her legs, kneading her taut calf muscles, tickling her ankles with the back of his nails, pinching the fine skin on the inside of her thighs. Again his fingers touched her, and her hands moved to guide them.

Again they withdrew, leaving her weeping in frustration. "Please," she cried, trying to capture his hands once more.

She felt him kneel between her legs and widened herself even more, arching her back, raising her hips into the air, presenting herself to him. She reached for him, but he eluded her grasp, taking her wrists in one hand and raising them above her head. Centimeter by tiny centimeter, he sank into her, filling her until she was sure she could take no more, sinking further until there was nothing of him left to give. And then her hands were free to touch him and she gripped his hips, wrapping her long legs around him, holding him imprisoned deep within her.

For moments neither moved. His thick shaft, embedded deeply inside her, pulsed with his heartbeat, sending her vaginal muscles into convulsions that in turn contracted around him. The friction of her spasms sent tremors through both their bodies until there was no him, no her, only a single being that erupted in one searing orgiastic finale, leaving them both weak and breathless.

Still he didn't leave her, allowing her to relax, her arms and legs unfettered, his own body held rigidly above her. Slowly, as they regained their collective breath, he once again seduced her delicious breasts, sucking, licking, suckling, until they, and she, responded once again.

"Oh," the thought presented itself when she could think once again. "I can hear him." Relieved that he hadn't deafened her with the ear buds and white noise, she concentrated on the low voice that murmured against her breasts. His voice!? It was the first time he had spoken to her in the whole time she'd been confined. NO! It couldn't be. "Joe?" she whimpered his name, but got no response. Instead, she felt him harden inside her once more, filling her with the most delicious sensations as he gently rocked within her, tipping her over the edge again and yet again.

"I love you, Jillian." His whisper was almost lost beneath the sound of her rapid breathing, panting as she lay boneless beneath him.

"Joe?" she really didn't have to ask this time. She would've known that voice anywhere. "Oh, Joe," she wrapped her arms around him, holding him as if he might disappear. "Oh, Joe!"

Her blindfold was lifted, but the face was the same as the one she had seen before, the rich, luxurious mustache, the thick, dark beard circling the chin and lining jaw, the same mask covering his face. "Joe?" she reached up gently, pushing the mask from him. And she gasped and cried when she saw the bandages and still dark bruising around the eyes. "Oh, Joe," she sobbed. "What have they done to you?"

She watched his smile appear among the whiskers, heard his deep throaty chuckle, knew it was her very own Joe no matter how different he looked. Her fingers gently circled his bruised eyes. "Are you all right?" Her concern was all the more real for the fact that she didn't yet realize that she had been the one to make such grave changes to his face.

He nodded, smiling into her eyes, leaning to gently bite her chin, licking upwards to take her lower lip between his teeth, sucking gently. "Hi," was all he said before measuring himself inside her once more and sending her skyward in an all consuming climax. "Miss me?" he asked.

When she had regained control of her breathing, she sought to dislodge him, pushing against his shoulder, but she couldn't move, trapped by his big body. "Joe!" she cried. "Let me up!"

"Nope," he mumbled against her neck. "I like you just where you are."

"Stop it!" she demanded, sucking in her breath a moment later when his hand caressed her fine golden mound.

"Do you really want me to?" he whispered against her shoulder, the tip of his tongue scoring a fiery trail to her breast.

"Yes!" she groaned. "No," she admitted. "Oh, Joe," she moaned softly as his fingers found her once again. "Please stop," she begged, then gasped when he closed his mouth around her already swollen nipple. "Unh . . ." was all she could say. She forgot that she had told him to stop, didn't want him to stop, wanted what he was doing to her.

"Still want me to stop?" he asked, his hand pressing against her, a single finger sliding through the damp, curly hair to the velvety softness inside.

"Oh, God," she cried out, thrusting her pelvis against his hand, spreading her legs again to allow him access to her innermost being. "Please," she begged, this time for more of him. "I want you inside me," she admitted, not knowing or caring what she was saying.

And he drove into her again, taking her by the hips and sliding her whole body up over his thighs until she was astride him, facing him, impaled upon him. Her breath left her in a single cry of fulfillment as he twitched inside her and sent her over the top once again. She screamed and moaned, her body convulsing in repeated orgasms, twisting and writhing against him as climax followed climax until it became a continuous, tumultuous fireball, consuming them both.

She slumped against him, unable to think, unable to breathe, able only to feel. After moments while he held her limp body against him, he leaned forward, gently laying her on the pillows, sliding down beside her, holding her tucked safely against him.

"Joe?"

"Yes?"

"What happened?"

"Just now?"

"No, I mean all of it?"

"What?"

She sat up, surveyed her own bedroom and realized she was no longer being held captive. She looked down into Joe's innocent brown eyes, and suddenly she knew. "It was you all along, wasn't it?" she asked. "You had me kidnapped! Do you know how scared I was? Do you have any idea how I felt?" She tried to sit up, but his arm across her body was too strong and she found herself gazing inches from his wounded nose.

He grinned, hoping against hope that she would forgive him, but now not very sure at all. "Are you going to be really angry with me?" he asked.

"Yes!" she answered sharply. "Maybe," she said after a moment. "Probably not," she admitted a moment later. "I probably should be," she warned him.

He nodded, rising to prop his cheek on his hand. "I wouldn't blame you," he said. "But, if it makes any difference, you've pretty much already paid me back."

"What? What are you talking about?"

He pointed to his face. "This," he said. Sitting up, he showed the other bruises, the yellowish remains of those that had been heretofore covered by the spray-on tan. "And this," he said.

It took her only a moment to remember the dark, the man and her knees meeting his testicles and his face. "That was you?" she asked.

He nodded.

"Serves you right," she harrumphed.

Again he just nodded, waiting for the explosion he was sure would come.

But she didn't blow up. She sat, pensive for a moment. Then she asked, "And you still came back and made love to me?" It was more of a statement than a question. She had already surmised the rest of the story. "Why?"

"Because I love you," he said. "Because I wanted you to enjoy loving me."

"I've always enjoyed loving you," she argued.

He cocked his head in askance. "I wanted you to enjoy making love to me," he explained.

"Well, mission accomplished!" And now she laughed. "You've turned me into a nymphomaniac! I can't think beyond the next time you'll touch me. Did you know that? When I go to bed at night, I sleep with my hand between my legs so I won't feel so empty. You've created a monster, Joe. Now what do we do?"

"Well," he said, his face taking on a truly lecherous grimace. "How about we fuck?" he said, reaching to take her ripe breast in his mouth once more.

"Joe!" she batted at his hand even as she arched her back to give him better access to her breast. "We can't do this twenty four hours a day!" she moaned as he nipped and licked his way to the other breast. "We have to stop!" She protested one more time before succumbing to the wonderful sensations that surged through her body.

"Okay," he mumbled, his mouth still full of her engorged nipple. He pushed gently against her ribs, laying her once again on her back. His hand traced her hip bone, drawing shudders from her as he grazed across her pelvis. "Now?" he asked, the tip of his tongue gliding down her belly, his whiskers just abrasive enough in contrast to create the impression of fire and ice as he took her in his mouth, suckling, nipping, biting and thrusting until she came once again.

"Now?" he asked, sliding up beside her once again.

"Never," she told him, wrapping her arms around him, sure that there could be nothing better in the whole world than being loved by her man.

JOE

WHEN JOLYN LEFT, it took all the courage that Joe could muster to return to the bedroom and his bound and blindfolded wife. Dr. Summers had given him a rough estimate of about how long the medication would last and he was already pushing the limits. He donned the black mask, shed his clothing and sat beside her on the bed, sighing once more before he began to move his hands across her lovely, outstretched body. It didn't take long for her to awaken. He could feel the tension before the cries began.

"She's going to hate me," he said, but he never ceased the gently probing of her delightful form. Kneading, teasing, tickling, he traced every quadrant of her until she ceased to fight her bonds and began to respond. "Thank you, Lord," he prayed under his breath. When she began to struggle against the straps around her ankles, he reached down and swiftly released them, rewarded by her renewed efforts to meet his roaming hands.

He could barely contain himself, but he was determined to wait until she was pleading with him, sure that that would be the only way he could ever convince her that he had done everything out of love for her. When he released her wrists, he held his breath, hoping she would do as she had before and not reach for her blindfold. Again he sighed with relief when she accepted her covered eyes, seeking only completion.

When she reached for him, he held her arms over her head until she stopped struggling; kissing, touching, sucking until she was begging him for release. Still he teased her until he could stand no more, finally smoothing her thighs apart and sinking slowly inside her, smiling to himself when she wrapped her long legs around him and pulled against his hips, holding him captive deep within her.

He didn't fight the sensations that tore the juices from him, holding her imprisoned beneath him while they both recovered, sighing against her hair, whispering his love. Without releasing her, he bent to her breasts, suckling once again, nipping and licking them into engorgement once more. He softly murmured his words of love, of contentment, of his ardor. And when she said his name it inflamed him once again, making him harden inside her, rocking against her gently until he felt her slip over the edge again and again and yet again.

"I love you, Jillian," he declared tenderly, waiting until she responded and called his name. He took a deep breath and lifted her blindfold, terrified of her response. He couldn't have expressed his relief when she reached up and lifted his mask, crying out his name, worried about his bandaged nose and still bruised eyes. He smiled, barely able to say "hi", happy that here, at last, he could tell her the truth.

He chuckled, nodded to her questions, leaned to kiss her, nipping her chin, following the tip of his tongue to her lip, taking that delectable morsel between his teeth. He felt his blood stir once more, grew stiff and strong, and measured himself inside her, dragging a gasp from her, moving against her and within her, driving her until she was once more lost in ecstasy. "Miss me?" he asked softly against her ear, munching on that tasty tidbit while she lay panting and exhausted beneath him.

And then she tried to rise, pushing against him, telling him to let her up, but he'd decided his course of action before he'd started and now he was determined to follow it. "Nope," he said. "I like you right where you are."

When she would have argued, he leaned down to take a mouthful of scrumptious breast into his mouth, worrying the nipple, sucking delightedly at her until she moaned. "Do you really want me to stop?" he asked, sliding his hand down her belly to her golden mound.

Even while she tried to stop him, she responded, moving with his hands, arching into his mouth, her hands smoothing over his flesh, keeping him excited and erect. And, finally, he heard the words he'd hoped for when she begged to have him inside her. He was only too happy to oblige, plunging deeply, groaning with need, moaning with desire. Each thrust sent her into spasms of orgiastic rapture, growing closer together as he quickened until he sent them both upwards into an earth shattering finale that left them boneless and complete.

When he finally was able, he moved to lie beside her, his arm resting just beneath her breasts, his fingers tracing designs on her ribcage. And he could have wept with joy that she was calm when she asked him if he had been the one who had arranged to kidnap her. Still he couldn't bring himself to answer her directly, but only asked whether she was very angry with him.

When she waffled, first saying yes, then maybe, then saying she should be, he told her she had already paid him back, pointing to his face in explanation, then showing her the greenish-yellowish remains of the bruises around his scrotum. He didn't argue when she told him it served him right. He had already told himself that many times. He waited, hoped, held his breath.

"And you still came back and made love to me?" she asked, filling him with a euphoria far beyond what he could possibly have hoped for. Her "Why" gave him the opportunity to explain, something he had been sure he would never have. "Because I love you and I wanted you to enjoy loving me," he said, telling her his most sincere desires in that one simple sentence.

Her misunderstanding allowed him the rest of the explanation. "Because I wanted you to enjoy making love to me," he said.

Her reaction was so far from what he had expected, he was totally flabbergasted. "Well, mission accomplished," she told him. When she told him she had become a nymphomaniac, he was delighted. When she told him she slept with her hand between her legs, he was elated. When she asked him what they were supposed to do, he couldn't contain himself. He used a word he'd never used before in her presence. "How about we fuck," he said and leaned to her breasts once more.

Her protests were feeble at best, growing less and less as her arousal grew until she was begging for him once more. The last few weeks had taught him that he could make love to her repeatedly over the course of a couple of hours, but he did have his limits. Instead he slid his tongue down her belly, kissing, licking and biting, taking her with his mouth and pleasuring her senseless.

Sliding back up beside her, nestling her in his arms, he asked if she still wanted him to stop. He chuckled when she hugged him, shaking her head, loving him.

All he wanted was to go to sleep with his lovely wife in his arms, but a glance at the clock told him that he needed to hurry with the rest of the surprise if they were going to make it to Jolyn's in time for dinner.

JOLYN

"**D**O YOU THINK I should call them?" Jolyn asked Kate, when she glanced at her watch for the fifth time in as many minutes.

"I don't know if we should," Kate said. "I sure would like to be a spider on the wall in their house right now, though."

"Wouldn't we all," Tom laughed, giving his brother-in-law a gentle punch in the arm.

"I don't think I want to know what they're doing," Kyle admitted, turning to Kate's husband. "What about you?"

"Hey," Eddie laughed. "I'm just an innocent bystander in all this. But I keep thinking what I'd feel if my parents had done this."

"And your conclusion?" Kate asked.

"I don't think I'd want to know about it," he admitted.

"And I'm sure Mom wouldn't want us to know about it," Kate added.

"You got that right," Jolyn told them. "Dad was really adamant about not letting her know that we had any inkling of what they were up to."

"Then why did he tell you?" Eddie asked, curious.

"Because we're the ones who talked him into it," Tom told him. "We've both seen first hand how well it's worked for other couples. And neither one has ever made any bones about the fact that she hated sex."

"It's amazing she ever had kids," Eddie commented.

"Well, that part of it she liked," Jolyn told him. "Mom loves babies. Doesn't matter whose, either. She just didn't like what it took to get them. She said that when the doctor told her she shouldn't have any more, it about broke her heart. And she's always done whatever Dad wanted, within limits. She's just never enjoyed it. Before."

"And now she does?" Kate asked.

"Oh, yes," Jolyn answered, stressing the word 'yes'. "It's like she's come alive in the last few weeks. She's like a horny teenager."

"Ugh," Kyle said, covering his ears. "Too much information."

Laughing, Tom reached over and patted his youngest brother-in-law on the back. "It wouldn't be too much information if it weren't your parents we were talking about," he joked.

"Yeah, but it is," Kyle protested. Looking at his watch again he groaned. "Do you think they're going to show? Maybe they're having a fight. Could be. She might be so mad at what he did to her, she's letting him have it."

"You might be right," Kate worried. Looking up at her older sister, tears in her eyes, she said the one thing that had worried her all along. "What if she gets so mad at him, she leaves him?"

"Can you imagine Mom ever getting that mad at Dad?" Jolyn asked, giving her sister a warm hug.

"I can," Eddie put in. "If she ever finds out we know, she'll quit talking to all of us, including him."

"I think you may be right about that," Tom said. "So we'll just have to make sure she never finds out."

"Well, Dad's cover story about an artists' colony should be a good enough. She's done some really fantastic drawings."

"Which are all of your father . . . naked." Tom told her. "She sure isn't going to want us to see those."

"He's not naked," she protested. "He's nude. Besides he's wearing clothes in some of them."

"Yeah. A few. If they weren't of your Dad, I might be tempted to buy one or two, though. They're some of the best drawings of the male figure I've ever seen. They'd look great in our office."

"Oh, no you don't," Jolyn scolded.

Tom laughed. "No, I won't. But I will go see the show that Zachery's has promised to have for her."

"Zachery's? That's that really exclusive art gallery in 'Frisco', isn't it?"

Jolyn nodded. "Someone from there is supposed to be at the house tomorrow to look them over. Isn't that great?"

"I think it is," Tom cautioned. "But will your mom think so?"

She just shook her head, glancing once more at her watch.

JILLIAN

"**Y**OU REALLY DON'T need to do this," Jillian protested, her hands out in front of her to keep from walking into a wall. "Please, Joe. Let me take the blindfold off." She wasn't sure why he would want to keep her eyes covered, didn't really care. She just wanted it off. "I'll keep my eyes closed," she promised.

His voice was low and seductive in her ear, his hands gentle but firm as he led her from the bedroom. "Trust me," was all she heard. She felt his hand on her abdomen, stopping her, then one hand lifted her foot, pulling it down onto the top riser of the stairs. She reached out for the handrail, grasping it firmly as she groped with her foot for the next step, then the next. Finally at the bottom of the stairway, he guided her around the end of the banister and down the hallway, stopping her after a few feet.

"Ready?" he asked softly, his hands on her shoulders, kneading the muscles, tantalizing her.

She couldn't stop herself. She leaned her face to his hand, caressing his knuckles with her cheek. "Yes," she breathed. "I'm ready." She had no reason to expect anything other than what she had been conditioned to for the last month, so was doubly surprised when he lifted her blindfold in front of the double doors to the den, stepping around her to open the door.

Jillian looked around what had previously been the den, amazed at the work that had been done in her absence. "When did you have time to do all of this?" she asked, tucking her hand into the crook of Joe's elbow. Tears threatened to spill, but from happiness, not sadness.

"Between feeding you and loving you, there was a lot of time for me to come home and work on it," he said. "Do you like it?"

"Like it? Oh, Joe. This is something I've always wanted and you know it." She pulled on his arm, bringing his face nearer for a kiss. "I guess I just never thought of making the den into a studio."

"Well, it's not being used at the moment," he told her. "It was a great playroom for the kids when they were little, and it was a good TV room when they were teenagers and wanted a little privacy, but they're all grown and gone, so now it's a good studio."

She looked around the room, noting the new floor with large, ceramic tile squares instead of carpet, all in colors she would've picked herself had she had the choice. "I almost hate to get anything on this floor," she said.

"But that's the beauty of tile," he replied. "It's easy to clean up. Even oils will just wipe clean. No need for a drop cloth or anything. And this wall is that stuff you have in the studio at school where your students are always pinning up their papers to work on them." He ran his hands over the smooth, soft covering on one wall. "That's what you like best, isn't it? Drawing against a wall where you don't have to worry about the size fitting an easel or anything?"

"Yes, you know it is," she said, her own hand covering the surface. "But it doesn't look the same."

"It probably will after a while," he said. "This one is just brand new. Never had a pin in it yet."

"And the work bench," she said, going to the wheeled cabinet. "How did you ever find one?"

"I got permission to order it through your department," he admitted. Turning her so he could see her face he asked, "Do you really like it?"

"How could I not like it? It's every artist's dream." She threw her arms around him, hugging him fiercely. "How can I ever thank you?"

"I can think of a few ways," he said, raising his eyebrow in a lecherous leer.

"I can't thank you enough for that, either," she admitted, fitting her body to his, her head tilted for a kiss. "What a wonderful husband I have."

"Who has promised his children he'll have their mother there for dinner and is going to be late if we don't hurry," he said glancing at his watch.

"And just where did you tell your children we've been over the last month," she said as she followed him out the door.

"You've been sequestered in an artists colony. I've visited you a few times and spent a few days getting my nose fixed."

"You're going to scare Little Joe," she warned, pointing to his still bandaged nose.

"Nah," he said. "The kids know I've been doing the room over for you, so they've dropped by a couple of times. Kyle, Eddie and Tom all helped me at some point or other. So both the babies have had a chance to get used to their grandpa looking bruised and battered."

"And very sexy," she purred, snuggling as close as the bucket seats permitted.

"Hmmm," he growled, encircling her shoulders with his right arm, pulling her close for a kiss.

"It's all so wonderful," she purred, happily snuggling across the console to get nearer. "I've always thought you were the best husband in the world. Now I'm absolutely sure of it. Thank you, again."

JOE

$\mathcal{J}$OE WAS AS jumpy as a long tailed cat in a rocking chair factory, waiting for the men from Zachery's to arrive. He hadn't told Jillian who they were, only that they were from a gallery and were going to assess the drawings and discuss options. They had spent most of the morning pinning them up around her new studio, sorting them by style and media so that there seemed to be a progression from sketches to finished work.

He almost jumped out of his skin when the doorbell sounded, hurrying to the front hallway, all but wringing his hands. He hadn't been expecting Case, did a double take before stepping back to allow the three men entry. One glance at the second man convinced him that it had been the right move for the young doctor to come. Although there wasn't a real resemblance between the two, it was obvious they were cut from the same cloth.

"Hi, Joe," Case smiled, extending his hand. "This is my uncle, Zach. And you remember my grandfather, John?" He moved into the hall, allowing the men to shake hands while he peered through the archway into the living room, getting a very good feel for the inhabitants of the large, comfortable home by the warmth he found inside.

"Uh, she's in the den . . . uh, studio," Joe said, stepping back to give them all room to step inside while he closed the door. Leading the way down the hall to the double doors of the studio, he called for his wife, wishing now that he had warned her a little better about their visitors. "Visitors," he called out. "You remember Dr. Summers?" He waited until she came to the doorway before continuing. "This is his uncle, Zachary Summers and his grandfather, John." He took her by the arm, pulling her into the hall.

He was saved from further explanation by Case, who reached out to shake her hand, already talking. "Uncle Zach has the art gallery that I told Joe about. He's already seen a couple of your pictures and is interested in maybe helping you set up a show. Do you mind showing him some more?"

Joe watched his wife's face go from anticipation to anger then reluctant acceptance. She glared at him for a brief moment before leading the men back into her new studio. "Thank you for taking the time to come see them," she said graciously, her hand waving through the air to indicate the picture laden walls. Joe swallowed, asked if anyone would like coffee and was relieved when all three men said yes. It gave him a moment to escape.

He was surprised when John followed him into the kitchen. "She wasn't expecting Case, was she?"

"No, she wasn't. Actually, neither was I." He gave a wry grin, shook his head. "I'm gonna have a lot of explaining to do."

"I don't think so," John's wide smile belied his age. "By the time we get back in there with the coffee, the boys will have already charmed her into acceptance. Especially when Zach tells her he has an opening on his calendar that he wasn't expecting and he can arrange her show by October. His gallery is usually booked up three to four years in advance, so that's quite a coup."

"October? That's wonderful!" Joe was so excited he missed the cup and poured a little coffee on the counter. "Oops," he chuckled, wiping the mess. He set the mugs on a tray, opened the fridge for some half and half. "I hope she's as thrilled as I am," he said. "She's had to arrange shows for her students and knows how to set them up and everything, but she's never had one of her own. At least not since she graduated."

"Slow down, Joe," John said, taking the tray from him and setting it on the table. "Let them talk for a little while longer before you go back. Give them a chance to work their magic."

"It'll really be magic unless she can get over the fact that Case was in on the fake kidnapping," Joe muttered.

"I think it'll be fine," John's smile was comforting, as was the gentle pat on the arm. "I've never seen those two boys fail."

Joe laughed heartily. "That's the second time you've called them 'boys'," he said. "Your grandson is, what? Forty five? And how old is Zachary?"

"Actually, Case is, let's see . . . forty-nine," John answered. "And Zach turned seventy in March."

"Seventy?" Joe was stunned. "I figured him a little older than I am, but . . . seventy? You're joking. Aren't you?"

"Not at all," John said. "He and his twin brother were born in nineteen thirty-eight. I was seventeen."

"That's right," Joe said. "You told me you were eighty-seven. I even find that hard to believe. Neither one of you look your age, that's for sure."

John smiled, knowing that he'd managed to make the anxious man forget about being worried, which, of course, had been his intention. He now steered the conversation back toward his son and the gallery, carrying the tray as he followed Joe back toward his wife's new studio. They stopped just outside the double doors, eavesdropping on the conversation going on just ahead.

"Would you rather pick the matting and frames yourself, or will you trust me to do it?" they heard Zach ask.

"I . . . I don't have any idea," Jillian admitted. "I . . . that is . . . uh . . . we . . . really can't afford to put elaborate frames on all of them. I just don't know what to tell you."

"Tell him to do it himself," John said, sailing in with the coffee, offering some first to Jillian, catching her eye and winking before setting the tray down. "He can afford it and he stands to double any investment he might have to fork out." He looked up at one wall of pictures, turning to get a good look at those pinned to all four walls, finally turning back to her. "They're wonderful," he proclaimed. "Congratulations, young lady," he leaned to give her a hug.

"Uh . . . thank you," she said, allowing the hug, her hands just resting lightly on his upper arms, confused as to who this elderly male might be.

"Dad," Zach cautioned, laughing, "she might object to having a complete stranger manhandle her."

"Nonsense," John argued, turning on his son. "It's not often you get to be in on the introduction of a completely new artist who just happens to be very, very good as well. Too many of the youngsters these days are into all of that weird stuff."

Now both Case and Zach had trouble containing their laughter. "Sorry," Zach said after a moment. Seeing the looks on both the faces of Joe and Jillian, he decided an explanation was in order. "Have you ever been to my gallery?" he asked.

"I'm sorry. I don't think so," she said.

"Probably because she doesn't know which gallery is yours," John reprimanded him.

"Oh, yeah," Zach chuckled. "I have a few around California, but my biggest is Zachary's in San Francisco and that's where these will go."

"Zachary's? Oh, my goodness. I didn't realize . . . I mean . . . Zachary's? No, No, we've never been able to get up there, although I've always wanted to." Jillian admitted. "I've heard of it, of course. As a matter of fact, you have a couple of pieces in your collection that are in the current text book for one of my classes."

"You're talking about Daphne," Zach replied. It wasn't a question. He was well aware of the fame of that single piece of sculpture around which the rest of his collection centered.

"Yes, I am," Jillian said. Suddenly her head snapped up, her eyes locked on those of the elderly gentleman who had just hugged her so warmly. "John Summers!" she blurted out without thinking, suddenly making the connection.

"Last time I looked," he admitted.

"Oh, my God." Her hands flew to her mouth. "I love that piece!" she said.

"Good," he chuckled. "Now, let's see what we need to do to have *your* pieces join mine at the gallery."

And it had been just that easy for Joe. The Summers males had carefully packed every one of the pictures and left, leaving a euphoric Jillian and a relieved Joe. He gathered the cups onto the tray and headed for the kitchen, escaping before she had time to get over the excitement of having her own show and start thinking once again about Case Summers and her captivity.

JILLIAN

*T*HE SECOND TIME she dropped the pushpins, Jillian was ready to scream. It was one thing to draw for herself and her family. It was quite another to have someone from an actual gallery come to judge them. She couldn't say anything to Joe, though. He was so proud that he had found a gallery where she could show her art that she didn't have the heart to say anything. She nervously rearranged a few of the pictures for the fifth time, standing back to see how they looked juxtaposed as they were. She was about to tell Joe to call them and tell them the whole thing was off when the doorbell rang.

She froze, waiting in her new studio until Joe called from the hallway. She went from anxious to furious in a heartbeat when she saw Case Summers, but she managed to hide her anger, graciously shaking hands with the three men while mentally firing daggers toward her husband. She sighed. There wasn't anything she could do about any of it, so she led the way into the studio, relieved when

Joe offered coffee. She didn't want to see him right now. She would deal with him later, she decided.

"Amazing," Zach Summers said, wandering around the room, examining each picture in turn. "You were right, Case," he said. "These definitely should be shown. Thank you for bringing them to me."

Jillian couldn't say anything. The lump in her throat threatened to choke her. It had been easy to be angry at Dr. Summers. Joe had explained that the clinic where she had been held captive was part of his domain and the idea of kidnapping her had been his. When she had seen him just now, she had wanted to scratch his eyes out. Now she discovered that she owed it to him that she might be having her very first art exhibit. She didn't respond immediately when Zach spoke to her and he had to clear his throat to get her attention.

"I asked if these are all of them," he said gently when she looked up.

"Yes, they are. At least these are all I've done lately and they're by far and away the best things I've ever done."

"It's too bad there aren't more," he sighed. "I could probably sell three times this many. And I'm going to have to do some tall talking to keep my wife, Alexa, from confiscating a few to keep on display. Do you have any problems with signing a contract? It's customary that the gallery receive a percentage of your sale and a contract will spell out everything."

"No, no. I don't have any problems with a contract. But . . . are you sure?" she asked timidly.

"Sure? There isn't any doubt in my mind that I want to have you under contract. As for these," his hand swept the room, "I can promise you that they will fly out of the gallery. They're wonderful."

"Listen to him," Case instructed. "He never tells anyone anything good. I've never heard him rave like that before. I thought they were very good, but it's better coming from him." His thumb pointed over his shoulder toward his uncle, but his eye caught and held hers.

"Thank you," she said, lowering her eyes. Angry as she had been at the conspiratorial doctor, she had to admit that he was the one who had given her this chance. It was hard to keep her anger sharp when she thought about that. It was also hard to be angry with him when he smiled so winningly at her. "Why would you be angry anyway?" her alter ego asked. "He was right! It worked! I've become a sex maniac!"

The conversation turned to framing and matting, making her endeavors presentable to the public. She hadn't even considered how much it would cost to have all of them framed and said so, relieved when the man agreed to shoulder the cost, including it in the contract that she had agreed to sign.

She was also relieved when Joe and the doctor's grandfather returned with coffee for everyone, blushing when the elderly gentleman served her first. She watched with apprehension as he walked slowly around the room. Somehow, his opinion seemed to matter most. When he complimented her and hugged her, she wasn't sure just how she should respond, so merely laid her hands gently on his bicep.

She couldn't imagine why the other two men laughed at his comments until she was told the name of the gallery where her own work would be on exhibit. "Zachary's?" She couldn't believe her ears. Her work would be on display at the single most prestigious gallery in the whole state. She tried to think of something appropriate to say and could only come up with the fact that she was familiar with it through one of the text books she actually used in her classes.

It hit her like a bolt of lightening. "John Summers!" Oh, Lord. She was talking to John Summers, one of her all time favorite sculptors, and he had just given her a hug and complimented her work. She was speechless. Fortunately, the three men seemed to be used to her reaction and went about dismantling her little exhibit, packing the pieces away in cases that they brought from their van, ignoring the fact that she had become almost mute.

She stumbled to the doorway to see them off and went in search of her husband. She found him loading the coffee mugs into the dishwasher. "Did you know he was talking about Zachary's?" she asked.

"Uh . . . yeah," he said, avoiding looking at her. "Didn't I tell you?"

"No," she shook her head, leaning against the doorframe, her arms folded, head tilted. "You know you didn't tell me," she accused. "Joe." She waited while he wiped down the counter, waited while he cleaned the sink. "Joe," she purred softly, waiting until he turned toward her to go on. "You didn't tell me because you didn't want me to know about the relationship between him and Dr. Summers, did you?"

She waited for his barely perceptible nod, knowing exactly what was going through his mind. "And you didn't want me to reject out of hand because it would be associated with him. Right?" Again she waited for the nod.

"Thank you," she said. "You were right. When I saw him, I was so angry I thought I would blow a gasket." She straightened and walked toward him. "But that wasn't fair, was it? I mean, all he did was teach you how to make me enjoy something I should have been enjoying all along. Right?" A third nod, accompanied by a brief shrug.

"And he just happened to have a connection with one of the most prestigious art galleries in the United States. Right?" Another nod. She took a last step toward him, sliding her arms around him, burying her face in his shoulder. "Thank you," she whispered. She leaned away so she could see his face and almost smiled at the look of relief she saw there. But she couldn't hold the angry pose, couldn't help the smile that escaped. Finally, she laughed. "I'm going to have an exhibit at Zachary's! Me! Can you believe it?"

"I always thought you were the best," he told her, holding her tightly. "Yours are every bit as good as the ones we saw in Case's office, and they were done by his other grandfather. Someone else you might know. Pedro Valenzuela."

"Pedro . . . ! You're kidding! He's one of the reasons I started working with pastels in the first place."

"I know," he said, finally relaxing enough to give her a crooked grin. "He's the one who went with me to buy the art supplies I left for you at the clinic. He had a pretty good idea of what you'd need, and I didn't have a clue."

"You met him?!" She was stunned.

"You told me about him a long time ago, when we first got married. It took me a couple of times before I remembered where I'd heard his name before."

"Where'd you get a chance to meet him?"

"He and John have been doing their morning drill at the clinic, so I've gotten to see them almost every day."

"Oh, it's John, now?" she kidded him, still overwhelmed at all the information she'd learned in the past hour or so.

"He told me to call him that," Joe answered defensively.

She laughed at his discomfiture. "Don't worry, Joe," she said. "I'm not mad. I'm just jealous as hell. Two of my favorite artists are in the building and I'm locked in a room with a sex maniac." She thought for a second. "No, that's not quite right. I was locked in a room becoming a sex maniac."

"Mmmm . . ." Joe growled, leaning to nibble on her ear. "I kinda like that part," he murmured.

"Joe!" she smacked feebly at his chest, not really trying to fend him off, but giving token resistance. And that didn't last long at all.

JOE

JOE SMELLED THE deliciously combined aromas of bacon and biscuits the minute he opened the door from the garage. "Mmmm," he said, smiling. "Smells wonderful." He strode across the kitchen, giving Jillian a kiss on the back of the neck, his hands kneading her shoulders. "Thought you were going running while I went to the gym for morning drill," he murmured against her ear, his hand slipping inside her robe, capturing one delightful breast, tweaking the already full nipple.

She clicked off the burners and turned in his arms. "I did," she said, her arms going up around his neck. "I got back early enough to take a shower already. It was too wet to get in a full run." He captured her lips with his own, pulling her tightly against him, his hands capturing her firm, round bottom in his hands.

"How long before they're done?" he asked, peeking over her shoulder at the food still simmering on the stove. He shoved the pan off the burner, just in case.

"When ever you're ready," she whispered.

"I'm ready now," he growled, rubbing his throbbing erection against her belly. He hit the light switch, ridding the room of unnatural light, darkening it to match the rainy and gloomy day outside.

"Joe!" She batted against his chest, but he just chuckled low in his throat. "I had an idea," he said, holding her against him as he walked the few steps to the door of the refrigerator. He didn't have to look far to find the little squeeze bottle of chocolate syrup, holding it up for her as though it were a grand prize.

"Oh, no you don't," she said, struggling feebly. "No! Oh, no," she gasped as the cold chocolate hit her, sliding down inside her robe and over her breast. He moved quickly, pushing the cloth aside to capture the sweet semi-liquid with his tongue, lapping against her in the process.

"Mmmm," he growled again. "Almost as sweet as you," he said softly. He held the bottle upside down and squeezed it again, allowing the brown goo to ooze lower, sliding over her belly. "I could get used to this," he slurped, lapping at the syrup, sucking at the fine muscles of her abdomen. He followed the drizzle down, down, smiling when he felt her hands on his head, pushing urgently.

Standing upright, wrapping his arms around her, he lifted her off her feet and carried her the few steps to the kitchen table, setting her on the edge, his big body firmly planted between her legs. "Want to try?" he asked, holding out the bottle. He was surprised when she took it from him, even more so when she inverted it and squeezed some out on his chest. He shuddered at the dual sensations caused by the cold chocolate and her warm tongue, shivering with delight when she suckled his nipple.

He leaned her back on the table, allowing his sweat pants to fall to his ankles, wrapping her long legs around him, pulling her toward him until he could fit himself into her, both their hands groping for him, guiding him. Neither was aware of knocking the bottle from the table and accidentally squeezing chocolate syrup in a long splash across the linoleum. It didn't matter to either of them. All that mattered was their bodies, now a single entity, joined together, locked in place by the lust that consumed them both.

He loved hearing her groans and moans as he drove into her, her deep throaty grunts as she strove to meet him, her screams of ecstasy as first one climax hit her, and then another. He almost came, but forced himself to hold off, knowing she was still ready, still capable of yet another fantastic trip into the rising sun.

He didn't hear anything beyond the guttural, nonsensical syllables coming from his lovely mate as she crested yet another sensual wave. He didn't hear the hurried steps behind him, or the man who grabbed him by the shoulders, tearing him from his wife. Off balance, tripping over his pants, he had no recourse but to fall in the direction he was pushed, striking his head against the corner of the refrigerator on his way to the floor. He struggled to rise, shook his head against the encroaching darkness. Unable to clear his vision, he sank into oblivion, his last clear thought the sound of Jillian's panic stricken voice.

"Jack! No!"

JILLIAN

*E*XCITEMENT COURSED THROUGH Jillian when she heard the overhead garage door begin its slow climb. Joe was home! Yes! Her face lit with a wide smile. She could only think how wonderful the last three days had been. Her pictures were going to be on display at one of the most prestigious galleries in the country. She had signed a contract that spelled out the amount of money she could expect should all of her drawings sell and found that there should be enough to pay off the house if she only sold half of them! And, best of all, she was in her own home but still had her mystery lover. She was literally dancing with joy. How could anything be any better?

She had finished her morning run early. The last two days of rain had turned part of her route into a quagmire, so she had bypassed it, returning home in time to put biscuits in the oven, take a shower and start the bacon before Joe got back from doing morning drill at the clinic. Now, in a loose, flowing robe with nothing but a hint of perfume beneath, she waited in front of the stove for Joe to come in from the garage.

She turned off the burners as soon as she felt his breath on the back of her neck, tilting her head to present her lovely neck for his kiss. When he showed her the container of chocolate syrup, she was appalled for just about two seconds before giggling, accepting the idea, cringing from the cold of the syrup, burning as his tongue lapped it from her breast. When he offered her the bottle, she couldn't resist, squirting it onto his chest, lapping up the combination of sweet, chocolate and male skin, sucking every last drop from him.

She could barely contain her impatience when he laid her back on the table, her hand meeting his as they both reached to position him for entry. Eyes tightly closed, she was lost in a dream world of electricity, fire and ice, groaning, moaning and, finally screaming as climax followed climax, squirming to achieve yet one more when she heard the scuffle and felt him leave her.

Her eyes flew open, her vision filled with the furious face of her eldest son. It hit her instantly. He didn't recognize his own father! "Jack! No!" She screamed, scrambling from the table, grasping her robe around her as she knelt beside her husband. She could see the streak of blood on the refrigerator and understood immediately what had happened.

"Call 911!" she instructed. Looking up, she saw that her son had made no move, indeed was staring as though she had lost her mind. "Jack!" she shouted. "Call 911! Now!" That got him moving, although not nearly fast enough for her.

"Turn on the light!" she yelled, her fingers feeling through Joe's hair for the cut she knew had to be there. It didn't take her long once the lights came on and she grabbed a hand towel from the drawer to place against the long, deep gash far back on the left side of his head. "What did you think you were doing!" she demanded of Jack, who had yet to say anything to her.

"Saving you," he muttered, still unsure of the identity of the man on the floor. "Sorry," he said, pointing to the dark splash of chocolate. "There, on the floor. It looked like blood. I thought you were being attacked. I, er, I thought he was r . . . r . . . raping . . . you."

"You thought your father was trying to rape me?" she asked, unable to believe her ears.

"Dad?" he choked. "Oh, shit! Is he really . . . Is he all right?"

"He's unconscious!"

Another pair of hands moved over Joe's body, up his neck, around his head. They disappeared for a moment, returning with another towel from the drawer. "I'll take him," a soft feminine voice told her. "Jack, help your mother."

"Who . . . ?"

"Mom, this is Janie. It's okay. She's a nurse." He helped Jillian to her feet while the exquisite young Eurasian woman sat on the floor, placing Joe's head on her lap.

"You might want to get some clothes on before the paramedics get here," she told Jillian. "Jack, see if you can pull your father's sweats back up." Her firm, calm voice steadied the two of them and they both hurried to do as she said. By the time Jillian returned to the kitchen, Jack had gotten Joe's pants tied around his waist and had brought a blanket from the sofa to put over him and a throw pillow to place beneath his feet.

Still crouched beside his father's prostrate form, he rose when Jillian came through the archway, all but running to her. "I'm so sorry, Mom," he started, but stopped when she placed her hand over his mouth. She slipped her arm around his waist, pulling him over to where Joe still lay.

She knelt beside the young lady who had taken charge, taking one of Joe's hands in her two. "Is he all right?" she asked.

"His heartbeat and breathing are just fine," Jane assured her. "He's just out cold." She gently touched the bandages on his nose. "He doesn't seem to have had a very good time lately, does he?"

"Yes and no," Jillian said. "His nose was broken long before I ever met him. It seemed a good time to get it fixed."

"Mom," Jack touched her shoulder, causing her to look up at him. "What's going on?"

"What do you mean?" she bluffed.

"Oh, come on," he huffed. "He's got a beard, short hair and not a hair on his body. When I left he was clean shaven, long-haired and furry all over." He ran his hand through his hair, unsure of how to ask the next question. "And, if it wasn't rape, why were you screaming?"

"Jack!" Jane stopped him cold. "You of all people should be familiar with the sounds a woman makes when she's having good sex. Shut up!"

Jillian blushed a deep shade of scarlet, her hands flying to cover her face, while Jack's face turned even a darker shade of red. Both were still spluttering when they heard the sound of the paramedic's siren. Jack turned and ran for the front door, thereby escaping any further comment.

"Sorry about that," Jane said to Jillian. "Sometimes I say things without thinking them through."

"No, no, that's quite all right," Jillian patted her on the arm. "You were right, but it's a totally new concept for our children."

"I guess I shouldn't say anything more. But I've already put my foot in it, so I'll just tell you that Jack has commented on your attitude about sex before." She giggled, returning Jillian's pat on the arm. "I'm not sure what he was talking about, though. That was definitely the sound of a woman having the time of her life."

Their conversation ended with the arrival of the paramedics who took over, checking Joe's vitals, feeling for any other injuries. The story that he tripped over a chair and fell backwards into the refrigerator was close enough to actual events that they accepted it without a word. While one returned to the unit to gather the gurney, the other talked with the three of them, telling them where they were taking him and any other information they might need.

"We'll follow you in our car," Jack told his mother. "You'll want to ride with them."

JOE

*J*OE COULD HEAR the sirens and feel the sway and bumps of the ambulance, but it was as though through a long tunnel. He groaned, rolled his head to the side then wished he hadn't. "Shit!" The word escaped even before he got his eyes opened. He blinked against the light, taking a while to focus. When he finally did manage to keep his eyes both open and steady, the first sight he saw was the worried face of his terrified wife.

"Hi," he croaked, unsure whether he should try to say anything more, absolutely certain he didn't want to try to move again.

"Oh, Joe," she smiled through the tears that flowed in a steady stream down her face. "Just lie still," she instructed.

"I don't think I have much choice," he grumbled. "What the hell happened?"

"Jack," she said.

"What?!" he started to sit up, thought better of it. "Jack?"

"He evidently decided to surprise us," she told him, giving a half hearted laugh which ended in a long sniffle. She wiped at her nose with the back of her wrist. He thought you were attacking me."

"Huh?" He couldn't wrap his mind around that statement. "Why?"

"Oh, Joe," she sighed, giving him a real smile. "You do look quite different, you know. And he evidently couldn't tell the difference between my screams of pleasure and those of terror. He thought you were some stranger . . . raping me."

"Greaaat," he couldn't be angry. It was the culmination of all that had happened in the last month. He started to laugh, but his head hurt so bad it ended in a groan and he squeezed his eyes against tears of pain.

He lay still and allowed the doctors in the emergency room to poke and prod, unaware of what else was going on in the waiting room. It wasn't until Dr. Summers poked his head through the curtains for the second time that he had any inkling that something else in his world had gone terribly wrong.

Jillian

FOLLOWING THE GURNEY into the emergency room, Jillian was stopped by a nurse and sent to a nearby waiting room. Jack and Jane came through the doors just as she turned back and she hurried to them, telling them what little she knew at that point. They found seats together in a more or less private section of the waiting room and tried to settle in and relax, but she couldn't. She kept popping up to pace around the small space, her eyes on the double doors where she had last seen her husband.

They hadn't been there more than a few minutes when Case Summers found them, promising to check on Joe and return with any news. He wasn't gone more than five minutes when he came sauntering out the double doors with a big smile on his face. "They're going to take him down for x-rays, but it doesn't look too bad. They'll probably keep him overnight for observation though."

"Oh, thank God," Jillian sighed, collapsing into one of the freeform chairs.

"He said he had a fight with the refrigerator and it won," Case told her, sitting down beside her, his arm across the back of her chair. "Haven't you two gone through enough the last month?"

"That's just it, Dr. Summers," Jillian confided in a low voice. "We were experimenting with chocolate syrup on the kitchen table when Jack surprised us with a visit. He didn't realize it was Joe and grabbed him from behind. His pants were around his ankles and he tripped over them and hit the fridge."

Case could barely restrain his laughter and had to put his hand over his mouth to keep it inside, but his eyes sparkled with amusement. She realized immediately that he was laughing and would have laughed with him if she hadn't been so worried about Joe. She did, however, blush a bright shade of crimson.

"Sorry," Case told her, still having to work to control bursting out in laughter. "I know it's scary, but I really think he'll be fine. He does have a headache, but he seemed in pretty good spirits." He looked over his shoulder when the outside doors opened, smiling when he saw who had come in. "Tom and Jolyn are here," he told her.

She jumped to her feet and ran to meet Jolyn, flying into her arms. She tried to explain what had happened, but couldn't figure out how to tell them without explaining all that had gone on before. She settled for telling her that he'd tripped and hit his head.

"It's okay, Mom," Jolyn said, giving her a strong hug, her arms around her, rubbing her back. "Jack told us what happened," she said.

"Oh," Jillian turned her face away, so embarrassed she couldn't speak. But Jolyn didn't let go of her, keeping her arm around her and leading her back to the seating area.

"I can't believe he told you," Jillian whispered.

"I can't believe he caught you," Jolyn whispered back with a conspiratorial smile.

"Jolyn!" she didn't know how to react. She glanced at the doors to the emergency room again, catching sight of Tom and Case talking. It occurred to her that they knew each other well . . . very well. When Kyle and Kate hurried through the doors she turned back to Jolyn. "Did Jack call you?" she asked.

"Yes, and I called them," she said, indicating her two siblings who hurried over to them.

"Then how did Dr. Summers know?" Jillian asked.

"Tom knew he was on call and would be here this evening and he asked him to meet you until we could get here."

"They're pretty good friends, aren't they?" she asked, although she had a pretty good idea of the answer. Anger began to build inside her as she thought about the extremely private things which had occurred over the last month and the idea that her *children* were evidently privy to the information. "How could he have told them?" she wondered, growing more and more irate by the minute.

"Yes, Mom," Jolyn sighed, something not lost on her mother.

"And?"

"They work together," Jolyn admitted. "Tom is doing his residency under Dr. Summers. He works in the clinic with him."

"But I thought you were working with Tom while you were doing your research," Jillian prodded, now realizing that they would be aware of everything that had happened to her during her captivity. She was beyond embarrassed, she was humiliated.

"I am," her daughter told her, watching the change in her mother's demeanor.

"So you already knew everything?" Jillian asked calmly, although she felt anything but calm.

"Well, some of it," Jolyn admitted hesitantly.

"How much of it?" Jillian persisted.

"Just that you were at the clinic," Jolyn said. "Dad made all of us promise that neither one of us were to be part of your therapy."

Now she was furious. Joe had known all along that her daughter was working in the clinic and was aware of all the things they had done. He'd not only kept it from her, but had assured her that the kids were in the dark. She could barely control herself as she asked the next question. "But you've seen others who have gone through this 'therapy'?"

"They have to be monitored, Mom, and Case has to sleep sometime."

Jillian stood abruptly, went to where Case and Tom seemed to be in conference. "When will we know the results of the x-rays?" she asked with barely concealed rage.

"They should be bringing him back up any minute," Case said calmly, realizing that his former patient was ready to blow.

"I'll go check," Tom offered, also aware that his mother-in-law was angry, not sure why, but happy to have some place to go to escape her possible wrath.

"You do that," Jillian purred, a sound that all her children recognized as a precursor to an explosion.

"Mom . . ." Jolyn came up behind her, reaching to take her arm, but Jillian jerked it beyond her grasp, now so furious that she could barely contain herself and not wanting to be touched by anyone connected with her betrayal.

"When you have some news of my husband will you please call my cell phone?" she asked, handing him a piece of paper with the number on it.

"Of course," Case said, looking astonished. "You aren't going to wait?"

"No," she told him, turning away, her eyes surveying the room until she found Jack. Hurrying over to her older son, she took him by the arm. "Take me home," she instructed.

"But, Mom . . ."

"Don't but, Mom me," she said. "At least you weren't in on the whole thing from the first. Please. Take me home now."

Jolyn had followed her across the room and now offered to drive her to the house.

Jillian didn't even look at her. "Now, Jack," she demanded.

"Yes, Ma'am," he said, looking around at the others and shrugging his shoulders. He followed her from the building, still unsure of what had just happened, but quite certain that his mother was as angry as he had ever seen her. He wisely kept his mouth shut as he escorted Jane and his mother back to the car for the short drive home.

"Go back to the hospital," Jillian instructed, stepping out of the car on their front walk. "You'll want to see that your father is all right."

"Don't you want to know?" he asked, his voice taking on just a hint of the child he had been.

"No," she said, turning her back, walking to the front door and letting herself in. She didn't turn to make sure he had left. She simply slammed the door with a finality that said he wasn't welcome.

As soon as she saw the car pull away, she gave vent to her anger, picking up the first thing she came in contact with and hurling it across the room. "Damn," she said aloud. "That was my favorite vase." She crossed the room and began to pick up pieces of porcelain, but tears that she'd managed to contain before now blinded her. She sat heavily in the middle of the floor and wept, not just angry but hurt beyond belief. She felt embarrassed and betrayed, humiliated to think that something so private would be public knowledge.

"How could he?" she cried. "It's not enough that the doctor knew. My children knew! My children!" She laid full length on the floor and sobbed, thoroughly soaking the carpet. She didn't move until she heard her cell phone ringing. She ran for her purse and dug out the offending instrument, almost throwing it as she had the vase, but she had to know Joe was okay.

"Jillian?" the deep voice of Dr. Summers came loud and clear over the tiny device.

"Dr. Summers? Is my husband all right?"

"He's fine," Case answered. "A few stitches and an overnight stay and he'll be ready to come home."

"Glad to hear it." She forced the words from her, trying to hold herself together for just a few more minutes.

"Would you like me to come pick you up?" he surprised her by asking. "I understand you don't really want to talk to any of us right now, but you might want to visit Joe for a few minutes. I didn't think you'd feel like driving."

"You're right," she answered. "I don't feel like driving. But I don't want to come back to the hospital. Right now, I don't want to see Joe either."

"Want to talk about it?" he asked.

"No. I don't want to talk about anything. And I don't want to talk to anyone. I just want to be left alone."

"Uh . . . wait a minute," he said and she could hear someone else talking. "Tom wants to talk to you."

"No. Goodbye," she said and folded the phone closed, ending the conversation.

JOLYN

"**W**E ARE IN deep shit," Tom said when his wife told him that his mother-in-law had already left the hospital. "She's figured out that we knew what they were doing all along and she's pissed."

"That's for sure," Jolyn said.

"But she can't stay away," Kate wailed. "Doesn't she care about Dad?"

"Not at the moment," Jolyn assured her. "Right now she's about as close to erupting as a person can be without blowing into a million pieces."

"Well, don't say anything to Dad," Tom told her. "He's got enough of a headache."

"Is he okay?"

"Probably. We won't know until the x-rays come back, but I think he'll be fine. It'd be funny if he hadn't ended up in the hospital and Mom hadn't figured out that we already knew about what went on at the clinic." He chuckled. "Hell, it's funny anyway."

"Tom!"

"Well, it is. Jack said his pants were around his ankles and he was going at it like a damn bull. And your mother was screaming as though she were enjoying every minute of it. Only he didn't realize that was why she was screaming when he first heard her. He said the lights were out and there was chocolate syrup on the floor, but in the dim light it looked like blood and he thought some stranger was doing her. He grabbed your dad and pulled him away from her and his legs got tangled up in his pants and he fell. Now, you couldn't have written that in a script, Jolyn. It's damn funny."

She giggled, coughed, almost choked. "I know, honey. It really is funny. But it's not. And Mom sure isn't laughing."

"That isn't why she's mad, Jolyn."

"No, I know it isn't. She's feeling like we're all ganged up against her."

"I think she feels like we all betrayed her," Tom disagreed.

"And lied to her," Jolyn added. "I don't think I've ever seen her that mad before."

"I know I haven't."

"What are you two talking about?" Kate asked, coming to sit with them. "Where'd Mom go?"

"Mom figured out that we all knew where they'd been for the last month and what they've been doing. She's really pissed."

"I told you she would be, if she ever found out," Kate told them. "But, where'd she go?"

"She went home," Jolyn said. "But I don't know what she'll do now."

"She wouldn't leave Dad at a time like this, would she?"

"I think she'll wait until she's sure he's okay before she decides what else she wants to do, but she isn't going to allow any of us near her for a while."

"But she's our Mom!" Kate wailed.

"Let's hope that's enough for her to forgive us," Jolyn told her, holding up crossed fingers. "'Cause that may be the only thing we have in our favor right now."

The outside doors whisked open and Jack and Jane came back in, looking perplexed as well as unhappy. "She's home," Jack said. "But she isn't a happy camper. Someone want to tell me what that was all about?

While Jolyn filled them in, Tom went back into the emergency room. He got back just as she finished talking, chuckling at the look on Jack's face. While Jane had no compunctions about laughing at the disaster that had occurred earlier, she fully understood the mortification that had sent Jillian rushing from the hospital.

"You should have told her," she told Jolyn. "She's probably feeling like you all are laughing at her, much less ganging up on her." She looked at the floor, then back up. "Sorry. I shouldn't have spoken. It's not my place."

"Well, your place or not, you're right," Jolyn said. "We should have told her."

Tom slipped his arm around his wife, announcing to everyone that Joe was doing fine and that they would be taking him up to a room for the night. They could all go up and tell him good night.

"What about Mom?" Jolyn asked.

"Case called her," he said.

"And?"

"And she said she was glad he was all right."

"And?"

"And nothing. She hung up."

"She must be madder than we thought," Kyle spoke for the first time.

"She's beyond mad," Tom said. "Case told her he would go get her, but she said no. Then he tried to give me the phone and she hung up."

"Now what do we do?" Kate asked.

"We go see Dad and we go home. She won't want to see any of us tonight. Maybe tomorrow," Tom suggested.

"Or next year," Jack said under his breath.

JOE

*J*OE HAD HAD to endure a lot of teasing when his students showed up for the first day of practice. First, he still had the mustache and beard. Second, it was obvious that he had had his nose fixed, and they razzed him unmercifully about having plastic surgery. That ended after the first hour of calisthenics when they were all staggering with fatigue and he made them run a mile. It wasn't that they didn't want to run, or that they didn't all feel they'd been put through a wringer. It was that he was doing everything right along with them and wasn't even breathing hard.

By the first game, they were in the best shape of any team in their league and they knew that they had him to thank for it. That they played better was a foregone conclusion. That they won didn't surprise them. That he didn't seem to share their joy bothered them. Those who were returning players knew that he was the kindest, most considerate coach they had ever had. He was still kind and considerate. He just wasn't happy, and that worried them.

After their fourth win in a row, Kyle met his father in the locker room when most of the students had already left. "C'mon, Dad," he coaxed. "Come with us. We're all going over to Kate's and have pizza."

Joe just sighed and nodded. He would go with his kids because he loved them and wanted to see the grandkids, but he wasn't really in the mood. It seemed he was never in the mood any more. He missed Jillian. He wanted her home. It had been almost three months since he'd gotten home from the hospital to find her gone.

No note, no phone call, nothing. Her clothes were gone as were some of her favorite things from the house. She had taken some stuff from the kitchen . . . utensils, pots, pans, dishes, silverware. Just a few of each. Just enough for a single person to set up her own apartment. And she had taken all of her art supplies from the den, but whether she intended to use them or burn them he had no way of knowing.

It had taken him weeks to find out where she was. When she didn't show up at the school, he had gone to the dean only to find out that she had taken a leave of absence. She hadn't taken her cell phone, so he assumed she had gotten another one, but again he had no way of knowing. She hadn't talked to any of the kids except Jack, and only then when he promised not to tell anyone where she was.

It had been Jane who had finally told him. She had come to his office one afternoon in late August after he had finished with morning practice and while Jack was at work. "Jack promised," she had said. "I didn't." She had given him Jillian's address, but had warned him that he shouldn't go unless she called him first. "She's hurt," she had explained. "Give her time to get over it. She still loves you and she loves her children and she really misses all of you, especially the grandkids, but she isn't ready to forgive anyone yet."

"When do you suppose she'll be ready?" he had asked, sounding pathetic but unable to stop himself.

"After her show," she had advised. "She'll want someone to share her success with. I think everyone should go to her opening."

"What if she still doesn't want us then?" he had wondered.

"She already does," she had said with a smile. "She just doesn't know it yet."

So he dragged his oversized body to Kate's, wanting to spend time with those he loved, but knowing he wasn't much fun to be around. With the baby already down for the night, he didn't even have her bubbly personality to bring him out of his funk. Finally, he made his excuses and returned to his big empty house, wanting nothing more than to get on the freeway and drive up to San Francisco to Jillian's apartment. He wanted to see her, to touch her, to hold her. He didn't feel whole without her.

He'd made the trip three times since Jane had given him the address. He'd sat outside her apartment, waiting until she left, following her. Once she had gone to a Catholic school and he'd found out later that she had gotten a job teaching there. Once she'd gone to the gallery and once she had gone for a run. He hadn't had the nerve to try to confront her. He'd simply followed her, watching her with a longing he couldn't have described. He didn't have enough words.

JILLIAN

*I*T HAD ONLY taken Jillian a couple of days to find a job teaching in a small private school. The principal had been only too happy to hire someone with her credentials for the paltry sum that she had to offer, and Jillian had spent the remainder of the summer preparing a curriculum for some five hundred students ranging in age from five to thirteen. From the first day, she realized the overwhelming task of bringing some kind of order to their chaos was exactly what she needed to keep her mind off her family.

It had taken her a couple of days longer to find an apartment, set up a checking account and get herself settled in San Francisco. She found she didn't need much, didn't really care about her surroundings. She used her tiny living room for a studio and the bedroom for when she collapsed from fatigue. She also found several different routes to run every morning and alternated them with the days of the week.

She also found herself gravitating to the art galleries that abounded in her area, wandering in and out of room after room, wondering why some of the objects on display were called 'art'. It took her two weeks to get up the courage to visit Zachary's and she was relieved when Zach greeted her with unadulterated enthusiasm. His superbly sensitive wife, Alexa, took one look at the lovely, lonely woman and took her under her wing, mothering her without suffocating her.

After that first encounter, not a week went by that the Alexa didn't call to invite her to a gallery opening or a dinner party or to accompany her on a shopping spree. And she allowed Jillian the time to talk out her frustration and humiliation without seeming to pry, encouraging her to express her hunger for her family and ultimately helping her to see the humor in her situation.

"I know I should call Joe," Jillian said after a couple of months of self-imposed isolation. "But now I'm half afraid to. He's got to be hurt that I wasn't there to take care of him when he came home from the hospital. And he might not even want me back. I don't think I could handle that."

"I happen to know he still works out at the clinic every morning," Alexa assured her. "Zach went with his dad one morning and Joe was there. Want me to have Zach find out what's going on with him? It'd be kinda fun. You know. Playing private detective."

"Oh, no," Jillian said, shocked. "I couldn't do that."

"Why not?" Alexa had said with a wink. "If he could keep secrets from you, you can do a little spying on him. Turn about fair play, and all that."

"But I couldn't involve you in something like that," Jillian had protested.

"My husband and I are both seventy years old," Alexa had proclaimed. "There isn't much we haven't seen or done in that time, so something a little offbeat like that would be fun for us. Besides, you are much too sad. Even when you smile, you're sad. You miss your husband and your family, and I'll bet they miss you, too. You can't spend the rest of your life in that tiny apartment teaching finger painting to a bunch of hooligans. Not with your talent."

And that had been the beginning of Jillian's recuperation. She had waited breathlessly for every detail that Zach could glean from his encounters with Joe, not to mention what Case was able to tell him about Jolyn and Tom. And Jack kept her up to date with Kyle and Kate, including pictures of the grandchildren taken at back yard barbeques or the park. When Joe's team won game after game, Jack brought videos to share his triumph with her, trying not to notice the tears that threatened when the camera panned on their handsome, but very somber, coach.

"He doesn't look very happy," Jillian told Alexa.

"He isn't," Alexa assured her. "Case says he does their morning drill with more determination and less joy than anyone he's ever seen."

"What am I going to do?" Jillian cried.

"Have your opening," Alexa advised. "Make sure Jack tells them all when and where, and that they should all come. I think they've been suitably punished, don't you?"

"I didn't do this to punish them," Jillian protested.

"No, darling, I know that," Alexa said patting her on the hand. "But you've managed to do just that. And you've punished yourself in the process."

"Punished myself?" Jillian asked. "What ever for?"

"For learning to enjoy something that you've spent your whole life thinking should be taboo," Alexa replied gently.

Jillian could only nod her head. That had been one of the hardest parts of all that had happened, but she could barely believe the perception with which her new friend could look into her past and come to the least obvious conclusion. She had barely come to terms with the idea of sex as imminently pleasurable when she had been confronted with the idea of sex as public knowledge. It had overwhelmed her. It had been too private. She had balked at sharing her most intimate moments with her family, and had fled them all.

JOE

*J*ACK BURST OUT laughing even before Joe reached the office, leaving his father perplexed. "What's so funny?" he asked, dropping his gear on his desk and leaning to close the door behind his son.

"You don't even notice them, do you?" Jack asked his bemused father.

"Notice what?" Joe asked.

"All those sexy coeds swooning over you when you walk down the hall," Jack elaborated.

Joe colored slightly and shook his head. "That's just your imagination," he told Jack. He sat on the edge of the desk, folded his arms and asked, "So, what's up?"

Jack stuttered a little, but finally got his question out. "Are you going up to 'Frisco for Mom's opening?"

"You're late," Joe chuckled. "Everyone else has already asked me."

"And?"

"And I have no idea what to do," Joe admitted. "I really want to go, but I'm not sure she wants me there. That doesn't mean you all shouldn't go. She won't feel like it's a success unless she has her family to share it with."

"And that includes you," Jack pointed out.

"Jack, this is between my wife and me," Joe began.

"No, it isn't," Jack said. "It's the whole family. She wasn't mad at just you, you know. She was angry because all of her children knew what had been going on in that clinic . . . except me, of course. Jane says she's such a private person, it's hard for her to accept that someone would know what she was doing."

"Jane is a very perceptive young lady," Joe observed.

"I think so, too," Jack said with a smile.

"And?"

"And, yes, I've asked her to marry me," Jack said. "And she said yes."

Joe stood and wrapped his son in an enormous bear hug that might have swallowed a lesser man, but Jack was every bit as tall as his father, albeit somewhat leaner. "Congratulations," he said. "So when's the big date?"

"This weekend," Jack said.

"What?!" Joe wasn't so much surprised as shocked. "Why so soon? Doesn't she want a big wedding with all the trappings?"

"Nope," he said. "She says she just wants me. And, since I just want her, it makes it pretty easy. Besides, we're already expecting, so we'd like to get hitched as soon as possible. This weekend everyone in our family is already going to be together up in 'Frisco, so it seemed a good time. And Father Timothy has a friend who will let him use his church up there."

"That's pretty slick, Jack," Joe said, shaking his head. "You just slid that little tidbit of information in there, kinda off hand, didn't you?"

"Seemed like a good idea," Jack said. "Look, Dad, you already knew we were living together. It can't be a surprise."

"No, I guess not," Joe said. He waited a heartbeat before going on. "So, you've blackmailed me into going up to San Francisco with you this weekend, haven't you? You knew I'd never be able to resist seeing you married off."

"I was hoping you wouldn't look at it like that," Jack said. "I just wanted everyone to be together and happy. We all used to be happy whenever we got together. I wanted it to be like that again."

"You're right," Joe said. "And I realize it's my fault we haven't been happy these last few months."

"That's not what I said," Jack bristled.

"No, it isn't. But it's the truth. If I hadn't been so determined to change your mother's outlook on sex, none of this would ever have happened."

"And she might never have had the chance to have her own art show," Jack argued. "Dad, you can stand there and feel guilty about everything that's happened, or you can see the good side of it all. I don't know about your sex life, but what I heard in the kitchen makes me think you were very successful in that regard. The thing all of you seem to have overlooked is the art itself."

"What?" Joe asked, not understanding. "Jack, what are you talking about?"

"Jane pointed it out to me," Jack said. "Remember the other day when we were going through some of Mom's old paintings to find something for our apartment?"

"Yeah, and . . . ?"

"She didn't like any of them," Jack had to confess. "I mean, they were okay," he stuttered. "But she got a look at a few of those Mom did of you and she said the old ones lacked the spark of the new ones. She said there was a sensuality to the ones she did of you that was missing from the others." He hesitated. "She said whatever she learned in the clinic was what made the difference."

Joe just stood, mouth agape. He'd never thought of it like that. It hadn't occurred to him at all. Finally, "What does your mother say about that?"

"She agrees," Jack said. "We had taken a couple of her old ones with us up to visit with her, and she showed them to Mr. Summers. He says the same thing. Her old ones lack that certain spark that makes the more recent ones dynamic. As a matter of fact, he told her that he would never have arranged her show for those."

"Wow," Joe said. "That was pretty harsh. She's always been a very good artist. Her earlier ones aren't all that bad."

"No, they aren't," Jack agreed. "They're really good, and he said that. He also said they lacked passion. They're just not outstanding. But the new ones have that, Dad. They have passion and then some. They're really great. And he said he only shows those that are really great. That's why his gallery is so successful."

"And he considers the ones she did at the clinic great?"

"And the ones she has done since then," Jack told him.

"She's still working, then?"

"Hell, yes. Wait 'til you see them, Dad. She's been working from photographs of the family. The ones of the babies are truly wonderful."

"Now I have to go," Joe said. "I don't have any choice, do I?"

"Nope," Jack chuckled. "Want to ride up with us?"

"You and Janie are going to want a little privacy, aren't you?"

"We *do* live together," Jack pointed out. "It's not like she's a blushing bride who's never been kissed or anything." He hesitated. "Kyle is riding up with Jolyn, Tom and Little Joe, and Kate and Eddie and the baby are going to follow them up. We already have hotel rooms near Mom's apartment. You could bunk out with Kyle."

"You already have it all worked out, don't you?" Joe asked with a grin.

"Pretty much," Jack admitted. "It was mostly a matter of getting you to agree."

Joe nodded, looking pensive. Then, for the first time in more than four months, he broke out in a true smile. "All right," he said. "I agree."

JILLIAN

*J*ILLIAN FELT AS though her skin was too small and she would burst out of it at any moment. She hadn't been this nervous since the day she'd gotten married and that was only because her mother had been so flighty; Jillian hadn't cared what happened as long as she could have Joe forever.

"What ever brought that thought on?" she asked herself now, but she already knew. Joe. None of this was as important as Joe. If she couldn't have him, she didn't care about any of this. She had wanted him to be beside her forever. Nothing that had happened since she had walked away from the home they had made together was worth one second of the time they had shared. She wanted nothing so much as to run outside, jump in her car and drive to where ever he was.

"Ready?" Alexa peeked in the door, entered and handed her a cut crystal flute of champagne. "The gallery is already packed," she told her. "It's a great exhibit, Jillian, and everyone out there is totally enthralled." She waved her arm at the tinted one way window that separated the office from the rest of the gallery, pointing out the packed house just beyond the door.

She could see all the people milling around, the men in tuxedos, the women in brightly colored evening gowns, their gold and diamond jewelry sparkling as they moved into and out of the intense spotlights. "I don't think I can go out there," she whispered.

"Do you want me to stay beside you the whole evening?" Alexa asked gently. "Or would it be easier if you had one of your family members with you?"

She shook her head softly. "I drove them away, Alexa," she said, her eyes glistening with unshed tears. "I can't just ask them to forget everything and ride to my rescue." She inhaled deeply, straightened, shoulders back, head erect. "Okay," she began, "I'm read . . ." The face just outside the window took her breath away. "Joe?" she whispered, her voice catching even as she tried to say his name. "Joe!" she shouted, dropping the flute and running from the room around the corner and into his arms. "Oh, Joe," she buried her face in the silky lapels of his tuxedo jacket, trying to burrow into him.

"I'm sorry," she whispered into his ruffled shirt. "I am so, so sorry," she said. When he seemed to push her away, she clung harder, not wanting to let go, afraid he would turn and walk away. She barely heard him say hey, but she was sure when he said he wasn't going anywhere. She sniffed, looked up and fell in love all over again. His warm brown eyes were full of the same adoration that she had come to take for granted over their twenty five years of their marriage. She couldn't take it for granted now. She could only weep with gratitude.

"Saying I'm sorry isn't enough," she told him. "But it's all I have."

"You don't need to say that," he said. "You don't have anything to be sorry for." He handed her his hankie, catching a stray tear with his thumb. "I'm the one who should be sorry. I should never have done that to you."

"No, you were right. It was wonderful," she admitted for the first time. "I just had trouble with having the kids know everything."

"They still do," he cautioned. "And they're here. They'd like to congratulate you."

Her head whipped around, looking for her children, but she couldn't find them. It wasn't until she turned back to Joe that she spied them. Her whole brood waited just beyond her husband's broad shoulders. She looked into his dark, dreamy eyes again, seeing only love. He stepped aside, his hand on her back, propelling her toward her babies, and she hurried forward, met after that first step by smiling faces, outstretched arms and warm embraces.

"I don't want to interrupt," a melodic male voice intruded on their all too brief reunion. "But there are a whole lot of people who are waiting to see the brilliant artist who created all of this." Zach's arm swept the open space around them, indicating the growing crowd that circulated from room to room, their collective gazes concentrated on the drawings that lined the walls. "I'd like to get the introductions over before the pictures are all sold out," he chuckled.

"Sold out?" Jolyn asked, excitement highlighting her face, roughening her voice.

"See all those little red dots?" Zach asked, pointing to the nearest wall. "Whenever you see one of those that means the piece is sold."

"But they all have dots on them," Kate said, her hands going to her mouth. It was the first time she had seen any of them and she was caught between the beauty of the drawings and the fact that they depicted her father. Embarrassment lost out to awe, though and she gushed her approval. "They're awesome, Mom!" she said loudly enough for those nearby to overhear.

Amid twitters and whispers, Zach led the family to the raised dais in the center of the main gallery. His introduction was short and to the point and he motioned to Jillian to join him on the dais. Still clinging to Joe, she had to be coaxed to climb the two steps amid loud, though gracious, applause. She had been nervous earlier, but now she was too rattled to do little more than stammer. "Thank you all for coming," she managed. "Please, enjoy the evening." It was all she could think of before looking to Zach for rescue.

"This from a lady who stands in front of a classroom and teaches all day," Zach joked, bringing warm laughter and more applause. He went on to talk about the exhibit, the amenities of the gallery and enjoined the glittering crowd to take advantage of the dance band playing softly in the main exhibit room. A few questions popped up from the appreciative audience and Zach fielded them for Jillian who had fled back to the safety of her husband's arms.

"Introduce us to the model," one matronly woman suggested to the hoots and catcalls of many of the otherwise staid women in the audience.

Zach looked pointedly at Joe, asking with a raised eyebrow and extended hand. Reluctantly, Joe stepped up beside him and was greeted by enthusiastic applause which grew when he pulled his wife up beside him. Neither said anything, just stood and held each other while the crowd clapped their approval of both. After the introductions, they were stopped, questioned, praised and complimented and could barely make their way through the gathering without receiving some accolade.

After one complete circuit of the interlinked galleries, Jillian followed Joe back to the little office, giving her a chance to catch her breath and finish greeting her family. Although little Megan, dressed in a fancy, lacey dress, had fallen asleep on her father's shoulder, Jillian couldn't resist taking her in her arms, holding her against her breast, loving even the feel of the tiny girl.

"Thank you. All of you," she was able to say after a moment. "I've behaved badly and I don't deserve this, but I am grateful."

"You haven't behaved badly," Jolyn assured her. "We should have let you know as soon as you got home that we knew where you'd been. It was wrong of us."

"Yes, it was," Jillian agreed. "But just having you know was too embarrassing for me to cope with. I've had a few months to think about it, though, and I know now that I overreacted."

"Shhh," Joe said, taking her in his arms. "We're just glad to have you back."

JOE

*J*OE FIDGETED WHILE Jolyn adjusted his bow tie, uncomfortable in the fancy dress-up clothes that he had to wear for the opening of Jillian's exhibit. "Are you sure this is necessary?" he asked for the tenth time. "Why a tuxedo?"

"It's Zachary's," she answered again. "It's a big, black-tie occasion, Dad. Don't you want to wow them?"

"I just want your mother happy," he replied, honestly.

"Well, if she isn't happy with how you look now, she never will be. You look great!"

"Thanks," he said absently. "Oh, hey. What about the kids?"

"They're going with us," she told him. "They'll probably fall asleep, but they should be there for their grandmother's big day, don't you think?"

"And Jack's," he reminded her. "You don't think your mother will be upset about their plans, do you?"

"It all depends on how she reacts to all of us showing up," Jolyn reminded him. "I hope she'll be happy to see us."

"I do to," Joe answered, biting his lower lip. He had worried enough for all of them over the past week, still unsure how Jillian would react to their presence and especially to seeing him. No matter that both Jack and Jane had assured him that she was ready to make amends, he still worried.

"Everyone ready?" Tom called from the hallway, herding the rest of the family in front of him. "We're going to be fashionably late already."

"I was hoping for a few other people to be there first," Joe told him, emerging from the room he was sharing with Kyle. "That way we can sort of blend in with the rest of them."

"Dad," Kate laughed. "You and Jack couldn't blend in, no matter how many other people might be there. You're both taller than most people and you're much better looking. She'll notice you just because everyone else will be looking at you."

"At least all the other women," Jolyn agreed.

"That's quite enough," Joe blustered, thoroughly embarrassed by his daughters' compliments. "Let's go."

The number of glamorous people milling around the brightly lit courtyard of Zachary's was nothing compared to the crowd inside the opulent building. The lump in Joe's throat kept him from being able to do much more than grunt in reply to the running commentary coming from his children as he followed them inside. He barely heard Kate's comment about the ladies they passed and but Jane's reply got his attention.

"What'd you say?" he asked, unable to believe his ears.

"I said we needed to keep you and Jack close or one of these ladies was going to kidnap you," Jane told him.

"Okay," Joe said with a sigh. "That's enough of that."

"What?" Jane asked innocently.

"I don't need you to keep telling me I'm good looking. I have a mirror. I know exactly what I look like."

"You don't have a clue," Jane argued with a giggle. She turned, seeking affirmation from Jolyn who nodded vehemently, then to Kate who just rolled her eyes. "And Jillian hasn't seen you since you got your bandages off. She's gonna freak."

"Stop already!" he hissed, trying to keep his voice down while making sure all of them heard him. "See if you can find your mother," he commanded, looking over the heads of those nearest him, frustrated that he couldn't see her anywhere. His anxiety rose exponentially with each person he saw who wasn't Jillian. He'd almost given up finding her when she suddenly appeared, flying into his arms.

"Hi," he said, wrapping his arms around her tightly, his lips against her hair. He breathed in her fragrance, wound his fingers through her hair, closed his eyes with relief and thanksgiving. He wanted nothing more than to pick her up and carry her out of there, away from the prying, curious eyes, but he took her by the shoulders and pushed her gently from him. When she clung even tighter, he said, "Hey, it's okay. I'm not going anywhere."

The sparkle of unshed tears made her already beautiful eyes seem luminous. He could barely believe her apology, offering one of his own instead. "I should never have done that to you," he said, astonished when she disagreed. When she tried to explain that she had been embarrassed that her children knew all that had happened, he reminded her that they still did, but that they were here and hoped she would allow them to congratulate her. The look she gave him melted his heart, but not his resolve. This was her night. They could talk later about what she planned for the future.

He stepped aside, loath to give her up, but anxious for her to see their family who waited just behind him. He couldn't express his happiness when she ran past him into their outstretched arms. Over her shoulder, he caught Jane's wink and Jack's nod and he knew his family was once again together, no matter how long it took to get her back home.

Zach's interruption wasn't welcome, but they knew this was why they were all there and they followed him to the dais where he introduced his newest artist, allowing her to say a few words before taking back the microphone and extolling her artwork, asking his patrons to be sure to enjoy the exhibit and to take advantage of the music of the orchestra and try a few steps on the dance floor. Of all people, he knew that tonight was more than a gallery show. To some of these people, one of his openings was the highlight of their social season and he wanted to make sure it was a memorable evening.

Joe, Jillian and their offspring made a swift, obligatory circuit through the rooms of the gallery, fielding questions and comments, anxious to find some place private where they could talk. After what seemed an eternity, but was really only fifteen or so minutes, they found themselves back in the office. Joe relinquished his hold on his wife long enough for her to take little Megan from her father, cuddling her sleeping form against her breast. When she gave her up, it was only to take Little Joe up into her arms, commenting what a big boy he'd become. The women all had a good cry and even the men had tears in their eyes at some point, but they were tears of joy, and by the time Alexa knocked on the door, they were ready to go back out to meet and greet.

JILLIAN

*J*ILLIAN HAD THOUGHT she would enjoy her grand opening, but she was anxious to have it all over with until Joe escorted her back into the gallery. Demonstrating his support by his constant touch, he gave her the nerve to stand making small talk with the beautifully attired denizens of the art world. After a few minutes, she was able to relax and enjoy the admiration of people whose extravagant lifestyles were so different from her own.

It wasn't long before she became aware of his fingertips tracing slowly down the inside of her arm as his hand sought her own and the tingle sent shivers throughout her body. Tucked against his tall, powerful frame, she felt secure, cherished and . . . oops, horny. "Oh, my God!" she thought. "I can't believe this. How am I ever going to get through the evening?"

Now his hand was at her waist, seemingly innocent, anything but. She could feel his thumb gently etching the outline of her ribcage, his fingers tightening fractionally on her body. His other hand rested lightly on her shoulder, under her loose, flowing curls, kneading tight muscles, his thumb tickling her neck.

When they turned to talk to another dazzling couple, he shifted, his left hand rubbing lightly up and down her upper arm, his right hand resting lightly on her hip. She could barely follow the conversations swirling around her, wasn't aware of the secretive smile that lit her face. And it occurred to her that no one around them was aware that he was subtly seducing her there in front of God and everybody.

After half an hour, she had a slight sheen of sweat on her temples and between her legs, and wanted nothing more than to drag Joe into the office and have her way with him. Her skin burned where he touched her, froze where he hadn't. She quivered with excitement. Her eyes sparkled, her smile widened and she leaned into her husband every chance she got. Still his fingers worked their magic unobtrusively and her whole body smoldered with anticipation.

She went up on her toes, whispered in his ear. "Please, Joe," she begged. "Now!"

"Now, what?" he asked innocently.

"Oh, Lord," she sighed. "Make love to me."

"I am," he answered with a grin, turning her around to greet yet another patron of the arts while he continued a gentle, subtle seduction of every part of her within reach.

JOLYN

*J*OLYN AND TOM wandered around the beautifully
illuminated gallery, followed closely by the rest
of the family. Shaking her head, she turned to the
others, commenting with more than a little wonder.
"Did you ever think that Mom could do something
like this?"

"They really are great," Jack agreed. "I don't
think I've ever seen anything quite like them."

"That's why I wanted to have her exhibit them,"
Case told them. "As soon as I saw what she was
doing, I knew Uncle Zach would want to show
them." He turned to his uncle for confirmation.

"And I have you to thank for one of the most
successful shows of the season," Zach told him.
"I've never before seen anyone who could depict
such power and sensuality in such simple lines. It
isn't just that Joe looks sexy, although that's certainly
part of it. It's that Jillian was able to capture it on
paper."

Alexa nudged Zach in the ribs and went up
on tiptoes to whisper in his ear. He glanced at the

attractive couple that would be the center of attention even if they weren't artist and model. Snickering, he turned to Case, pointing out what Alexa had told him. "He really took everything in your manual to heart," he said.

"That isn't in the manual," Case informed him, watching Joe's slow, subtle seduction of Jillian. "He's doing that without coaxing," he observed, "and it seems to be working."

Tom followed Case's glance and chuckled. "We're going to have to add *that* to the manual," he said. "I'm not sure he even knows he's doing it," he added.

"*She* sure does," Jolyn nodded toward her mother, smiling. "She looks like she's ready to jump him."

"She looks like she's enjoying whatever he's doing," Jane whispered in Jack's ear.

"What is he doing?" Kyle asked, confused.

"Oh, Kyle," Jolyn rolled her eyes. "Jack, would you like to fill him in?"

"Nope," Jack laughed. "Have Tom tell him. I had to find out the hard way."

"Gee thanks," Jane smacked him in the ribs with her elbow. "I didn't realize it was difficult for you."

"Well, no," Jack admitted. "I had a great teacher," he leaned to give her a kiss on the forehead. "A really great teacher," he whispered in her ear.

"Oh, all right," Kyle gave in. "I get it. I may not know everything, but I get it."

"Unless you want your married life to be as chaste as our parents' has been, you need to learn," Jolyn cautioned him.

He put his hands over his ears. "Euuu," he said. "I don't want to hear about our parents' sex lives."

"But you can wander around a gallery full of drawings of your father in all his glory and it doesn't bother you?" Eddie kidded him.

"I just don't look at that part," Kyle admitted.

"Prude!" Jack kidded him.

"Not me," Kyle said. "Unless it has to do with my folks. I don't know about all of you, but I don't blame Mom for freaking out about everyone knowing about her and Dad. I wouldn't want all of you to know whatever I'd been doing."

"So that's why you already moved out and got your own apartment?" Tom accused him.

"Right," Kyle grinned.

"Kyle!" Jolyn squealed.

"Well?" he replied defensively. "It's none of your business."

"Hey," Jack blurted, looking all around the large room. "Where'd they go?"

"Probably in another room," Tom offered.

"Yeah," Eddie agreed. "A private room."

JOE

*H*E COULD FEEL her quiver under his fingers, loved it when he ran his hand down her back and felt her shudder. He only hoped her reactions weren't repulsion, but he couldn't be sure. Everything he did was gentle, subtle, hidden. He didn't want the people they were speaking with to catch on. He didn't want anyone else to figure out what he was doing. He only wanted to turn her on, because if he did, he could be sure he was forgiven.

He could feel her reacting, could see the moisture on her brow, watched her tongue languidly licking her lips. When she leaned into him, she rubbed her firm little bottom against him and he sprang to attention, grateful now that he had had the foresight to wear tight underwear and loose fitting trousers. After half an hour, he was having to work hard at maintaining a smile and harder still at following a conversation.

He was almost faint with relief when she went up on her toes to beg him to take her somewhere . . . now, but they couldn't just walk off. It took a few more minutes to extricate themselves from the present group of admirers and even longer to work their way around to the little office. She all but dragged him inside, barely getting the door closed before wrapping herself around him, groaning in anticipation.

"Wait," he whispered into her hair.

"I can't," she moaned.

"Yes, you can," he said, keeping his arm around her waist while he made sure the door was locked and the blind pulled over the little observation window. He lifted her, carrying her pressed full length against him across the room to the far side of the desk.

"There really isn't any place for us here," he said. "Maybe we should wait."

"Oh, please, no," she whimpered. She leaned against the desk, raising her floor length skirt above her hips. Her panties were all that separated her from the front of his trousers. "I've already made us wait too long," she sighed, reaching for his zipper.

His lips curved slowly into a smile. He reached down, hooked his fingers into the sides of her panties and very, very slowly lowered them to the floor. Straightening, he took her by shoulders, turning her around and slowly pulled down the zipper on her dress. Again he turned her, sliding her dress off her shoulders, pulling it down to her waist, then beyond, allowing it to puddle on the floor at her feet. He leaned over, picked it up and spread it on the desk, creating a silky bed on which to lay her.

Slowly he lowered his zipper, trying to negotiate his fully tumescent erection through the opening without catching it on the sharp metal teeth. He thought he was prepared for her, but he wasn't ready to have her grasp him greedily, pulling him toward her. He shook his head, capturing her hands and holding both her arms above her head with one hand while he guided himself to her with the other.

Still he hesitated, prolonging her agony. When he finally touched her, she gasped, wriggled closer, begged him for release. And he gave it to her, sliding full length in one smooth motion, releasing her arms to grasp her hips, holding himself buried deep within her. She groaned, arched her back, closed her eyes, the material of her skirt bunched in her clenched fists.

He waited, watching her with adulation while her breath sucked in, her body went rigid and she slid over the summit. Waiting until her breathing evened out and her eyes opened, he slid his hands down her legs, pulling them around his waist as he leaned over her, lifted her onto him. Turning, their bodies still connected by his throbbing erection, her legs wrapped around him, he rested his bottom on the edge of the desk. He supported her with his hands on her back, allowing her to control her own movements.

And she began to push herself up and down against him, riding him, head thrown back, back arched. Her hands dug into his shoulders, leveraging herself until she achieved the perfect position and the perfect orgasm. Finally, she slumped against him, whimpering his name, telling him how much she loved him.

"Really?" he asked.

She could barely nod.

"Good," he whispered. "'Cause I'm not done."

Her head flew up and he chuckled at the shock that registered in her widened eyes. He smiled and measured himself within her, drawing a soft moan from her. With agonizing slowness, he moved, sliding deep and withdrawing, his hands on her bottom moving her up and down in rhythm with him. Her breathing quickened, her eyes closed once again and she moved on her own, freeing his hands.

He slid them around her thighs, his thumbs seeking and finding her most fragile, most sensitive inner being. As her groans increased in volume, he found he needed one hand to cover her mouth to keep her shouts of ecstasy from filtering past the door. Still he drove her as she drove him, together reaching that shock of release as he surged a final time, driving her over the edge once again.

He was loath to release her, but, finally reached around to grasp her legs, straightening them and lowering her to the floor. When she swayed against him, he smiled, kissing her hair. "Hey," he said tenderly. "We need to get back out there."

She groaned, but opened her eyes. "I can't," she whispered.

"Sure you can," he assured her. "Go clean up," he said, pushing her gently toward the little bathroom. "I'll wait here."

She moved slowly, but she went, and he breathed a true sigh of relief. "Thank you, God," he said, lifting his eyes upward. He took a deep breath, stuffed himself back into his shorts and zipped his pants. He looked around to make sure that they hadn't disturbed anything, spying her panties on the floor just beneath the desk. Gathering them up with her dress, he went to the closed bathroom door and rapped softly.

"Just a minute," she called. A moment later she opened the door, looking radiant. "I seem to have lost . . ." she started, but didn't even need to finish. She reached for her panties now dangling from his forefinger, but he drew them back. Kneeling in front of her, he held them for her to step into, pulling them up slowly. Then he held her dress for her to step into, turned her around and pulled the zipper into place.

"Ready?" he asked.

She shook her head. "No," she told him.

"Yes you are," he said. "C'mon."

"I can't," she insisted.

"Yes, you can," he assured her. "You can do anything you set your mind to."

She gave him a look of disdain which turned rapidly to adoration. "If you say so," she breathed against his lapel.

"I do," he promised, meaning something completely different from what they had been discussing.

"I do, too," she smiled brightly, understanding just what he was saying.

"Let's do this," he said, leading the way to the door. He opened it a crack, making sure the coast was clear and that they weren't being observed. He pulled it the rest of the way and escorted her back out into the glittering mob, keeping her close but trying not to touch her. After a few minutes, he gave up, settling for holding her at the waist, trying to be on his best behavior.

JILLIAN

$\mathcal{B}$Y THE TIME Joe agreed to accompany her to the little office, Jillian was so horny she could barely negotiate through the crowd. "I can't believe I feel like this," she thought, then quit thinking, turning to throw herself at him, burrowing into him when he lifted her and carried her to the desk.

She had no coherent thoughts. It was all she could do to keep herself upright. She hadn't worn any underwear beyond a pair of lace panties. The dress was too overwhelming, too heavy. She hadn't wanted anything else beneath it. Now she was grateful as she lifted the long skirts above her waist, unsure how she could get her panties down while holding onto her dress. Fortunately, Joe had two empty hands and helped her, although he moved much too slowly for her. "Hurry up," she thought, but didn't say. She didn't want to say or do anything to make him go away. She wanted him here, now, inside.

When he lifted her, laying her back across the desk, she reached for him, but he stopped her, capturing her hands. It took her muddled brain a few moments to realize that she couldn't have helped him without having to take all his clothes off, something she would have preferred, but not now. It would take too long.

"Please hurry." The thought repeated itself, running amuck through her brain. But he seemed to be moving underwater, slowly approaching her, slowly touching her, slowly sliding into her until she was filled with him. "Oh, Lord, but that is wonderful," she thought, wriggling to increase the sensations that were wracking her body until she found the ultimate position, the glorious sensation that sent her skyward, fulfilled, complete, entirely whole for the first time in months.

She had barely caught her breath when he lifted her onto him and turned, now resting his buttocks on the desk while holding her pierced by his wonderfully throbbing shaft. She tightened her legs around him, increasing the depth and the pressure, rising against him, grinding into him until she could reach that pinnacle of perfection that blew her apart, fracturing her mind, capturing her body in that state of explosive energy that only Joe could bring her to.

She slumped against him, totally exhausted, nerveless, complete. "I love you, Joe," she whispered. "You'll never know how much."

"Really?" he asked.

She nodded against his lapel, smiling.

"Good," he whispered against her temple, his lips on her hair. "'Cause I'm not done," he said.

Her head whipped up. Her eyes gazed into his, finding only total love, complete adoration and a twinkle as he lifted her then drove into her. "Oh, my God," she whispered, her body responding immediately. Already tender inside, the new onslaught brought her to climax in minutes, her vaginal muscles contracting around him, wringing his fiery spurt from him at the same moment.

Exhaustion took her. Not only was her body spent, but her mind as well. She wanted nothing more than to remain as she was; still joined to the one man she had loved almost her whole life. Beyond that she was unable to think.

Fortunately, Joe *was* able to think and lowered her until her feet touched the ground, propelling her toward the bathroom. As her scattered thoughts coalesced, she realized she was naked but for her shoes. At the same moment she heard a light rap on the door and she popped it open a tiny bit.

She didn't have to say a word. Joe stood with her panties hanging from one finger, but, instead of handing them to her, he knelt in front of her, holding them open for her to step into. He pulled them up slowly and she thought, no, hoped, he might want to fool around some more. She was almost disappointed when he simply spread out her dress for her to step into also.

All zipped up and in order, he guided her with one hand at her waist to the door, which he opened just enough to peer out at the milling crowd. Once he was sure they wouldn't be observed, he escorted her out into the gallery. This time he simply stood beside her for a while, but it didn't last long. Soon his hand rested at her waist, holding her close without trying to seduce her. She couldn't have expressed how thankful she was, not only that he was there beside her, but that he wasn't doing those things with his hands that turned her mind into mush.

It was almost closing time when they returned to their family, huddled all together at the doorway. "Are you leaving?" she asked.

"We're on our way to the church," Jolyn explained.

"Church?" she asked.

"The priest has agreed on a midnight mass for Jack and Janie," Kate told her.

"Jack and Janie?" She turned to Joe for an explanation.

"They didn't tell you?" he asked.

"Tell me what?"

"That they're getting married," he said.

"Married? Now? Really?"

"Really," Joe told her with a kiss on the cheek. "I thought you knew about it," he confessed.

"No, I didn't," she said. "But I think it's a wonderful idea. They're so cute together."

"And she's *so* pregnant," Jolyn told her.

"Pregnant?!"

"Well, shit," Joe exclaimed. "They didn't tell you that, either."

"No, they didn't," she said. She looked around at her children and her husband, sighed and then smiled. "But now I'm even happier that they've decided to get married."

She didn't see the looks of relief and disbelief that were passed between her children and her husband.

She merely smiled, giving all of them kisses and telling them she would see them in a little while. As soon as the door closed behind them, she turned to Joe. "I deserved that," she said.

"What?" he asked, perplexed.

"I wasn't privy to information that the rest of the family already knew because I had excluded them all from my life. Thank you for coming to get me. I knew I'd made a mistake a long time ago, but I didn't know how to extricate myself."

"I don't know if it was a mistake," he disagreed. "I understood why you left. I just didn't know whether or not you would want me to try to talk you into coming home."

"I guess I should've let you know where I was, though," she said.

"Janie did," he admitted. He held up his hand to stop her from saying anything. "She said Jack promised not to tell me, but she didn't promise anything. She thought we were both too sad, so she let me know where your apartment was."

"And you didn't come?"

"Oh, well, yes, I did. I just didn't come in. I spied on you, though. I sat in my car and watched you." He looked at his shoes, at the walls, at anything but his wife. Finally, he met her eyes, shrugged. "I missed you," he said.

She melted against him. "I missed you, too," she admitted. "You'll never know how much."

JOE

*J*OE STARTED LOOKING at his watch long before people started leaving the reception. Jack had already waved from across the room, letting him know that he and Jane were on their way to the church. And he could see the kids gathering near the wide courtyard doors. He gently pulled Jillian with him as he negotiated the room, weaving around groups of brilliantly gowned dowagers and their tuxedoed husbands, careful not to step on any of the long wide trains that trailed away from their dresses.

When they reached the kids, his tension started all over again. Jillian didn't know about the wedding! He'd never imagined that they hadn't told her. It had never occurred to him, but he could understand. They preferred the whole family minus one rather than the one minus the rest of the family. Jillian seemed to understand that as well, telling him that she had deserved to be excluded.

He was on pins and needles for the next twenty minutes while the gallery emptied out in preparation for closing. They both stood with Zach and Alexa at the doors, shaking hands and thanking everyone for coming. They still had almost an hour to make it to the church, provided they could find it. Jack had thrust the directions into his hand just as they had entered the gallery and he'd never had a chance to look at them.

When the door closed behind the last guest, he pulled the paper from his pocket, showing it to Jillian and asking her if she knew where the address was. When she told him no, he turned to Zach.

"Sure," Zach said. "Would you like a ride over there?"

"But I'd have to leave my car here," Jillian protested.

"Okay. Then you can follow us."

"Wait. Follow you?"

"Sure," he laughed. "Tom asked Case and me and our wives if we'd like to attend. Even if we weren't pretty crazy about your family already, we'd go. Tomorrow's Sunday and this will count as mass."

Joe chuckled and nodded, his hand never leaving Jillian's waist. While Zach and Alexa turned off lights, set alarms and closed up, he pulled her close, his lips at her temple, feeling her heartbeat. "Ready?" he asked.

"Certainly," she answered, but he could see that she wasn't really happy.

"Are you all right?" he asked.

"Yes and no," she told him. "It's been such a rollercoaster today. My first show and I was so scared I couldn't talk myself out of the office. Then I saw you and I forgot all about the show. All I could think about was you. You and the kids. I was so happy to see you. Then all I could think of was sex. Me! And now I find out my eldest son is going to get married. And he's going to be a father. And I realized something. I realized all of this," she swept her arms to include the walls of the gallery, "isn't worth one moment lost with all of you."

"But it's a great accomplishment," he argued.

"But I missed so much," she told him.

"Not yet," he said. "But, if we don't hurry we might." He gave her a quick squeeze.

He took her keys, started the car and waited until the big Mercedes pulled to the driveway. He followed closely, afraid he would lose them, but it wasn't far and they pulled into the church parking lot with plenty of time to spare. Inside, they didn't have to look far to find their children who occupied the front pews of the otherwise empty church.

"What about Jane's parents?" Jillian asked as they hurried down the aisle.

"There are several reasons they aren't here," Joe explained when they were seated. "The first is that they live in Japan." He paused. "But I don't think Jane told them. She said they weren't happy about her and Jack. We're Catholic. They're Buddhist. He's American, they're not."

"Does it bother them that he's white?" she asked.

"Her mother is part French, so, no, it doesn't bother them." He paused. "Does it bother you that she's not?"

She looked at him blankly. "Of course not," she blurted. "She's a darling girl and will be a wonderful addition to our family." She looked at her hands, looked up and caught his eye. "I just feel badly that she won't have her family around her." She sniffed. "I know how painful that can be."

He pulled her against him for a moment, but he had something he had to do. He rose and strode back down the aisle to find the priest. The young man all robed in white seemed enchanted with the midnight ceremony, but had to herd the single altar boy to light the candles because the child was almost asleep on his feet.

"Excuse me, Father," Joe began.

"Jack's dad, I presume," the man said with a handshake. "He certainly favors his father. I'm Father Timothy. I want you to know I'm enjoying this immensely. They're a wonderful young couple. Did you know we were going to baptize Jane tonight, as well?"

"No, I didn't, but it doesn't surprise me. She's certainly asked me enough questions about our faith. But I thought she had to go through RCIA first."

"We had a few private lessons," the priest admitted. "She's a very determined young lady and very quick. She has a better grasp of our faith than many people who are raised within it."

"You may be right about that," Joe said, wondering how to change the subject, but he needn't have worried. The young cleric seemed to realize there was something else on his mind and asked what he could do.

"It's kind of difficult to explain," Joe answered. "But is there any way my wife and I could renew our vows?"

"Sure, why not," Father Timothy said with a shrug. "Before or after?"

"Um . . . I don't know. Whatever you think."

"We'll play it by ear," he assured him. "I'll see what Jack and Jane want to do. It may be that they would rather not. Would that bother you too much?" When Joe shook his head, he smiled then checked his watch. "Better take your seat," he admonished. "It's time to start." And with that he disappeared through a side door, leaving Joe to return down the aisle alone.

JILLIAN

*J*ILLIAN WATCHED JOE walk away and felt her heart go with him.

"Where'd he go?" Jolyn asked, leaning over the sleeping form of her son.

Jillian could only shrug. "I don't have a clue," she admitted. She gently scooped Little Joe from the pew and held him tenderly in her lap. Looking up, she caught Jolyn's eye. "You don't mind, do you?"

"Of course not," Jolyn said, scooting closer. "He's missed you. We all have."

"And I've missed you, too," Jillian said. "I really must have been out of my mind to have run off like that."

Jolyn's arm slid around her mother, giving her a squeeze before she could decide what to say. "We all understood, Mom," she told her. "But it's been hard on all of us not to have you around. I think Kate has missed you the most. She's always been the tenderest of all of us. But I feel guilty. It was my fault that Dad took you to meet Dr. Summers in the first place. I'm the one who talked him into it."

"You?" Jillian questioned, then thought about it for a while. "Of course," she said. "It would've been either you or Tom, wouldn't it? You're the ones who have seen the results of Dr. Summers' unique therapy. I guess I should have thanked you instead of being angry."

"No. I should have found a way to let you know before this. I am sorry," Jolyn said, resting her head on her mother's shoulder.

"I love you, you know," Jillian whispered into her hair. "I'm so glad you came tonight. I was almost ready to leave the gallery and go home until I saw your dad. I don't think there are words to express how I felt when I saw all of you." When Jolyn sat erect, peering intently at her mother, Jillian pointed out one other fact. "And I wouldn't have gotten to see Jack married."

"But we're all together now," Jolyn said, a single tear leaking slowly down her cheek.

"Yep," Jillian said. "We're a family again. And we're evidently going to be adding a couple more to our clan in the immediate future." She winked.

"Three," Jolyn told her.

Jillian raised one elegant, expressive eyebrow in question.

"Little Joe is getting a sibling," Jolyn confessed. "Sometime around Easter."

Jillian almost dumped Little Joe on the floor reaching for her eldest child to embrace her. "Oh, Jolyn, how wonderful," she murmured in her ear. "What a wonderful ending to an almost perfect day."

"Almost?" Jolyn asked playfully.

"Well, yes," Jillian admitted. "I guess I'm still uneasy about your father. Did you know he spied on me?"

"No more than you spied on him," Jolyn pointed out.

"What?"

"Did you think we didn't know about Zach and Case keeping an eye on Dad for you?"

"Ha," Jillian burst out, quickly covering her mouth and looking around to make sure no one had overheard her. She blushed a rosy shade of pink to realize that everyone in the church had heard. Fortunately, Joe chose that moment to return to her side and she forgot her embarrassment when he slid his arm over Jolyn's and squeezed her shoulders, tucking her against him.

"Want me to hold him?" he whispered in her ear, reaching for Little Joe.

"Please, no," she said. "It's been too long. I have a lot of time to make up for." Before she could say anything more, the priest crossed to the altar, followed closely by Jack and Kyle. Just before Jane started down the long aisle, the Wedding March sounded from the high organ loft and they all rose to their feet to greet the newest member of their family.

Jillian watched as the rites of baptism were conferred on Janie, delighted to see that she would not only be joining their family, but the church as well. And there were tears in her eyes when the young priest introduced the younger couple as husband and wife. She was ready for them to march together back down the aisle when Janie came to her, taking her hands and pulling her to her feet. Jack, beside her, held out his hand to his father, and the two encouraged his parents toward the altar where Father Timothy waited.

"We are thrilled that we can celebrate not only the introduction of a newly baptized woman to our small congregation, and her joining together with her new husband, but we are able to celebrate a renewal of vows, as well," Father Timothy announced to the gathering. Motioning to Joe and Jillian, he positioned them directly in front of him. Quietly, he asked Joe, "Are you sure this is what you want?" When Joe nodded, he turned to Jillian. "And do you wish to renew your vows, as well?"

"He loves me!" she thought to herself. "He's telling me he wants to marry me all over again!" She could barely respond, nodding her head as he had, unable to speak. But, as he went through the ceremony, she found her voice and when he asked if she would love, honor and obey, she said loud and clear, "I most certainly do."

She didn't hear the giggles from the ladies present, didn't care about anything but Joe, only waited to hear his own profession. "I do." That was all she cared about; his promise to love her and honor her and cherish her.

And then it was all over and they were all congratulating each other, hugging, kissing and smiling. "I would say welcome to the family," Jillian whispered to Janie. "But you've been in their midst while I've been on the outside."

"You haven't been on the outside," Jane told her. "You've just been on holiday. And I'm so happy to be a part of your family."

"My family," Jillian echoed, dreamily. "My family. What a dope I've been."

JOE

*I*T HAD BEEN a long day and even longer night and Joe was pooped, but he was sure the kids would want to celebrate their nuptials. He had already made up his mind that he would do whatever they wanted, so was pleasantly surprised when they announced that they wanted to wait until breakfast the following morning for their celebratory meal.

"We're all beat," Jack told them. "We'd just like to go back to the hotel and sack out until maybe noon. We can all meet for brunch or a late breakfast, if that's all right with everyone."

No one wanted to disagree, especially Kate and Jolyn, whose children had already slept through the whole thing. "How about we meet at eleven in the hotel lobby," Jolyn suggested. "We can decide where we want to go from there."

With agreement all around, Joe and Jillian kissed their children goodnight. "You can enjoy the room all to yourself," Joe told Kyle. "I'll stay with your mother at her apartment."

"Did I invite you?" Jillian asked, her voice and look both telling him she was teasing.

"Nope," he said. "I just assumed you wouldn't want to sleep with me in a room with your son in the next bed."

While everyone laughed, he put his arm around her and led her from the church, guiding her to the car and opening the driver's side for her to climb in. "You know the way better than I do," he told her. He went around, got into the passenger seat, fastened his seat belt and watched as she smoothly negotiated the short drive back to her apartment.

"I wasn't expecting company," she told him when he took her key and unlocked the front door.

"That's okay," he quipped. "I like to think I'm not really company." When she hit the light switch, he understood what she'd been telling him. The front room was filled with her drawings and her paraphernalia was spread everywhere. A couple of old sheets serving as drop cloths were smeared with bright colors, another sheet covered her easel, hiding whatever it was that she had been working on.

He wandered around the tiny room, going from picture to drawing to painting, nodding and smiling. His children smiled back at him from the array, running through the sprinkler, playing with various puppies, kittens and snakes, picking forbidden flowers, all memories of the life they had lived for the last twenty-five years. "How come Zach didn't put any of these in the exhibit?" he asked. "They're every bit as good as those you did of me."

"He wants to have another show next year," she said, matter-of-factly. "These are so different from the others, it's almost like a different artist. He said there would be a whole different clientele for these." She gave him a slow smile. "And he said the ones of you are so sexy that it would be obscene to show these with them."

Joe laughed, agreeing with that assessment. Still, he could barely contain his admiration. "You've really blossomed as an artist," he told her, crossing the room in a few swift steps to give her a quick kiss. "Do you have any idea how proud I am of you? The whole family is."

"I have you to thank for that," she murmured. "If you hadn't taught me how to really love, I might never have found that depth of feeling that makes my art so much better than it was before."

"Jillian, you've always known how to love," he argued. "You've just never known how to express it as well as you do now." He nuzzled her hair, breathed in her scent, wanted her. "I don't know about you," he said. "But this has been a long day and I'm bushed. Are you ready for bed?"

She giggled. "I'm tired, too," she admitted. "C'mon," she took his hand, leading him from the bright colors of her studio to the more subtle shades of the rest of her apartment. One glance at the tiny kitchen told him that his wife hadn't changed completely. Clean and shiny, everything was in its proper place, including a scented candle in the middle of the counter. "Are there sheets on the bed?" he asked.

"Of course," she replied, the look on her face telling him that she was astonished he would ask.

"Good," he said. "At this moment that's the most important thing. I'm so tired, I'm reeling."

Her low chuckle sent little shivers down his spine. "Just how tired are you?" she asked.

Slowly, his grin widened. "Well . . ." he answered, allowing her to tug him into the bedroom. Before he could reach for the first button, she began to undress him, batting his hands away when he tried to undo his tie himself. He sighed and relaxed. He was tired, but not that tired. He allowed her to strip him totally. By the time she got to his trousers, his dick had turned to stone and was ready to go. She petted him, caressed his balls, turned for him to unzip her dress, holding her hair out of the way.

He divested her of her clothing once again, running his hands up her legs as he straightened. Again he waited for her to take the initiative, allowing her to lead him to the bed, waiting while she pulled aside the comforter, letting her push him back onto the mattress and follow him into bed. He was both surprised and delighted when she turned her back on him, snuggling her firm bottom against him, pulling his arm around her and taking a firm grasp on his hand.

"Do you mind if we just sleep?" she asked, wriggling against him into a more comfortable position.

"Uh, sure," he agreed, torn between wanting to sleep and wanting . . . her.

Try as he might, he couldn't make himself relax, was still hard as a rock. He tried to stuff it between his legs, but it sprang from his hiding place, erect and throbbing. When she looked over her shoulder, he shrugged. "Sorry," he said. "It seems to have a mind of its own."

"I've got an idea," she said, reaching between her legs and taking his penis in her hand. She tucked it between her legs, but that didn't seem to do the trick. Again she adjusted her position until he slid inside just enough for both of them to be able to enjoy the subtle sensations. Unable to stop himself, Joe began a gentle rocking motion, stirring reciprocal feelings in his sleepy mate. "Sorry," he whispered again. "It just won't behave."

"I think it behaves just fine," she murmured, her bottom moving in rhythm with him.

It wasn't fireworks or volcanoes, no eruptions, no electricity. It was slow, simmering, comfortable. Gentle probing met with sweet acceptance. And it was the most wonderful completion either had ever felt.

JILLIAN

*J*ILLIAN GNAWED AT the inside of her mouth while Joe perused her most recent paintings. Above all else, she wanted him to approve of her depictions of their children. When he praised them, questioning their omission from her exhibit, it gave her a chance to tell him about her next show, something she hadn't known how to do before. She was relieved that he seemed pleased with them and even more so that he didn't react negatively to the idea of a repeat performance.

It wasn't until he told her that he was tired, that she admitted to herself her total exhaustion. It had been a roller coaster of a day for her, huge ups and swoops, her worries over the acceptance of her show, her feelings of desperation before her family arrived and her elation at seeing them.

She had felt both thrilled and depressed that her son was going to be married. Thrilled for the addition of the lovely young woman to her family, depressed that they hadn't let her know beforehand. She hadn't let anyone know how she had felt about that, except Joe. And she hadn't even told him how hurt she had been that her one family member with whom she'd had communication had withheld that tidbit of information from her. Her mind had understood. Her heart had hurt.

And repeating their vows had taken her completely by surprise. Yes, she had wanted that. No, not that. She had wanted Joe. And his willingness to marry her all over again after childishly running away from him, had bowled her over. Her stomach had barely calmed down from one high to only to climb to another, but it had left her exhausted. It was as though he were reading her mind when he told her he was ready for bed.

"Bed?" She could barely negotiate the trip through the tiny kitchen to the bedroom, her mind flying in several directions at once. She was afraid that if she didn't want sex, he would be angry, so tried to be seductive, undressing him, touching him, and holding her hair out of the way for him to undress her. She was grateful that he didn't play with her, that he allowed her to make all the moves. And once in bed, she snuggled against him spoon fashion, pulling his arm around her, but hanging on to his hand so he couldn't use it to arouse her.

When he didn't seem to make any sexual overtures, she found the temerity to ask, "Do you mind if we just sleep?" and was gratified that he agreed. She felt him wriggling behind her and suddenly became aware that the erection she had discovered when she'd removed his trousers hadn't diminished.

She had to laugh, softly, to herself. He was apologizing to her for being turned on by her. "I've got an idea," she said and reached between her legs to grasp him, tucking him between her legs. When that wasn't quite comfortable or right, she adjusted her position until he slid just inside her warmth, loving the feel of him, loving him.

She forgot her fatigue when he rocked softly against her, giggled at his second apology in as many minutes. She found this gentle probing comfortable and she moved lightly to his rhythm. There was a sweetness to this that had been lacking before, a calmness and a tenderness that made her feel cherished. Even the finality was tender as he held her to him, helping them both achieve heaven.

And she had an epiphany. This was what he had been trying to teach her all along. This was what she had missed all those years. This was what he had meant when he called it making love.

And she looked forward to the years ahead when they would make slow, sweet love in their empty nest.

About the Author

*A*s an avid reader with a degree in literature, a degree in Fine arts, an insatiable curiosity and love of language it was a natural extension for me to begin writing. A lively imagination, an intense curiosity about people and places, and opportunities to travel extensively have given me an enormous volume of possibilities for characters, locales and situations. Retirement on with my husband of 44 years on the shores of Lake Erie has finally given me the opportunity to bring everything together with the written word.